T0277549

YORÙBÁ BOY RUNNING

YORÙBÁ BOY RUNNING

A NOVEL

Biyi Bándélé

HARPER

An Imprint of HarperCollins*Publishers*

HarperCollins books may be purchased for educational, business, or sales promotional use. For information, please email the Special Markets Department at SPsales@harpercollins.com.

Originally published in the United Kingdom in 2024 by Hamish Hamilton.

On p. 271, Anglican bishop Samuel Àjàyí Crowther and his son Dandeson, c. 1870. Photograph by Sydney Victor White.

FIRST U.S. EDITION

Library of Congress Cataloging-in-Publication Data has been applied for.

ISBN 978-0-06-341708-3

24 25 26 27 28 LBC 5 4 3 2 1

PUBLISHER'S NOTE

This novel is typeset from the revised manuscript sent by the author Biyi Bándélé to his editor Hannah Chukwu, following their last editorial discussion, on the eve of his death in August 2022. Apart from some standardisation of names and signposting of times and places as part of our copy-edit, the text is as we believe the author intended it.

Dedicated with warmth to the memory of
my grandmother,
Victoria Táíwò Ìbírónkẹ́ Thomas,
matriarch, businesswoman, cat-lover,
who went to sleep, and joined the ancestors,
on July 19th 1981.

And to my grandfather,
John Adéníji Babátúndé Thomas,
engineer, avid hunter,
who took wing, of a snakebite, and hastened,
far too young, to the realm of the ancestors,
on April 1st 1944.

And to Adéníji's father, recaptive and returnee,
a liberated slave who came back home,
much like the hero of the narrative
you are about to read.

This morning when I arrived at the working place, I met a woman who was waiting for me with her little boy about eight years of age: she requested me to take the boy under my care altogether as she was willing to give him up to be brought up by me. I told her I was not in a condition to receive him just now as I was busy building, but when I have removed to my new house and the school shall be opened, she might send him to school as other children . . .
This is an evidence that the faith of the people is being shaken in the gods of their forefathers, which cannot be better shown by anyone in this country than by asking the priest of a foreign God to look after the life of one of these children whom they almost idolise.

Reverend Samuel Àjàyí Crowther (c.1809–1891),
journal entry, Abẹ̀òkuta, January 31st 1847

INTRODUCTION: A TRIUMPH
OF RESILIENCE

Among the framed homilies and early black and white photographs
on the sitting-room walls of my childhood home was the unsmiling
portrait of a black figure in Victorian attire. As was customary at that
time of British colonial occupation, the subject struck the formula
pose beside a desk, looking slightly sideways, almost with a hint of
defiance, at what would have been the hooded camera. It all sig-
nalled membership of a select coterie of men of culture and learning,
business or profession of a colonial era. A short walk from that missionary home located in Aké, Abẹ́òkuta, within an enclave known
as St Peter's Parsonage, was the Anglican church to which that compound owed its name, the Anglican church of St Peter. That edifice
also had its portraits, only this time as implants on stained-glass
windows. Dominating the altar was St Peter himself, and he was
flanked by two prelates, complete with names, resplendent in clerical
robes, crozier and other symbols of the Christian order. One was the
Reverend Henry Townsend, the other one Reverend Hinderer – that
grouping is faithfully acknowledged in my childhood biography,
Aké: The Years of Childhood.

The first-mentioned figure was not featured among the stained-
glass icons. That was the Archbishop Samuel Àjàyí Crowther, a
black prelate. The other two – Townsend and Hinderer – were, of
course, European. All were prominent actors in the Christian mission in my hometown Abẹ́òkuta, and of course further afield, in the

great evangelising mission of the Christian church across my Western bulge of the African continent, prelude to the even more imperious mission of colonisation.

As a child, attending St Peter's School, and even warbling as a chorister in St Peter's Church, I had not the slightest knowledge of the intertwining of the careers of those three figures – Townsend, Hinderer and Crowther. Christians all, serving the same deity, but evident occupants of different rungs in the hierarchy of godly service – including its politics. As confessed in my childhood biography, however, my fertile imagination never failed to spin fantasies around those images, most persistently that last, Àjàyí Crowther. That was predictable, from the moment I learnt that he actually once occupied the adjoining compound to ours, a two-storey colonial structure that, at least, was a concession to his status within the Anglican church. The other two – Hinderer and Townsend – became fused with the colourful ancestral masquerades against whom, ironically, all three were united in demonising as products of pagan superstition.

We all knew the Àjàyí story, of course – right from elementary school. Kidnapped as a child and sold into slavery. Rescued by British warships and deposited on a settlement called Sierra Leone. Eventually restored to his home in present-day Nigeria a quarter of a century later, after life-and-death escapades plus, thankfully, immersion in intellection waters. That last produced numerous translations and original works, such as *The History of the Yorùbás* – a pioneer work on that subject, and still a seminal reference work for scholars and students.

Biyi Bándélé's literary thrust – a mix of the anecdotal, archival and inquisitional – in this posthumously published work, parts company with the slave narratives to which we are more accustomed. It disorientates, yet inducts one, at a most primary level of intimacy, and even self-identification, into the realities of capture, enslavement and displacement; eases one deftly into a milieu of the slaving occupation as an existential norm, and one that was near inextricably intertwined with the trajectory of colonialism in West Africa. This was Bándélé's last work, and I find it highly commendable that his publishers have opted to leave it exactly as rendered by that vividly reconstructive mind and its creative empathy. Penetrating through to character retrieval from time past, in the context of nations in the making, takes history out of dry pursuit and immerses us in the passions, motivations and even banalities of men and women of power and influence. This joins other works in the endlessly fascinating drama of the imperial adventure in its motley guises, a phase over which, one would wish, a final curtain has been drawn.

Alas, today, what we are confronted with is nothing less than its resurgence, albeit under different guises, at the hands of new players, and powered by both subtle and crudely violent mechanisms. For us in this part of the world, there is a grave resonance of a historic replay, near eerie, provoked by several incidentals and perspectives of this narrative. Here is a quick sample that must send shivers down the spines of today's inhabitants of the West African subregion, from Burkina Faso to the creeks of the Niger Delta:

from hamlets on the Atlantic coast and villages and towns in the rainforests and the savannah and cities at the edge of the Sahara Desert, thousands – tens of thousands – had been abducted and sold into slavery by marauding squads of Filani soldiers, mercenaries whose most versatile weapon was stealth and surprise. In the early days, such raids had been carried out in the name of God, but the raiders themselves, most of whom were not yet born in those early days, had long ceased to use the pretext of jihad as justification. They were born into plunder as a way of life and bred with beggar-thy-neighbour as the first rule of survival, as were their fathers and their fathers before them. To these men, being a plunderer was a trade no different than being a weaver or a cattle-rearer; it was just a lot more rewarding.

Now place that passage beside the following:

The kidnapping of school children, wholesale traumatization of community and nation appear to be their core concept of spiritual submission — indeed, to them belongs the discredit of the inauguration of a twenty-first-century slave trade. These are the seasoned practitioners of commercial partnership by direct coercion; by this I mean straightforwardly that these new slavers force others — governance and the governed, you and me — into partnership, whether we like it or not. In my view, they even imbue their centuries-old predecessors with a spurious respectability. Those past practitioners took risks in their hunt for that human commodity. Today's raiders simply wait until defenceless children are gathered together in one place at the behest and/or compulsion of governance, parents and guardians, for the purpose of learning. The hyenas swoop upon the unsuspecting prey, cart them off, sequester them in forest and other holding pens, then call on families and governments to come and negotiate for them. The world, including its global institutions, had better wake up to the fact that the slave trade is back on African soil with a one-sided ferocity, all the more obscene and blasphemous for being camouflaged as a religious mandate.

INTRODUCTION

The first passage, from Bándélé, refers to 1821; the latter, from a 2022 publication in my Nigerian series, *Interventions*, narrates the present: that is, a full two centuries after Àjàyí's capture and sale, commerce does not appear to have faltered, and aspiring nations – dedicated to the enthronement of godhead in sublime perfection – thrive on this defilement of the human essence. It would be an affront to our human sensibilities to adopt the solace, albeit sometimes offered by some of the enslaved themselves, that, despite the trauma and degradation, the slave experience has nonetheless produced distinguished men and women of global stature – Phillis Wheatley, Frederick Douglass, Olaudah Equiano, Wilhelm Amo, etc. – indeed an endless list of manifested talent, even genius. The answer to that is obvious – men and women of acknowledged accomplishment have emerged even more robustly from the norm of freedom. However, the extraction of the heroic virtue, and the capacity for resilience and survival despite inhuman odds, captured in such narratives, dedicated to the triumph of the human spirit, do not pall. Even as Àjàyí ran and ran, arriving eventually in freedom, as long as the ensuing narratives succeed in compelling us to keep in step with his strides, humanity remains an ultimate beneficiary of such inspirational passages.

The humanity hidden behind the unsmiling portrait in the Aké family parlour comes to life for this reader – combative, learned, warmly human, even with a touching sense of humour. It has taken a writer armed with a matching diligence to flush him out.

Wole Soyinka

PART ONE

1821

Run, Àjàyí, Run

One

On the night before the Malian swordsmen swept into Ọ̀ṣogùn, chanting, 'God is great, God is great, God is great,' as they laid waste to the town and corralled its inhabitants into barracoons, all twelve thousand of them, and herded them down to a mosquito-infested backwater on the coast, an obscure fishing village christened Lagos by the Portuguese merchants whose trade in human cargo had brought them there, Àjàyí had a dream in which he saw the god Ọ̀sanyìn hunched over, his notched and scarified, weather-beaten face drawn and dejected, gathering herbs in the dank forests sprawling beyond the six gates of the town's encircling walls.

In Àjàyí's dream, the healer god was blind in one eye, and had just one leg and but one arm. The god's left ear was big as a cassava leaf, but he was deaf in this ear. If he was deaf in his left ear, which wasn't quite as big as a cassava leaf, truth be told, spare a thought for his right ear, which was no ear at all. It was a dimple. Where others would seek out their right ear, Ọ̀sanyìn had a dimple. Where some had a dimple, Ọ̀sanyìn had his right ear. Needless to say, he was deaf in this ear too. And yet all he had to do was cup the dimple with the mud-encrusted fingers of his stubby hand and he could hear a moth on the wing.

In place of hair, a wild constellation of tousled beads on the òrìṣà's misshapen head shone like night light from a distant place. Beads of every hue sparkled on his head, and each time he plucked a healing herb on the forest floor it was as if he were harvesting the very beads on his head.

When Àjàyí arose from his mat the next morning, he knew exactly what to do about the dream. He would ask Ìyá what it meant. It was the only thing to do. There was certainly no point asking his sister, Bọlá. Bọlá would simply stare him down and say, 'Go away, child,' without actually saying 'child' or even 'go away'. She would simply stare him down.

There was a time when he could count on Bọlá as an ally, a partner-in-crime. But those days were long gone. Any such understanding between them ended the day Àkànní the hunter came asking for her hand. Since the day she became betrothed to the most revered elephant hunter in the land, Bọlá had taken to treating everybody – namely, the boys – like something Àkànní's dog Konginikókó dragged in from a hunt. It was not so much that Àjàyí faulted Bọlá's choice of husband. What was hard to stomach was that his own sister would choose to treat him, her flesh and blood, like a wastrel and a fool.

Better to ask Ìyá, he decided. Ìyá knows best.

In the unlikely event Ìyá didn't know, she would bring the matter to the attention of Ìyálóde. She would go to Ìyálóde's shrine and ask her. Ìyálóde was the òrìṣà of purity. There was hardly a question on the Maker's earth that Ìyálóde could not answer. She was, after all, the First Lady of the Universe.

Ìyálóde knew all there was to know about the land of the living, which is everything under the sun, and beneath the sea, and in the realm of the stars. And she knew all there was to know about the land of the ancestors, where all must go who depart the land of the living, as all mortals must do to reach immortality. And she knew all there was to know about the land of the unborn, the womb of all wombs through which the ancestors, deathless all of them, must navigate their way to the land of the living, where they occasionally must go because even immortals sometimes need a break.

Two

With the dream of the òrìṣà vivid in his mind, Àjàyí sprang up from his mat and headed to his mother's hut.

He stretched out flat on his face and bid Ìyá good morning. He would have gone to his father's workshop and done the same thing, but Bàbá had left home well before cockcrow that morning to tap his palm trees.

As he lay at Ìyá's feet, flat on his chest on the earthen floor, Àjàyí quickly sensed that his mother was in no mood to hear about his dream. Only the week before, he had told her about a dream in which the goddess Ọya had appeared to him with tears streaming down her face. 'I'll make tears stream down your face,' Ìyá had responded, 'if you don't go and fetch water for your father's morning meal.'

He knew he wouldn't fare any better today, but there was no harm in trying. As he opened his mouth to speak, Bọlá, who was running a comb through the dense thicket of Ìyá's shimmering black hair and palming òrí into it, took one look at him through the corner of her eyes and stopped him dead in his tracks.

'Mother,' she said, without once taking her eyes off Ìyá's head, 'your son has had another one of his dreams. I can see it clearly in his eyes' – she said this without even looking at him. 'He looks like a haunted rat. He always looks like a rat when he's had one of those dreams.'

Àjàyí swallowed hard, doing his best not to cast a spiteful look her way.

'If you do that again—' Bólá warned him, even though Şàngó knew, and Ògún knew, and all the òrìşà knew, that he'd done no such thing.

He'd had enough of her for one morning.

'I don't look like a haunted rat,' he muttered as he turned to leave, his eyes clouding with tears.

'Forgive me,' said Bólá. 'You're right. You don't look like a haunted rat.' She waited until he was by the door, before adding, 'But you do bear more than a passing resemblance to the grasscutter Lánre caught in the palm grove last night. Are you by any chance related?'

'Tell her to stop calling me a rat, Mother!'

'How dare you call my bàbá a rat, Bólá' – Ìyá called him her father because Àjàyí was the spitting image of his grandbàbá. 'How dare you. My bàbá is a prince, not a rat.' Her eyes were twinkling with laughter. 'Come here, my father,' she said. 'Don't mind your sister. Blame it on ojú kòkòrò.' Envy, sheer envy. 'I'm all ears. Tell me about your dream. Tell me all about it. Spare no details.'

And so, sitting at her feet, he told his mother about his dream of the healer god who looked sorely in need of healing and about his missing leg and his sawn-off arm and his sightless eye and his deaf ears and his hearing dimple and his many-coloured beads and his speckled herbs and, most of all, about the depthless sadness in the god's lonesome eyes.

Ìyá listened with rapt attention. Bólá did, too, until he mentioned the dimple. The dimple. Did he actually say dimple?

'Did you actually say dimple?' she asked him.

When he mentioned the dimple, Bólá's eyes narrowed down to a

7

squint, the better to contemplate his lips, which were surely not lying.

'We have heard of white men who turned the ocean into a high-way,' she gravely declared. 'But did you just say the òrìṣà could hear with his dimple? Is that what you said?' And now she bent over and began to make a strange sound, the sound of throttled laughter. 'Did your son actually say that,' she asked Ìyá, 'or have I lost my dimples and gone deaf?' And now she held her sides and shook, the tears streaming down her cheeks.

Ìyá patiently waited for her to finish laughing.

'Have you finished laughing?'

'But I'm not laughing, Mother.'

She waited until Bọ́lá had stopped laughing before turning, once again, to Àjàyí. 'You saw Ọsanyìn.'

'Yes, Mother,' Àjàyí replied.

'Ọsanyìn, the gods' own sorcerer.'

'Yes, Mother.'

'Ọsanyìn, the òrìṣà of health and well-being.'

'Yes, Mother.'

'And he looked unwell.'

'He looked as if he had ibà.'

Bọ́lá's eyes widened in disbelief.

'The òrìṣà Ọsanyìn has ibà?'

Ibà, the fever malaria.

'I didn't say he had ibà,' retorted Àjàyí. 'I said he looked like he had ibà.' He addressed this information to Ìyá, even though it was Bọ́lá who had asked him the question.

'Was Ọsanyìn pouring with sweat?' Ìyá asked.

'He was drenched in sweat, Ìyá.'

'That's a dead giveaway. He must have ibà.'

Àjàyí tapped Bọlá on the shoulder.

'Did you hear that? Ìyá thinks I'm right.'

'If you come anywhere near me again,' Bọlá said threateningly, speaking to the hand Àjàyí used to tap her on the shoulder as if the hand was a being separate from and independent of its owner. The hand beat a hasty retreat.

Àjàyí nodded in eager agreement to something their mother had said while his sister was threatening his hand.

'And he looked haggard and unhappy,' she had said.

'Yes, Ìyá,' he replied. 'He looked unhappy.'

Bọlá's sceptical eyes measured him from head to toe.

'Mother,' she pleaded. 'I must ask you at once to stop indulging this child. How could you tell it was the òrìṣà himself?'

'It was him,' Àjàyí insisted, his voice rising.

'You keep saying that,' said Bọlá, 'it's your word against Òsanyìn's dimple,' and that set her off again.

'Don't you mind her, Àjàyí,' Ìyá told him. 'Don't mind her at all. Did the òrìṣà speak to you?'

The blank stare in Àjàyí's eyes was all the answer Bọlá needed.

'Of course the òrìṣà didn't speak to him,' she sniggered. 'They never speak to him. They keep turning up in his dreams. And then they don't say a word. They ignore him.'

Ìyá ignored her.

'Did the Lord of the Leaves speak to you, Àjàyí?'

Àjàyí shook his head. 'No.'

'Not a word?'

'Not a word, Ìyá.'

'But he looked unhappy.'

'He looked unhappy,' Àjàyí said, looking unhappy, and wishing he'd had the presence of mind to ask the òrìṣà why he looked so unhappy.

Bọ́lá, who had a knack for reading his mind with unerring precision, now read his mind.

'It's no use being sad,' she told him. 'Next time you fall asleep and find yourself in the presence of an òrìṣà, open your mouth. Talk to them. They won't bite you. They might even talk to you.'

Àjàyí fixed his eyes on Ìyá and tried to pretend Bọ́lá didn't exist.

He clenched his lips firmly so that all the rich insults he so badly wanted to rain on her dried up in his throat.

Three

Ìyá looked off into the distance, her face clouded with worry. When she finally spoke, all she said was, 'I don't know the meaning of your dream.'

Then she drifted off again.

'See what you've done to Ìyá?' Bọ́lá said to Àjàyí. 'Your dream boggles the mind.'

Àjàyí ignored his sister. He shifted from one foot to another and waited for Ìyá to speak.

Finally, she came to a decision and said what he'd been hoping she would say: 'We shall have to go and ask.'

He knew precisely what that meant, he knew it could only be Ìyálóde, but he still had to ask.

'Who are we going to ask?'

Nudging him in the ribs, Bọ́lá asked, 'Who else would Afàlà, the high priestess of Ìyálóde, seek answers from? Your dimple?'

In all the land, Ìyá, whose name was Afàlà, was renowned as the chief priestess of the òrìṣà Ìyálóde. Devotees seeking favours of the goddess came to her from as far afield as Ilé Ifẹ̀ and Ọ̀yọ́ and Ìjẹ̀ṣà and Ẹ̀gbá and Ìjẹ̀bú and from as far away as Èkó and Badagry and Kétu and even Dahomí further down the coast.

'Go and fetch your morning water,' Ìyá said to Àjàyí. 'We shall pay Ìyálóde a visit when you return.'

The prospect of visiting Ìyálóde's shrine, his favourite deity of all, lit a fire in Àjàyí. A foolish grin settled on his face as he stood watching Bọlá braid Ìyá's hair.

'Shouldn't someone be somewhere fetching something?' Bọlá wondered out loud.

Àjàyí snapped out of his reverie and bounded out of the hut. In the compound he perched a pot on his head and set out for the river. He was almost out of the compound when he suddenly turned around and headed straight back into Ìyá's hut.

'He had a high-pitched voice,' he told her.

Bọlá stared at him.

'That's good to know, Àjàyí,' Bọlá said. 'Who has a high-pitched voice?'

'He means the òrìṣà Ọsanyìn,' Ìyá said. 'Did you mean the òrìṣà Ọsanyìn?'

Àjàyí nodded. Bọlá stared at him, arms akimbo.

'I thought you said he didn't speak to you.'

'He didn't,' Àjàyí replied. 'But I heard him cry.'

Bọlá and Ìyá exchanged looks.

'You heard Ọsanyìn cry,' Ìyá said, slowly. Àjàyí nodded.

'What else did he say to you?' Bọlá asked.

'He didn't say anything.'

'He just cried.'

'He simply sat there, hunched over, and cried.'

'Twice this month,' Ìyá said, thoughtfully, 'I put a question to Ìyálóde. And twice she has refused to answer my question. But now I realise I may have misread her response. She hasn't refused to answer my question. I mistook silent despair for mere silence. My father,' she said to Àjàyí, 'the god Ọsanyìn has revealed himself to you for a reason. You know that. He is your guardian òrìṣà. Are the òrìṣà aggrieved? Perhaps they are. What I don't understand is why anyone would be crying. Bọlá, go at once to Ìyá Ọkẹ's house. Tell her I need something for Ìyálóde.'

Àjàyí knew what that something for Ìyálóde was: 'Kola nuts,' he informed Bọlá.

'And what makes you think I didn't know that?' Bọlá asked him. 'I'll be back in no time,' she said to her mother. 'Àjàyí?'

'What?'

'The answer to your question is no.'

'I didn't ask you anything.'

'No, you can't come with me to Ìyá Ọkẹ,' she said, heading out.

'Who said I was going to ask if I could come? Who wants to go anywhere with you? I don't.'

'Good. Just as well. Because you can't.'

He paused for a moment, before yelling, 'Wait for me!' and ran after her.

Four

At the kola-nut seller's house, Bọlá and Ìyá Ọkẹ immediately settled down to spirited banter. Not once did Bọlá bring up the errand
from her mother. She hadn't forgotten, but it was the last thing on
her mind. Among her people banter was considered serious business. Every child knew, from mother's milk, that what comes after
six is more than seven; that a judicious whisper speaks louder than
ten big drums. Outsiders often would key into an exuberant
exchange, unaware that it was less than half the story, that the
meaning of the exchange was complete only when taken together
with the other, entirely unspoken, conversation going on beneath
the fireworks.

The tonal peculiarity of the language was another minefield: the
same word could mean utter chaos, for instance, or it could mean the
exact opposite, complete tranquillity. It was all in the tone; whether
you said ayéró, or whether you said ayéro. For outsiders, it could be
a maze of maddening contradictions. But to the Yorùbá mind, it was
contradictory only to the extent that the zeroes and ones written on
Ọpọ́n Ifá – the divination tray – could be said to contradict one
another. Like good and evil, they were pairs of opposites, but the
one binary digit did not negate the other; together they signified the
fullness of life in all its ugly-beauty.

After a suitably drawn-out exchange of these pleasantries, and having set the world to rights, Bọlá rose and announced that now she knew all was well with Ìyá Ọkẹ and her household, she would go back home and relay the great tidings to her mother. Only now, as she was leaving, did the real reason for her visit come up. Even so, it wasn't Bọlá who brought up the matter.

'You cannot come all this way,' Ìyá Ọkẹ declared, 'and leave without taking something back to your mother from me for Ìyálóde.'

She picked up a calabash of the most exquisite white kola nuts Àjàyí had ever set eyes on and pushed it into Bọlá's hands.

They took leave of her and headed back home.

Along their path were fallen trees, strewn everywhere, unmistakable evidence of the wrath of Ṣàngó, the god of thunder. Damaged houses were being repaired. Whole compounds swept away were being rebuilt.

They were halfway home when, suddenly, Bọlá stopped.

'You,' she said. 'Why are you following me?'

Àjàyí turned to see who might be following them.

'There's nobody following us,' he told her.

'There may be nobody following you,' she replied. 'I know that someone is following me. Why are you following me, Àjàyí?'

Àjàyí visibly blanched; he was speechless.

'I'm talking to you, Àjàyí. Why are you following me?'

'Following you?' His scrawny chest, of its own accord, puffed out. 'Who is following you? I'm not following you.'

'I'm relieved to hear that,' Bọlá said, all sweetness now.

Àjàyí eyed her suspiciously. He was right not to fall for it: 'I'm going home, which is this way,' she patiently explained. 'You're going to the river, which is the other way.'

She let that sink in.

'O,' he said. 'O,' he repeated; as if, finally, he understood the truly diabolical nature of her treachery. He knew it would be futile to yell, so he said, in the quietest tone he could muster under the circumstances, 'Why can't I go home?'

'Stop yelling,' she advised him.

'I'm not yelling,' he yelled.

'Yes, you are.'

He lowered his voice. 'Why can't I go home?' His voice had gone from a yell to a murmur.

Bọlá cupped her ear and leaned towards him.

'I didn't hear that,' she said. 'What did you say?'

'I said . . .' he began. Then he stopped and cried, 'What about the shrine?'

'Indeed,' she said. 'What about the shrine?'

'Ìyá said she wanted me at the shrine.'

'Ìyá said no such thing.'

'She did! You know she did!'

'She did not.'

'She did,' he yelled. 'You were there when she said so.'

'I was there when she told you to go and fetch water,' Bọlá said. 'Go and fetch water.'

She grabbed him by the ear and spun him in the right direction. She headed home, leaving him standing, with the pot perched on his head, a look of utter disbelief on his face.

She'd barely walked more than a few steps when she stopped.

'What's that sound?'

'What sound?' he asked suspiciously, trying to divine what new treachery she had in store for him.

'Listen.'

Àjàyí pretended to listen.

'Nothing.'

'That's because you're not listening. Listen. It's coming from Ìsẹ́yìn.'

Àjàyí knew that whatever it was she'd heard, it couldn't possibly be coming from Ìsẹ́yìn.

Bọ́lá rolled her eyes. 'The gate, not the town.'

The gate was called Ìsẹ́yìn because it was the gate where tolls were collected from traders coming from Ìsẹ́yìn. Each of the six gates was named after the town it led to.

Àjàyí listened. All he could hear was a bawdy exchange between two talking drums coming from the market, near the king's palace. One talking drum spoke in the aggrieved voice of a husband who was searching for his missing wife. The other talking drum responded in the voice of an exasperated merchant:

We know your wife tonight has died.
You have our sincere sympathy.

We also know the tale of the wife
who died at night in her husband's house
only to be spotted the following morning
stirring awake in her lover's arms.

But must you go around the market
with a lamp in your hand
in search of a dead person?
Must you come here looking for your late wife?

If you want to buy okra, buy okra.
If you want to look for the dead,
go and look for the dead.

But you must know that
this is a marketplace, not a graveyard.

Àjàyí smirked. 'That's not it,' Bọ́lá said, frostily. 'Listen carefully.' He listened. And this time, he heard it; it was a quiet rumbling that seemed to be coming from the bowels of the earth.

'I hear voices. Many voices.' He knew at once what it was, and his heart sank. 'It can't be the Malians, can it?'

'It can only be the Malians,' Bọ́lá said calmly.

Several times a year, the itinerant bands of slave-raiding warriors known as the Malians would float like a cloud of locusts through Òṣogùn on their mayhem-spreading, terror-causing expeditions to the hinterland. Days later, they would show up again, travelling the other way, marching back with their wailing bounty of captives in tow, with mothers shackled to daughters, fathers to their sons, foe to friend, neighbour to neighbour.

Àjàyí felt a knot forming in his belly.

'I wonder why they're here,' he said.

'They pass this way every time they're on their way to the interior.' Bọ́lá shrugged. 'It's the quickest route.' She saw the worried look on his face. 'Don't worry. They always pass this way, but they never bother us.'

This was true enough. But the reason the Malians never bothered Òṣogùn was because they were biding their time and even though no one said so, it was always at the back of everybody's mind. Òṣogùn was one of the richer pickings in this neck of the imploding empire known as Ọ̀yọ́, a vast realm that had held sway for almost a thousand years, and was now riven by civil war, a sputtering cinder that had erupted into a firestorm that would engulf the empire and devour it, body and soul.

The fire was still burning, the remains of the empire still in flames, seventy years later when British gunboats arrived and claimed the empire and its territories for their possession.

Long before the British arrived, and the French soon after, and all the other colonial powers, the first foreign invaders of the empire were jihadi armies from the north country. The Malians, as they came to be known, arrived at the very outset of the civil war and saw in the ensuing power vacuum and the breakdown in law and order an ideal opportunity to run rife through the empire, picking up towns and villages piecemeal, and flooding the seaside slave markets of Europe and the New World and the desert-valley riverside souks of Arabia with its sons and daughters.

'How come the Malians never bother us?' Àjàyí asked.

'Bother us?' said Bọ́lá in astonishment, the thought seemed inconceivable. 'Do you know how many òrìṣà we've got watching over us, not just at night but the livelong day? Why would they even contemplate such a thing? They know it would be suicidal of them. Ṣàngó would flail them alive. Ṣọ̀pọ̀ná would riddle their bodies with oozing pores. Èṣù would turn their day into night. Yemọja would drown them in their mother's milk. Ògún would strangle them with his bare hands. Ọbàtálá would kill them. And his only weapon would be kindness. Bother us? They wouldn't dare, those demon seeds of hyenas.'

Àjàyí had never seen his sister so angry.

'Many of them were born on this very soil,' she told him. 'Before they learnt to chant the verses of Mòhámọ́dù, they knew Ifá.'

It was true that the Malians were in fact not at all Malian. Some were Filani, from the land of the Awúsá in the north country. Others were Awúsá or Gàmbàrí, from Ìlọrin. Many more of the Ìmàle – known in the Ọ̀yọ́ dialect as Yorùbá – were native-born sons of the empire. Few if any of them hailed from the desert kingdom known as the Mali Empire. Sons of the soil who took up the new faith were called Malians because the faith they now espoused when they turned their backs on the gods of their ancestors was brought to the empire from Mansa Musa's Mali. And because Ọ̀yọ́ Muslims were called Malians, all Muslims were known as Malians no matter where they hailed from; to call a swordsman a Malian was merely to call him a Muslim. It was neither a pejorative nor was it said in mockery. An Ọ̀yọ́ man did not cease to be from Ọ̀yọ́ when he learnt the ayahs and surahs by rote and proclaimed himself a Malian. All it meant was that he prayed, five times a day, to a faraway desert deity, in a language he neither spoke nor understood, and that he now considered his people infidels and their deities idols.

The Malians were holy warriors, but their holy war was entirely a commercial enterprise: in the name of the one and only true òrìṣà, they abducted human beings and sold them; in the name of the one and only benevolent òrìṣà, they spread terror through the land.

The most feared of the Malians were not the Filani or Awúsá or Gàmbàrí strangers. The most feared of them were the ones who were born in Ọ̀yọ́; those who once were steeped in the vast oral literary corpus of Ifá; those who had learnt the verses of Ifá by heart and could recite all 256 verses of it, a total of 204,800 narrative hymns since each verse was a repository of 800 hymns.

In addition to the incantations associated with the divination system of Ifá, there was a separate canon of incantations dedicated to each of the òrìṣà. These hymnal recitations were prodigious in length. The chants of Ògún alone, the god of iron, could easily fill a book twice the size of the Holy Book of the Malians. So, too, would the verses of Ọ̀ṣun, the goddess of divination, and the poetry of

Ọbàtálá, Lord of the Earth, not to mention all the other deities, over four hundred in all.

There were some among the Ọ̀yọ́-born Malians who had grown up steeped in this ancient body of knowledge. And they, of all the Malians, were the most feared. It was said that their penchant for mindless cruelty stemmed from a deep vein of self-hatred. They knew, deep down, that their hearts and the hearts of the people they now called kèfèrí, heathens, were one and the same. They could scrub their bodies of all residue of heathen impiety five times a day but no soap existed yet that could wash a man's heart of his being. And so, they struck terror and visited misery on anyone who reminded them of themselves.

'There's nothing to fear from them,' Bọ́lá blithely assured her younger brother as the murmuring of Malian voices rose and fell from beyond the city walls. 'If you hurry up, you may be able to make it back home on time. Mother will wait for you. She always does. Sometimes I have a feeling you are her favourite child. Do you know why? It's because she says so all the time. Not that I mind. You are my favourite brother, after all.'

'I am your only brother,' Àjàyí pointed out.

'The problem with you, Àjàyí, is that you don't know how to take a joke.'

'The problem with you,' he retorted, 'is that it's difficult to know when you're being serious.'

Bọ́lá held her sides and rolled with laughter.

Then the earth rumbled again. They stared at each other. Now the Malians sounded like a swarm of bees.

'Hurry up, Àjàyí,' Bọ́lá said. The laughter was gone. A look fleeted across her face that was suspiciously close to fear. Àjàyí would never know. Long years would pass before he saw her again.

Five

One afternoon, a week before the Malians came, in the drummers' courtyard of the king's palace, a stone's throw from Àjàyí's household, the aludùndún beat out a rich, full-toned telegraph on his talking drum. It was the aludùndún's office as the king's talking-drummer to alert the palace to the presence of visitors. He did so using the talking drum as both his voice and its amplification, so that His Majesty the King, wherever he was, could tell who had entered the courtyard before the dignitary was formally announced.

The visitors, a young war chief and his second-in-command, were shown into the morning courtyard, where the king's guests were brought to his presence.

Fámórótì was but a child when he last stepped on Òṣogùn soil, the soil of his birth. When his father, the king's war chief – the akọgun – had been summoned to Ọ̀yọ́ by the king of kings, the Aláàfin, to lead troops of the imperial army to battle against the invading army of Ìlọrin, it was understood that the akọgun would be back in Òṣogùn as soon as the war ended. That was many years ago. The akọgun's formidable leadership skills on the battlefield had proved indispensable and the Aláàfin kept him in Ọ̀yọ́.

The Aláàfin's decision to keep Òṣogùn's topmost chief of war was met with joy and pride in Òṣogùn; it meant that in the scheme of things Òṣogùn counted, even if it was but a hamlet when compared to those of its neighbours whose chiefs of war had been allowed to return home. Take the Ìjèbú, whose mighty kingdom sat between Òṣogùn and the ocean. The Ìjèbú capital city was a sight to behold. It stretched as far as the eye could see, protected by a rampart eighty miles long and a thousand years old. The Ìjèbú were known for their facility to turn a profit where others would lose the gown off their back. And they were not to be taken for granted on the battlefield either. And yet while their chief of war had been let go by Ọ̀yọ́, tiny Òṣogùn had been told that her war chief was vital to the well-being of the empire.

Now, years later, Fámorótì, the famed war chief's only son, now himself an akọgun, was back in the land of his fathers. Fámorótì's journey home was to inform the king that his old army chief had lately fallen on the battlefield.

The akọgun's dying words were a message to his old friend and master: go home and tell my king they're coming back, he whispered to his son, tell my king they're coming back.

Memories came flooding back to Fámorótì as he stepped on to the palace grounds. It was right here in the morning courtyard those many years ago that he had watched two emissaries of a faraway sovereign present themselves to the king.

The emissaries, he remembered, were turned out in turbans and other accoutrements of the desert-farer. One of them, a tall, austere-looking man who called himself Ibn Sàídì, carefully and fastidiously unfolded a scroll of parchment filled with Arabic script, a letter from their monarch. As he read it out to the court, his companion, Ibn Àyúbà, translated in fluent but heavily accented Yorùbá.

'To sum up,' Ibn Sàídì declared as he came to the end of the letter. His carriage was haughty, his lips curled into a permanent sneer; he barely glanced at the scroll in his hand. 'If you respond to the oath of allegiance and to its conditions – namely, that you expel into the wild all those of our enemies who come to your land, and that you allow free passage to all the people of the kingdoms which lie beyond you who have come to enter into obedience to us – which is an obligatory duty for both them and you, then you and your subjects and your lands are safe and secure, protected by our mercy which shall guard you from all sides so that you shall not experience from our exalted abode anything which shall harm you or alarm you to the end of time, if it be the will of God; you shall be safe and secure, and you shall have support from our divinely victorious armies over your enemies. But –' he had been reciting intensely and fiercely but quietly; he was now doing so with a venom that cut through the bone '– if you refuse to respond and your bad judgement causes you to deviate from the path of success, then receive the glad tidings of our conquering armies aided by God and our extensive military forces made victorious by God, which shall pour over your land – if God wills – like torrential floodwater or the raging sea. You will think it a downpour flowing with ignominy and destruction, until by God's might, they shall reduce your land to a barren wilderness and bring you to the same plight as the erstwhile monarch of your neigh-bours, the Kitipa, whom they made to taste death and whom together with his kingdom they swallowed up, since he had disobeyed our exalted command. We have given you fair warning and notice, so choose yourself and pursue the path which your better judgement commends.' As he came to the end of the letter, he executed a perfect bow in the direction of the draped door of the king's antechamber, adding, with a flourish, one last word: 'Peace.'

Fámorótì remembered the charged silence that ensued as carefully and fastidiously Ibn Sàídì folded the scroll, tugging absent-mindedly at his sword and betraying for the first time his tension.

'Your Highness,' said Ibn Àyúbà, 'that is the message to you from our Lord and Master, His Exalted Eminence, Messenger of the Prophet, Defender of the Faithful, Master of Masters, Conquering Sovereign over sundry dominions, of whom it is said "the sandstorm is the answer to the man wearing a raincoat", because he descends upon his enemies with the blinding ferocity of a desert storm. He requires an immediate response.' He bowed deeply and said, 'He sends felicitations.'

Many years later the blistering silence that followed Ibn Àyúbà's speech still brought shudders to Fámórótì's body whenever he thought about it. His father, who was positioned nearest to the ante-chamber, leaned forward and listened to instructions from the king. The instructions were brief. The akọgun bowed and nodded; he turned to the visiting emissaries.

'Kábíyèsí, long may he reign, wishes to confer with you, Ibn Àyúbà,' he informed the visitors, pausing before adding: 'In camera.'

In the court that morning were ministers, guards, priests, enter-tainers and other courtiers, all watching, quietly, as the turbaned emissary walked into the antechamber, closely followed by the akọgun and two young warriors, one of whom was Fámórótì, to confer with His Majesty.

It was a remarkably brief conference.

'Kábíyèsí had a most lively palaver with Ibn Àyúbà,' the akọgun announced to Ibn Sàídì on reappearing sometime later. 'They talked about many things: the price of salt, the constellations, the Kingdom of Portugal in Rio de Janeiro. Ibn Àyúbà entertained Kábíyèsí with a joke whose punchline escapes us. Something about a Portuguese tailor. Or perhaps he said sailor. Let me assure you, though: Kábíyèsí was entertained.'

Ibn Sàìdì hadn't heard a single word.

'Ibn Àyúbà,' Ibn Sàìdì said. 'Where is Ibn Àyúbà?'

'Your brother-emissary,' the akọgun told him, 'desired a shave.'

'A shave?' Ibn Sàìdì swallowed hard, his throat suddenly gone dry.

'Yes, a shave,' said the akọgun. 'Fortunately for him, the royal barber was at hand. He stropped his razor, flicked it this way,' he demonstrated, 'and that way; just like his father and his father before him. And right before our very eyes, Ibn Àyúbà's beard was gone.'

The akọgun snapped his fingers and the young warriors appeared, carrying in their hands an object that made the court gasp.

The akọgun eyed the grisly, blood-soaked object and shook his head regretfully.

'So, unfortunately,' he told Ibn Sàìdì, 'was his head.'

The emissary clenched his fist to his mouth and emitted a quiet scream.

'And as you can see,' the akọgun continued, 'the beard is unlikely to grow back. Your master required an immediate response to his petition. Kábíyèsí is a courteous man.'

'Long may His Majesty reign,' chorused the court.

'Kábíyèsí loathes to keep people waiting,' said the akọgun. 'He wants you to take this head back to your master without delay. He begs you to pass on the following message: we know that the gods, in their great wisdom or for amusement, give nuts to those who have no teeth. But a joke is a joke. Should ever again your master take leave of his senses, should he ever slur our land with such discourtesy again, we shall walk all the way to his palace – pardon me, I meant to say *cave* – pausing only to pluck partridges from the sky. Kábíyèsí, you see, has a fondness for partridges.'

'He likes to kill them,' volunteered the palace treasurer.

'He likes to kill them,' the akọgun solemnly agreed. 'We shall retrieve your master from his cave – pardon me, I meant to say *palace* – drag him out on to the pestilential wilderness of his sand-strewn kingdom, and shave his beard for him. Ibn Àyúbà's clean-shaven chin will testify to the sureness of our touch. That is my king's message to your master, Ibn Sàídì. Saddle your horse, take some water – it's clean water. It was fetched this morning from the king's newest well. Do not look back.'

'It's bad luck to look back,' Fámorótì counselled him.

'Fámorótì fetched the water, Ibn Sàídì.' The akọgun noted, 'You could do also with a wash. But, as the traveller, dying of thirst, said to the soap seller he encountered in the desert: "If I cannot wash my inside, how can I wash my outside?"'

'It tastes of salt,' Fámorótì informed his father.

'The water tastes of salt,' the akọgun informed the emissary. 'Which is just as well. But do not drink it. Our people say that truth in discourse is like a dish that is spiced with salt. Go, Ibn Sàídì, and as you go, dwell on this truth which it pleases Kábíyèsí to share with you: this earth is great, and so is our kingdom.'

The akọgun would later tell his son that he thought the king's decision to have Ibn Àyúbà beheaded a reckless move, even if the kingdom's army was at the time second to no other in the land. In any case, Ibn Sàídì's monarch did not send the threatened army of invasion: in his thirst to conquer, the desert king overreached himself and came to grief in the rainforest.

Now, so many years later, Fámorótì, who had left Òṣogùn a boy, had returned a much-honoured man of war with a message from his dying father.

The message was this: the Malians are coming. There will be war.

Six

Fámorótì and Fúyẹ̀ were shown into the morning courtyard just before the afternoon meal. They were still there, with no sign of His Majesty the King, as the men of Ọ̀ṣogùn returned from their farms and children gathered firewood for their mothers for the evening meal.

The visitors were the very model of good breeding. They politely insisted on remaining on their feet when seats were offered to them. They did not decline it when a servant brought them a gourd of water, but the gourd remained untouched. When the servant, who had known Fámorótì when the young warrior was but a child, finally realised they had no intention of quenching their thirst, the old man rebuked them by permitting himself a faint smile and a shake of the head. He meant no offence, and none was taken by Fámorótì. The only indication that Fúyẹ̀ might have considered it an impertinence to his master was the agreeable smile that seemed suddenly to sneak up on his face; it was totally at odds with the cold glint in his eyes.

Fúyẹ̀'s name was Ọ̀tọ̀lórìn, but everyone called him Fúyẹ̀ because he was nimble on his feet and light as a feather. He was a powerfully built man with a long torso; on the battlefield his body had been known to become an elusive projectile whose dazzling speed made the whistling arrows of skilled marksmen seem leisurely and poorly aimed. Fúyẹ̀ had been Fámorótì's bodyguard since the tenth year of

their age and he took his office quite seriously; too seriously sometimes, it had been noted by some.

But he knew when to respond to a slight on his master and when
to let matters rest. This afternoon, he let matters rest; the warning
smile on his face vanished as soon as it appeared, and he continued
to wait for the king with his master.

At one point, Fámórótì felt they were being observed; raising his
eyes, he found one of the king's chief advisers, a burly, thick-waisted
man, staring at him with the speculative look of a hawk contemplat-
ing a fowl. This rattled him and he did something he had vowed not
to do as a dawn visit turned into a day-long vigil: he almost lost his
temper.

'Does Kábíyèsí know I'm here?' he asked the man, a shade more
abrupt than he had intended.

'He knows,' replied Olóyè Alábòsí Múgùwọlé, who was better
known, for reasons lost in the mists of time, as Òròmbó, which
means 'the Orange'.

Òròmbó was calm, suave, and unflappable.

'Will he be long in coming?' Fámórótì asked; it was almost a
rebuke rather than a question.

Fámórótì thought he heard a quiet chorus of short, half-
suppressed laughter coming from behind Òròmbó. The courtier
seemed as startled as the warrior by the tittering and he turned to see
who the culprit was.

Òròmbó had no neck; his neck had expanded, rather like the perquisites of office, and assumed the size of his ample shoulders, so that
it was no longer possible to tell where his shoulders ended and where
his neck began, and yet when he flicked his head, it moved with
the impersonal ferocity of a butcher's knife. The laughter behind
him died.

It had been coming from Òrombó's retinue of praise-singers: a chronicler and a poet laureate.

The chronicler's duty was to eulogise his master's ancestry. Since it was a well-known fact that Òrombó came from a long line of simpering, back-stabbing double-dealers, the chronicler kept his place by scrupulously avoiding the facts of his master's ancestry, which were all unsavoury, and making it up as he went along.

The laureate's role was to eulogise his master's accomplishments. Since Òrombó's greatest accomplishment was to worm his way to the top with a mouth as keenly sharpened as the dagger he always carried on his person, and he didn't care who knew about the dagger, the laureate's task was considerably easier than the chronicler's.

The chronicler and the laureate now stood with their heads bowed and quietly traded insults over who had been the first to laugh when the warrior spoke.

'If I hear another sound from you,' Òrombó told them, 'if I so much as catch you thinking of a pin dropping, and I imagine that I hear pím –' the smallest unit of sound in the universe '– your head and the pin will drop together.'

Òrombó's threat concentrated their minds and peace immediately broke out between the two men.

Fámórótì repeated his question to their master.

'Will Kábíyèsí be long in coming?' There was no hint of anger in his voice this time.

'Kábíyèsí,' announced Òrombó, 'will take as long as it takes for him to come.'

'We could come back later,' Fámórótì said, with a sidelong glance at Fúyẹ́. 'It's been a long journey and we haven't had a wash.'

'I share your interest in personal hygiene,' Òrombó declared. 'Have you tried Portuguese soap?'

'Olóyè Òrombó,' said Fúyẹ́, 'I don't believe Akọgun Fámorótì is acquainted with the white man's soap. His favourite soap is, I believe, Ọṣẹ dúdú.'

Òrombó's ears rang with astonishment. He stopped dead. It was as if he had gone to the market, minding his own business, and before he knew what calamity had befallen him an ape had approached and bid him good morning.

Clearly in shock, he addressed the ape without looking at it. 'I'm speaking to your master,' he said mysteriously, his voice humbled and pained, his eyes pleading to the world for understanding. He lifted his well-bred shoulders and indicated his praise-singers, with the dazzling polished rocks on his fingers. 'You'll notice,' he said to the ape, 'how quiet my minions are. They speak only when spoken to.' The praise-singers, who had resumed their squabbling, now took the cue from their master and froze in mid-word, so that their lips hung wide open, but nothing came out of their mouths. They were not clowning. It was an act of self-preservation.

Òrombó emitted a grave sigh, relieved he didn't have to kill anyone to make his point, and, swiftly moving on, turned his back on the impertinent ape and addressed its master. 'The white man's soap has a most agreeable fragrance,' he trilled, regaining his equilibrium, 'I don't much care for it myself. Too sweet. But my wives swear by it. Don't get me wrong, they haven't given up on the delights of our local soap. But when the occasion calls for something special, something befitting their standing in society, they will settle for nothing less than the sweet scents of Rio.'

Out in the drummers' courtyard, the aludùndún's bàtá drum flared up, waxing lyrical about the exalted lineage of a new presence on the palace grounds. The pre-announcement had a remarkable effect on the frozen praise-singers: it defrosted them instantly, and they cast nervous glances first at their master, then at the entrance to the morning courtyard, then back to their master. Òrombó stopped to listen. A dark cloud settled on his face.

'I must tell you about the sweet scents of Rio,' he told Fámorótì. 'But that will have to wait another day. In the meantime, there's nothing I can do about the delay, I'm afraid.' The sparkle was gone from his voice and his eyes were set on the entrance to the courtyard. 'Let it suffice to say, it is unavoidable. Kábíyèsí is attending to eminently pressing affairs of the state.'

He had barely finished speaking when Aya'ba Oyátómi swept in with her entourage. 'Affairs of the state?' she said, her voice shot through with incredulity. 'Did you say affairs of the state?'

Aya'ba Oyátómi was a woman of slight build. She looked even smaller standing next to Òrombó whose extraordinary corpulence had been immortalised by a versifier as being nothing short of a discernible manifestation of the miracle of good living, an epithet which would outlive both Òrombó and the prolific lickspittle who coined it. Well over a century later, in a land called Nigeria, this panegyric to portly abundance would for a while become a mantra, a sacred affirmation of wanton greed and conspicuous squander: a man in public office who didn't carry a great stomach before him was said to be devoid of evidence of good living and considered by some to be accursed.

Denizens of that land of the future would have taken one look at the small and thin Aya'ba Oyátómi and had her down as a Nigerian princess, meaning she was no princess at all but a swindler impersonating one. She would be considered not only a failure but a crook.

Seven

Aya'ba Ọyátómi was neither a failure nor was she a crook but her smallness was certainly misleading; packed within that small frame were infinitely dense, closely packed nerves of steel. It was no accident that she was the wealthiest trader in town and one of the most powerful people in the land. She looked harmless and unremarkable, but the graves of Òṣogùn were full of fools who had underestimated her. Òrombó was no fool and, although he would sooner die than admit it, he feared her. He feared and detested her.

'What Olóyè Òrombó means,' Aya'ba Ọyátómi informed the visiting warriors, 'is that Kábíyèsí, our dear king, is keeping his august visitors waiting while he attempts to insert his royal privilege into the comely virtues of a young maiden. Much ado, dare I say, over nothing. Were the king's penis a warrior – he wishes it were – it would have been beheaded long ago for persistent dereliction of duty.'

'Let me introduce you to Aya'ba Ọyátómi,' responded Òrombó with a glassy-eyed smile. 'Aya'ba Ọyátómi is a discarded mistress of His Majesty. I know she doesn't mind my saying so. She herself never misses an opportunity to bring it up in conversation. I don't blame her; it is the only remarkable thing she's ever done, her greatest achievement, to wit: she spread her legs for His Majesty, and he ejaculated between them.'

'It is well known in the seraglio,' Aya'ba Ọyátómi acidly replied, 'that, though the king never sleeps, his penis is forever nodding off.'

'Two of my own wives have had the rare privilege of supping with Kábíyèsí,' Òrombó declared. 'And upon their word – they have no reason to lie.'

'They lie,' Aya'ba Ọyátómi cut in, 'with every bondservant in the land.'

'Upon their word,' Òrombó smoothly continued, 'the royal manhood is as long as the sacred python.'

'Your wives may have lain with a snake, Olóyè Òrombó,' Aya'ba Ọyátómi observed, 'but not with the one between the king's legs. It is a worm bereft of limb flattered into thinking itself a reptile.'

'How dare you, Aya'ba Ọyátómi. How dare you.'

'I did tell your second wife, Kẹ́mi,' she continued, 'when she said she was marrying you, that you had not done badly with her, for she is radiant and so is her smile. You bedecked her with gold and bales of cloth. But I could see, from looking at you, that you could not satisfy her. What she needed, I told her, was a man who once he mounted her would not let off until the roof fell through. Not a glorified procurer who farms out his wives and daughters to curry royal favour.'

'It's called loyalty, Aya'ba Ọyátómi,' Òrombó shot back, 'which comes from good breeding. Have you heard of good breeding? Ah, there I go again. Forgive me. Just like me to forget you were bred in a bordello.' He swung, furiously, on his praise-singers. 'Don't just stand there, you good-for-nothing scroungers!'

They glanced uneasily at Aya'ba Ọyátómi.

'It is as your wives say, Olóyè Òrombó,' said the laureate, 'the royal python is long indeed.'

'We haven't had a chance to size it up.'

'But it's either very long.'

'Or it is as long as it is.'

Òrombó glared stonily at them.

'Long may His Majesty reign,' said the laureate, now addressing himself to the astounded visitors. 'His Majesty fathered a child in Ọyọ while emptying his testicles in Ìsẹ̀yìn.'

'When once Kábíyèsí took the royal snake for a constitutional in the marketplace,' said the chronicler, 'the royal thing sought the welcoming thighs of a barren woman.'

'The king entered deeply,' the laureate reported.

'Deeply,' the chronicler repeated.

'He moved this way.'

'And that way.'

'And then straight on.'

'Like a fearless hunter running.'

'Slowing down.'

'And then off like a duiker.'

'He entered deeply.'

'Deeply.'

'He touched the base of his cock. Was it asleep?'

'Was it fatigued?'

'He found that his cock, the fearless warrior, was not fatigued.'

'It was thrusting.'

'Thrusting.'

'Except for his testicles.'

'Except for his testicles, which were emptying.'

'Emptying.'

'You see?' Òrombó yelled at Aya'ba Ọyátómi. 'You see?'

'Kábíyèsí shivered and screamed,' said the laureate.

'The barren woman shivered and screamed,' said the chronicler.

'The woman shivered and screamed.'

'She birthed twins nine months later.'

'You see?' yelled Òrombó. 'You see?'

'She birthed twins nine months later,' said the chronicler, 'yet the royal thing still hung rigid, dripping thick, sticky tears.'

'Was it from joy?'

'Was it from pain?'

'When we asked it why it cried so, the king's cock said, "Crying? Crying? Who said I was crying? This is how we laugh, where I come from."'

'You see?' yelled Òrombó. 'You see?'

'I did not come here to listen to the idle prattle of a court jester and his minions,' said Aya'ba Oyátómi. 'As for the king – if you want my opinion – the problem with Kábíyèsí is in his penis. More's the pity, since he has no penis.'

'I'm warning you, Aya'ba Oyátómi!' Òrombó fumed. 'I'm warning you!'

'Run along now,' she advised him. 'I came here to see these strapping warriors for myself. We bid you welcome, great warriors. Your reputation precedes you like the crackling roar of a bush fire. And you, Akogun Fámorótì, you may remember a brave warrior named Àjàlá.'

Àjàlá had been to Fámorótì's father what Fúyẹ was to Fámorótì: his second-in-command, his right-hand man, his best friend.

'How could I forget our elder Àjàlá?' Fámorótì answered. 'Àjàlá was like a father to me. I was there on the battlefield with him when he gave his life to save my father's.'

'We did hear that you were with him when he breathed his last,' Aya'ba Oyátómi said. 'That is why I am here to see you. If you would care to honour my compound with your presence tonight, his daughter Oyíndàmọ́lá will be there waiting to thank you in person.' Then, eyeing Fúyẹ with a mischievous glint in her eye, she added, 'There's no reason why your gallant friend shouldn't come along. The more the merrier. I shall now take my leave of you. I will send someone to come and fetch you once Kábíyèsí has received you.'

'I dare not take offence, Aya'ba Ọyátómi, even if you take me for a stranger to these shores,' Fámorótì told her. 'But there is no need for you to send anyone to come and fetch me. I was born here. I know where you live.'

'Of course you do,' she said, 'of course you do! Pardon me. We shall be expecting you.'

'Mark my word, that woman is evil, evil!' Òrombó declared as soon as Aya'ba Ọyátómi was safely out of earshot.

Aya'ba Ọyátómi never failed to unnerve Òrombó; she seemed to have cut him to the quick this time. It was no doubt because she'd mocked him in the presence of strangers. 'Spouting such monstrous slander about our king,' he roared. 'It's nothing less than treason. Let me assure you that the royal penis is in rude health. I have it on good authority from no fewer than threescore and ten of our most comely maidens.' He paused, grimly, then he muttered to himself, 'I'll have that witch hanged someday.' He meant it.

'Even if it kills me.'

He meant every word of it.

Eight

As he made his way to the river that morning a week later, Àjàyí felt a tide of anxiety welling inside him, a feeling that something terrible was about to happen.

He did not linger at the river. He filled his pot and left immediately. On his way home, pulled irresistibly by the pulsing cadence of drums, the same drums he and Bólá had earlier heard, he allowed his ears to lead him up the path that cut through the market where the drummers, a blind couple called Gbèdurèmí and Àyángbèmí, had set up shop. He found a big crowd, spellbound and in stitches, gathered around the minstrels, the best-known amúludùn in all the lands of the empire.

Gbèdurèmí and Àyángbèmí were their praise names, not their given names. Nobody in Òsogùn could quite remember their given names. No one knew where they hailed from or how long they'd been walking the land. All that could be said for certain was that many in the audience were not yet born the first time Gbèdurèmí and Àyángbèmí played in Òsogùn. Àjàyí had never seen them perform. It was the second year of his age the last time they came to Òsogùn and that was a decade ago. It was said of the couple that there was no town in the land they hadn't set foot in, no hamlet in the empire they had yet to perform in. Gbèdurèmí was gifted with a voice that was said to be coated in honey and Àyángbèmí was known for his nimble footwork, but together their fame rested squarely on their bàtá drums.

Whether speaking as themselves, which they would deign to do only when playfully hectoring the audience not to be stingy with their gifts, or whether speaking as the characters in the earthy tales they often enacted, Gbèdurèmí and Àyángbèmí seldom spoke. They had no need to. Their drums did all the talking for them.

It was possible for them to use their drums in place of their mouths because Yorùbá was a tonal language; what they did with their talking drums was to perfectly mimic the tone and rhythm of everyday speech. There was no conversation too complex, no thought too difficult, to express with a talking drum. The human voice was beautiful beyond compare but it couldn't carry over long distances. This was why talking drums were invented, in days now so distant we may as well be talking about the first single-cell organisms who left the depths of the ocean and swam to the sun. They were invented in the court of Ṣàngó, the belligerent king who in death was deified and worshipped as the fearsome òrìṣà of thunder. In his always reckless and unfailingly irascible days as a mortal, before he hanged himself and was promptly deified by his equally irascible followers in a belligerent renunciation of his death by suicide, Ṣàngó was known to use the talking drum to summon thunderbolts to strike down his enemies. And for centuries after the god-king, the talking drum remained the privilege of princes and divinities. Gbèdurèmí and Àyángbèmí were not the first artists to take it out of the company of monarchs and the fraternity of priests and bring it to the commonwealth of the marketplace, nor were they the first minstrels to fully exploit its tailor-made potential for minting and unleashing the profane, but among the most renowned in their time they were first among equals.

'I came to your house. I met no one,' raged Àyángbèmí's drum. It spoke in the wounded voice of a man speaking to his mistress. The crowd hummed in anticipation. It was a tale they had heard many times, but it was a tale that never got stale.

'No one? Not even the dog?' purred Gbèdurèmí's drum, speaking in the weary voice of the mistress. The crowd chortled, on tenterhooks, for the man's wounded response.

'I met the dog,' curtly said the man. 'Nasty specimen of a beast. But I came prepared: I threw him some meat.'

'And the goat?' asked the mistress. 'Was the goat there too?'

'I met the goat also,' answered the man. 'He was yoked to a post. He brayed at me. I did not wish him well either.'

'And the fowl?' asked the mistress. 'Was the fowl there?'

'I met the fowl as well,' said the man. 'She was hatching an egg. She flared at me, thinking I'd come to steal her brood. I saw her off with a swipe of my gown. You know those gowns made for me by my second wife's younger sister. Her yarning skills are quite remarkable. Do you think I should marry her? But that is not the point I'm trying to make. The point I'm trying to make is this: I came to your house. I did not steal a goat. I did not steal a hen. I even fed your dog. But look at the scars on my back. Look at the welts on my arms. Look how your husband beat me so!'

The crowd erupted.

Àjàyí quickly remembered where he needed to be and hastened homeward. As he pushed his way through the crowd, the buskers launched into another crowd-pleaser, this one about the dog who climbed a rope to heaven during a famine to hide his mother while all the other creatures slaughtered their mothers and ate them up.

Ìyá ìyá ta'kùn wálẹ̀ ò
Àlù jọn jọn kí jọn

Gbogbo ayé pa yèyé rẹ̀ jẹ
Àlù jọn jọn kí jọn

Ajá gbé ti ẹ̀ ó dọ̀'run
Àlù jọn jọn kí jọn

Giddy with joy, the crowd sang along. Àjàyí quickened his pace, trying to make up for lost time. His anxiety had returned twicefold. He listened out for the rumbling voices from the Malian camp but heard nothing. Still he felt anxious. He looked at the faces around him, searching them for clues. Everyone appeared to be aware of the Malians' presence outside the town gates, but no one seemed to be in the least concerned about it.

Nine

As Àjàyí got closer to home, he stopped a few neighbours and queried them.

'Yes, they are outside Ìséyìn,' said Àkànbí when he saw Àkànbí and asked her if the Malians were still outside the town.

'I wonder why they are here,' Àjàyí said, searching Àkànbí's face for clues.

'They always go this way,' Àkànbí answered. She was on her way to fetch yams from her father-in-law's farm.

'Yes,' said Odédé when he ran into Odédé and asked him if he had seen the Malians. 'I saw them outside the north gate. It's clear they are on their way to Ìpétàdó. Don't look so worried. I went outside and sized them up. There are no more than five thousand of them. Do you know how many warriors we have? They are no match for our warriors. I should know, I am one of them.'

Odédé was on his way to the market.

'Yes,' said Omolúàbí when he ran into Omolúàbí. 'I saw them outside the south gate. I counted five thousand of them.'

'I wonder why they are here,' Àjàyí said, scanning his eyes for clues.

Omolúàbí shrugged and said, 'They always go this way,' before shifting his hoe from one shoulder to the other and going on to his farm.

'Yes,' said Ròobòdìyàn when he ran into Ròobòdìyàn, whose real name was Yíósìda, which means 'it will be well'. His parents gave him this name because he was born during a time of famine. But everybody called him Ròobòdìyàn, which means 'upheaval', because he was known to be short-tempered and loved nothing better than a good scuffle.

'I saw them outside the west gate,' said Ròobòdìyàn. 'There are about five thousand of them.'

'I wonder why they are here,' Àjàyí said, studying his face for clues.

'They always go this way,' was all Ròobòdìyàn would say. He was on his way to the shrine of Ṣọ̀pọ̀ná, the òrìṣà of smallpox.

'Yes,' said Ìjí when he ran into Ìjí. 'I saw them outside the east gate. I counted five thousand of them.'

Ìjí was Àjàyí's best friend. He was also, undoubtedly, the most ridiculous person Àjàyí had ever known. His name was Fáfunwá but he was called Ìjí because he walked like Ìjímèrè, the monkey.

'And they always go this way, don't they?' Àjàyí asked him.

'No, they don't always go this way,' Ìjí replied. 'They sometimes go through Dádà. They only go this way when they're going to Láfíàjí.'

'Are they going to Láfíàjí?' Àjàyí asked.

'No, they're not,' answered Ìjí. 'But I hear the place they're going to is near Láfíàjí.'

Àjàyí was not satisfied with Ìjí's answer but he knew that pressing him was a waste of time. Not only did he walk like Ìjímèrè the monkey, Ìjí had the attention span of Ìjímèrè.

Àjàyí was about to finish the conversation by asking him where he was going when he heard an almighty roar behind him. At first, he thought it was the minstrels and their crowd. But clearly this roar wasn't coming from the marketplace. It was coming from beyond the town walls. If that was bad news, there was worse to come: it wasn't just coming from beyond the town walls. It was coming, not from the south gate or the north gate or the west gate or the east gate or any one particular gate. It was coming from all the gates, all at once.

Àjàyí looked at Ìjí and Ìjí looked at Àjàyí. They looked solemnly at each other.

'What's that noise?' Àjàyí asked him, even though he knew exactly what it was. He only asked because he was hoping Ìjí would make that monkey face and say, 'It's nothing. Don't look so worried.' But that wasn't what he said. What he said was: 'I think we're being attacked,' which was exactly what Àjàyí was hoping he wouldn't say.

'Don't panic, Àjàyí,' Ìjí advised him calmly, before immediately saying, 'Run, Àjàyí, run!'

Then, leading the way, Ìjí ran the best way he knew how to, like a monkey, which was quite fast, but not exceptionally so.

Àjàyí quickly overtook him.

Ten

It was one week earlier, before the Malians came.

By the time Kábíyèsí finally deigned to make an appearance in the morning courtyard where his guests had waited for him all day and well into the evening, Fámorótì had already come to the conclusion that his father had sent him on a fool's errand. He had come bearing tidings of life and death. If there was nobody to receive it, there was no point in staying. He would cut short his homecoming and leave at once.

Before departing, however, there was the matter of Aya'ba Ọyátómi's invitation to consider. To honour the invitation would be to accept her hospitality and to accept her hospitality would mean having to spend the night in Òṣogùn. That was out of the question. He felt a need to put as much distance as he possibly could between him and Òrombó, the clown-prince of Òṣogùn.

His mind made up, he said to Fúyẹ́, 'Tell the men to saddle the horses. We're leaving.'

'Leaving?' Fúyẹ́ was aghast.

'I have no intention of spending the night here.'

'But if we leave, my lord, what about Aya'ba Ọyátómi? What about Princess Oyíndà? We gave them our word, my lord. Is it wise to depart without bidding them farewell?'

'It would be the wisest decision you've ever made,' said a booming voice from behind them. They turned to find Òrombó reappearing, his men in tow, after a lengthy absence for evening repast. In his best Aya'ba Ọyátómi impression, Òròmbó chirped, '"There's no reason why your gallant friend shouldn't come along. The more the merrier." It is clear, my dear Akọgun, clear as daylight, that Aya'ba Ọyátómi has taken a fancy to your slave.'

'Fúyẹ́ is not a slave,' Fámórótì coolly informed him.

'She's clearly taken a fancy to you,' Òròmbó told Fúyẹ́, giving no indication of having heard Fámórótì. 'Watch out, though. Or before you know it, she'll have you full-blooded and throbbing inside her. And before you know it, she'll have you wedded to her. And before you know it, you'll be her fifth former husband.'

'Her sixth, Olóyè Òròmbó,' the chronicler interjected.

'Her fifth,' said the laureate. 'The olóyè is right.'

'Of course the olóyè is right,' said the chronicler. 'And when he said it was her fifth, he was right. And I was wrong when I said it's her sixth, but it really is her sixth. One of them she married twice and twice divorced.'

'She has been married to five men,' Òròmbó informed Fúyẹ́. 'Two of her former husbands are friends of mine. I hear she likes to ride her men. It's the only reason I have never tasted of the woman's largesse. She's small but tasty. Small but sweet and juicy. But she likes to sit astride a man.' Turning to his men, he asked, 'Have you ever heard of such a thing?'

Òròmbó and his men were still rolling on the floor when the king made his appearance. But Òròmbó wasn't caught out. Power was to Òròmbó what blood is to a shark; he could scent it from half a mile away. He scented the king's approach well before Kábíyèsí actually appeared before him. By the time His Majesty lurched into the court-yard, sandwiched between the two hefty eunuchs propping him up, Òròmbó had already converted full-throated laughter into full-tilt

46

obeisance as he flung himself, prone, on the floor, drooling from the wildly intoxicating fragrance of the raw, undiluted pheromones of power oozing from the king; a powerful odour that reeked, to Fámorótì's far less attuned olfactory lobes, of sweet, frothing palm wine and Portuguese liquor.

Fámorótì was right. Kábíyèsí was drunk. Kábíyèsí was drunk by several orders of magnitude. Kábíyèsí was so drunk he couldn't tell whether he was coming or going. After two aborted attempts to leave while obviously under the impression that departure was arrival, and arrival departure, the eunuchs gently helped him make up his mind by carrying him to the throne and firmly planting him there.

'I salute you, my king,' Òròmbó piped, gasping for breath, from the floor. 'You are, like a needle, sharp at both ends. You pick your teeth with a sword. Any mortal who scoffs at you will use his teeth in place of a knife to peel cassava.'

A young maiden emerged from the antechamber. She stood quietly to one side and sobbed. Òròmbó was silent for a minute. He glared at her. Then he glared at the chronicler. The chronicler avoided his gaze. The laureate gazed at his feet.

'I am addressing you, my master,' Òròmbó said to the king. 'You are the swift warrior moving to battle in the enemy's bush path. You are the waddling warrior cautiously advancing in enemy territory. I pay you homage, my king. You are a torrent of rainwater: you go everywhere. You are the forest fire that destroys the undergrowth together with the mass of leaves under it. I salute you, my king.'

'Òròmbó!' roared His Majesty.

'Your Majesty.'

'Why do you inflict these passionless old bats on us?'

Even Òròmbó, whose depravity knew no bounds, was given pause for thought. But only briefly.

'Your Majesty,' he said, carefully choosing his words, 'she's only—'
He turned to the chronicler and said, 'How old is your daughter?'

'She . . . I . . . she,' mumbled the chronicler, shame oozing from
every pore on his face.

'Bísí is sixteen,' said the laureate, helping his friend out.

'She's only sixteen, Your Majesty,' said Òrombó.

'Only sixteen?' bellowed Kábíyèsí.

'Quite old, I must admit. Your Majesty, heaven forbid that I
should contradict your wisdom, which is infinite and – might I add –
incomparable, which is to say, it surpasses all others. I was merely
trying to say, I can vouch for her age. Her father here has worked
for me for many a year. How many years have you worked for me,
Ládèjo?'

'Many,' confirmed the chronicler, quietly, the life drained out of
his voice.

'She may well be your daughter, Ládèjo,' said the king to the
chronicler, 'she may as well be your own mother's mother. We need
young blood, Òrombó. Go and find us a winsome young virgin.'

'But of course, Your Majesty.'

'Go,' ordered the king. And with that command, Kábíyèsí glared
defiantly at the eunuchs and was lifted, immediately, off the throne
and out of the courtyard, airborne, his feet not touching ground.

Òrombó picked himself off the ground and said, coldly, to Ládèjo,
'Take her home.'

'You have disgraced us, Bísí,' the chronicler said, grabbing his
daughter by the arm. 'You have ruined the good name of our family.
We'll never hear the end of it. Wait till your mother hears about it.'

'All she had to do was lie back and think of your good name,'
noted Òrombó. 'Is that too much to ask of a daughter?'

'Father,' sobbed Bísí, 'I'm with child.'

'With child?' he said. 'With child?' he shouted.

'Father,' she cried.

'Take me to the wretch who did this to you!'

Òrombó stood still, the very picture of mortification. Then a fire sparked alight in his eyes. He turned to the laureate and said, grimly but gently, 'Ọmọlẹwà.'

The laureate blinked, several times, before saying, 'What did you say, Òrombó?' But it was obvious that he'd heard correctly; he wouldn't have dared to call Òrombó by name if he hadn't. Only sheer lunacy or virulent anger, or both, could bring a man to such self-murdering folly. He had seen Òrombó kill men for lesser slights. But instead of reaching for his dagger, Òrombó reached into his pouch and brought out his snuff-box.

He tapped a pinch of snuff on to his finger and said, just before he lifted it to his hairy nostrils, 'I am asking after the health of your daughter, Ọmọlẹwà. I saw her in the market the other week. I could not believe my eyes. She was only a child yesterday, and now she's blossomed. She's blossomed into a thing of rare courage. That is what I want to talk to you about. The exceptional courage of Ọmọlẹwà. It is so rare these days. Notice I did not say "beauty". I have nothing against beauty, mind you, but mere beauty is nothing. That is why I did not say "beauty". I said "courage". I want to hear all about it. Which is why you're going straight to my house with me. My tapper brought in fresh palm wine this morning. I left home without taking the time to taste it. We will go and taste it together. I insist. You will not say no. I will not hear of any argument against my generosity. I want to hear all about the courage of Ọmọlẹwà.'

The laureate followed Òrombó out of the palace, his head hung low, like a man about to be offered in appeasement to an angry deity who is deeply athirst but insists only water tapped from the veins of men will do for his parched throat.

As the two men left for Òrombó's compound, Fúyę turned to his master and said, 'If we leave now, we should be in Ìsęyìn before cockcrow.'

'Leave now?' said Fámoróti. 'And not bid Aya'ba Oyátómi farewell? We gave her our word. Your very own words. Let's go and see Aya'ba Oyátómi. And then we shall leave.'

Outside the palace, Fámoróti wearily mounted his horse, his eyes bleak and angry.

'Did he even notice us?' he wondered.

'I doubt it, my lord. His Majesty was in no state to notice anybody.'

'In a few weeks, these will all be gone,' said Fámoróti soberly, indicating the homes and farms around them. 'Everything. They'll take every living soul, then they'll burn down the town. They'll leave nothing in their wake.'

'And you think we really could do anything to prevent it?'

'Perhaps. Perhaps not,' Fámoróti replied. 'The Malians are able warriors. But there's no such thing as an invincible army. Can Òşogùn stop them? I don't know. This isn't the Òşogùn of my childhood. The decrepit old fool we met tonight, the buffoon who calls himself king, wasn't the man I knew when I was a boy.'

'Your father would spit on this man.'

'The man has gone to seed. His court has gone to seed. When I was a child, Òrombó and charlatans like him wouldn't be allowed within a mile of the palace. Now the charlatan has the run of the place.'

'He does act as if he owns the place.'

'He does own the place. And not just in Òşogùn,' Fámoróti said. 'There is an Òrombó everywhere you go, it's all across the land.'

They cantered quietly through the marketplace.

Eleven

A week later, a thousand turbaned men on horseback, all dressed in uniform pitch-black gowns billowing in the wind, poured into Òṣogùn. The horsemen sailed in through the north gates and the south gates and through the east gates and the west gates, crackling firebrands held aloft in one hand, steering their horses with the other, and chanting, 'Allahu Akbar, Allahu Akbar, Allahu Akbar.' As the cavalry entered the town, spilling in all directions, thousands of men on foot hared in after them, dressed also in dust-laden black, bismillahing and chanting, 'God is great, God is great, God is great.'

'We're not here to kill,' they assured the panic-stricken people. 'We want you alive.'

They had come to rustle, not to slaughter. A dead captive was worth nothing to them at the slave market. All the same, it was crucial to set an example, and so when they got to the marketplace, they immediately beheaded two men.

One of the men they beheaded was Rògbòdìyàn, who was on his way with an offering to the shrine of Ṣọpọná. Rògbòdìyàn told the Malians where he was going and refused to stop when they told him to. The man who cut off his head picked it up from the bed of cured tobacco leaves where it lay spurting with blood, and told it a joke about the supplicant who arrived at a shrine to offer an offering, little realising that he himself was the offering on offer. When the bodiless head did not respond, the man turned to the townspeople.

'I realise it would be asking too much to expect him to laugh,' he said to them, 'but he could at least smile.'

The leading horsemen were sons of the soil. Who else but a son of the soil could so confidently gallop through town and head straight to the king's palace without once stopping to ask directions? After they burned the palace to the ground, before turning their flaming torches on the shrines and then the market, followed by the homes of the people, a rumour quickly spread that the Malians had put the king and his entire court to the sword. This rumour was immediately quashed by witnesses to the arson, those who were there when a Malian identified as Lárúdú, the son of Bokúotẹ́ the leatherworker, who now went by the fashionable name of Sùlèmọ́nù, torched the thatched roof of the palace. As he did this, they heard him tell his fellow Malians to 'flush the rodents out of their hole'. And many rodents did come scurrying out of the sizzling tongues of flame. The king was not among them.

These witnesses in turn started another rumour, claiming that the reason the king was not inside the palace when the Malians razed it to the ground was because he had flown the coop the night before. He had received advance warning of the raid, they said, and abandoned his people, leaving them at the mercy of the invaders. He had fled with his wives and children, together with his servants, to Ọ̀yọ́.

'It's not true,' Ìjí said to Àjàyí in a hushed whisper. 'The king hasn't fled anywhere. The king couldn't have fled anywhere. He's in there in the palace, dead. He's been dead for many days now, but the palace has kept it quiet.'

Àjàyí fixed him with a dubious stare.

'Did your father tell you that?'

Ìjí's father was a guard at the palace.

'No,' answered Ìjí. 'Bàbá didn't tell me anything. They were sworn to secrecy.'

'Who was sworn to secrecy?'

'Bàbá and all the other guards at the palace. On pain of death.'

'Who swore them to silence?'

'Òrombó.'

'How come you know?'

'Bàbá told my mother. I wonder where he is.'

'Bàbá?'

'Òrombó.'

It was about three hours after the Malians entered the town; Àjàyí and Ìjí were crouched low behind a cluster of trees in a palm grove a short distance from Àjàyí's compound. From their hiding place, they watched as the Malians, wielding long, cowhide kòbókò whips, flogged people into a stupor, barracking them into quavering droves, like cattle being led to pasture. All around them, and as far as the eye could see, there were fires blazing from every compound, roofs belching with smoke.

Hysteria everywhere leapt and stung like sparks from the raging fires. Families fled their homes and ran in one direction, then turned and ran the other way. No matter where they ran, they ran directly into the hands of men in black. Mothers fled into the bush, with infant babies and toddlers strapped to their backs, and their four children, their five or six children running before them, fleeing after them, and their heads piled high with all their worldly belongings. It was all to no avail. At the best of times, the dense bush was barely navigable; now it was impenetrable. Even when it dawned on them to jettison the load and save their energy for the children, they still found themselves able to take no more than a few faltering steps before lassos dropped around their necks and around the necks of their children and they were led away.

Àjàyí and Ìjí had avoided capture thus far by sheer providence. It helped that they knew every inch of every backyard and every last contour of every undergrowth in the town, but so did many of the Malians. They were well aware that the odds were overwhelmingly stacked against them, that they would eventually fall into the hands of the invaders; the question wasn't whether they would, but when they would.

Everywhere you looked were men in flying black robes, drawing swords or sheathing them. For every single inhabitant of Òṣogùn, you could count almost two men in black. They were simply everywhere. Thus was the way of the Malians. They overwhelmed by dint of force.

Àjàyí and Ìjí had tried every way they knew to flee, but everywhere they went, they found Malians there. They had approached each of the six gates; five were firmly shut, with men in black standing guard. Only Ọ̀yọ́ was open, but the Malians had left Ọ̀yọ́ open for a reason: it was through this gate, the widest of them all, that they herded their captives out of the town. There were thousands of them clustered here, arguing fiercely but without rancour over who was entitled to how many captives, and apportioning the spoils strictly according to the tenets as espoused by such and such authority in Timbuktu or this lèmọ́mù or the other in Ṣókótó or Ìlọrin.

Àjàyí and Ìjí were under no illusion that they would escape capture. Their objective was to get back home, to reach their families and be with them when they were captured.

'I heard my father talking to my mother the other night,' said Ìjí, 'about what he saw at the palace.'

'Stop talking,' Àjàyí whispered.

'About how the king died. His Majesty wasn't satisfied with all those wives he already had. He had to have one more.'

'Stop talking,' Àjàyí whispered, fiercely. 'There's someone approaching.'

They sank lower into the ground, their eyes peering furtively at a pair of pungent, jiga-infested feet that planted themselves directly in front of their noses, briefly, before picking themselves up and moving on.

Ìjí didn't say another word until the feet had disappeared, the footfall gone. Then he turned to Àjàyí and said, 'Haven't you wondered why we gave in without so much as a fight?'

Àjàyí knew that the overwhelming magnitude of the attack, and its stealthy suddenness, brooked no reply, but even so, it did cross his mind that the resistance, such as there was one, was over almost immediately it began.

He turned to Ìjí and asked, 'Why did we give in without a fight?'

'I don't know,' Ìjí replied. 'But if I told you what Bàbá witnessed at the palace, you'd accuse me of lying.'

'What did he witness at the palace?'

'He was sworn to secrecy after it happened. All the guards were sworn to secrecy.'

'Who swore them to secrecy?'

'Òrombó. I already told you.'

'Tell me again,' said Àjàyí. 'What happened?'

'If I told you, you wouldn't believe me,' said Ìjí. 'So I won't tell you.' He was silent. Then he said, 'But before that, he almost killed Bàbá.'

'Who almost killed Bàbá?'

'Òrombó.'

'Why?'

'He said Bàbá betrayed him.'

'Did he?'

'I don't know,' Ìjí said. 'But Òrombó decided to spare him because he said even though Bàbá betrayed him, he was only telling the truth when he said what he said.'

'What did he say?'

'I don't know. But I think he said Òrombó killed someone.'

'Òrombó kills people all the time. Weren't you there the other week when he killed what's-his-name? Régbękę.'

'Régbękę.'

'And all the man was doing was minding his own business.'

'He said he did not like the way Régbękę looked at him.'

'How did Régbękę look at him?'

'I don't know. All I know is that he killed an innocent man for no reason.'

'Who did he kill this time?'

'Régbękę.'

'I know he killed Régbękę. I was there when he killed Régbękę.'

'I don't know who he killed this time.'

'You said your father said he killed someone.'

'Yes. He didn't say who it was.'

'So the king was dead.'

'That's what Bàbá said.'

'And Òrombó killed him?'

'I don't think so. Bàbá didn't say so.'

Silence descended upon them. The silence quickly became unbearable.

'Do you call him by that name at home?'

'Who?' Ìjí asked, his eyes narrowing.

'Your father,' Àjàyí said.

'What name?'

'Sly, Sudden Death,' Àjàyí replied.

'No,' Ìjí replied. 'Nobody calls him Sly, Sudden Death at home.'

'You call him Bàbá.'

Ìjí nodded. 'Only Mother is allowed to call him by name,' he said. 'But she only calls him by name when she's pleased with him.'

'I know.'

'Or when she's upset with him.'

'I know. It's the same with my parents.'

'Usually, she just calls him Bàbáa Fáfunwá.'

'I know. Why doesn't she call him Bàbáa Ìjí?'

'She didn't name her only son after a monkey.'

'But you don't look like Fáfunwá.'

'Who said I had to look like Fáfunwá? I am Fáfunwá.'

'You don't look like Fáfunwá.'

'How many Fáfunwá have you met?'

'Apart from you? None. But you don't look like Fáfunwá. You look like a monkey.'

Àjàyí froze. Through the corner of his eyes, he saw a man's feet. The man was breathing heavily. Another pair of feet approached. They came to a halt inches from Àjàyí's nose. The feet were unmistakable, their stench unforgettable. They were the feet of the man who had stood in front of them a minute earlier. They looked like giant tubers of dry-rot-infested yam.

'If you move,' said the man, 'I'll kill you.'

Àjàyí felt the sharp edge of a knife grazing the back of his neck.

'They have to move,' said the man holding the knife to Àjàyí's neck.

'Why?' barked the man with festering scabs on his feet.

'They have to move,' the knifeman repeated. 'They have to move for us to take them down to the barracoon.'

The jiga man refused to concede to the impeccable logic of his colleague's argument.

'If you move,' he insisted, 'I'll kill you.'

Àjàyí and Ìjí did not move.

PART TWO

1821

Dog Eat Dog

Twelve

Only four days earlier, Òròmbó had arrived at the king's palace with the urgent comportment of a man who had come bearing a message. An ensemble of acrobats with a troupe of drummers was about to embark on a command performance when Òròmbó stepped into the morning courtyard. The king glowered at the entertainers from his throne, bored to distraction, wearing the glazed-over look of habitual inebriation.

It was three days since Òròmbó had sat down under a full moon with his personal laureate and engaged in a long and exhilarating disquisition on the theme of courage in marriageable maidens in general and in particular the laureate's own daughter, Ọmọlẹ̀wà, on whom the gods had bestowed courage in splendid abundance. The gods had also endowed her with delightful looks, ripe hips and a fulsome bosom.

Three days after this wine-fuelled meeting of minds, Òròmbó woke up with his third hangover in as many days to discover that his laureate, the hack, had packed up the night before, with his entire family, including his courageous daughter, and left town.

As he had already gone to great lengths to put in place a private audience with the king for Ọmọlẹ̀wà, this cowardly betrayal left Òròmbó in a most awkward position at the palace.

If he was put out by this act of rank ingratitude, he hid it quite well when he breezed through the drummers' courtyard and headed straight into the inner chamber. He stood before the king and solemnly declared, 'When others drink wine, you drink blood, my king. When others plant yams, you're planting the heads of men. When others reap fruit, you're harvesting the breath of warriors.' He paused to catch his breath. 'I am,' he said, 'your most devoted slave, my warrior king.'

The king's glassy eyes swivelled in their watery sockets. With a barely perceptible movement of his bejewelled fingers, he dismissed the players.

'You waffle a lot, Òrombó,' he said. 'But there's salt and pepper in your waffle.'

'I bring you news, Your Majesty,' Òrombó boomed. 'I bring you tidings that will make your heart sing, your loins dance, and the seraglio roar at your hunting skills.'

'You have found us a maiden.'

'Not just any maiden, my king,' Òrombó warbled. 'One that dwells at heights unknown on the crest of beauty.'

'Does this gem have a name?'

'Her name is baked in honey, Your Majesty,' Òrombó declared. 'It is coated in honey, and to be relished like honey: Oyíndàmọlá. She does come with pedigree. You may remember Àjàlá, whose father was Ṣèkóní, whose father was Adéòtí. Àjàlá was the right hand of your very own chief of war, Fágbénlé, who we last saw when he left for Ọ̀yọ́ during the first war with Àfọ̀njá. Oyíndàmọlá is the child Àjàlá left behind with her deceased mother's sister, Aya'ba Ọyátómi, who has raised her as her own. She's bloomed, Your Majesty. She's bloomed into full-blown splendour. A purple star blown into our earth by the crack of lightning at dawn, Your Majesty.'

'Òrombó!'

'I mention the dawn, Your Majesty, because she is fresh like the dawn. Her face is fresh, her hands are fresh, her bosom is fresh – discretion prevents me from naming all other parts of her that are fresh like the dawn, Your Majesty.'

'Go on, Òrombó.'

'If you insist, Your Majesty. Her face is fresh, her bosom is fresh, even the swollen valley between her thighs is fresh like the dawn.'

'A virgin? And not spoken for?'

'Spoken for! Don't swear in the presence of His Majesty, Your Majesty! Spoken for! How can she be spoken for, when this very night Kábíyèsí will honour her with the royal veil? "Spoken for", Your Majesty!'

'All the same, has she no suitors?'

'The queue of noblemen knocking at her door stretches from here to Ìlọrin and Àkúrẹ́.'

'And she has said no to every one of them?'

'She hands out "no" to her suitors like alms to beggars. She likes to say no, Your Majesty.'

'You mean to say she's headstrong?'

'She likes to say no, Your Majesty. That is all I am prepared to say.'

'We like them headstrong. Slow, Painful Death!'

A tall, lanky figure stepped out from the shadows.

'Slow, Painful Death at your service, my king.'

'Fetch her. Fetch the maiden.'

'Right away, Your Majesty,' said Slow, Painful Death, now flat on his face before His Majesty.

'She shall sup with us.'

'She will be honoured, Your Majesty,' said Slow, Painful Death.

'As Your Majesty speaks, even her ancestors are dancing with gratitude.'

'You know we like them headstrong, Òrombó.'

'I am but your slave, Your Majesty,' Òrombó reminded the king. 'I dare not presume.'

Slow, Painful Death rose to his feet and swiftly departed.

Thirteen

Three days before Slow, Painful Death was summoned by the king to bring a maiden to sup with His Majesty, in the second most opulent household in the town, home of the adoptive mother of the maiden on whom this rare privilege was about to be forcibly conferred, Aya'ba Ọyátómi had welcomed two young warriors with great fanfare.

'Mothers, fathers, sisters, my workers,' Aya'ba Ọyátómi announced, and to much jubilation. 'It has been said of Èṣù, the god of fate: when he lies down, his head touches the roof of the house, and yet when he stands up, even an ant on the ground can reach out and touch his face. Èṣù slept in the house, but the house could not hold him. Èṣù slept out in the open, but the open could not hold him. Èṣù slept in the shell of a walnut – at last he could stretch himself! Does he not turn right into wrong? Does he not turn wrong into right? Would he not hit a rock until it bleeds? Èṣù threw a rock today and flying out of his hands struck a bird yesterday. Let me present to you the mighty Fámorótì. Fámorótì, whose every step is guided by Èṣù. Fámorótì, whose every deed is sanctioned by Èṣù. Fámorótì, you are the jewel of the trickster's eye. I address you, Fámorótì. Did you not drive back to their furthest frontiers the galloping warriors of our enemies? You worked havoc in the hinterland, stalking forth like a god aggrieved. You did not spare the cities, nor rivers, nor farms, nor markets. Your campaigns have been a matchless triumph in the path of our gods. You are our hero. You are – Fámorótì. We welcome you and your brother warrior, Fúyẹ́.'

'We thank you, our mother,' Fámorótì replied. 'You are the sea that cannot be emptied. The flood that struts through fire. The rope that drags the elephant along. The seed that holds a forest. The silence that births a song. We salute you, mothers of our land.'

Aya'ba Ọyátómi now turned to the girls who had all gathered to catch a glimpse of the august visitors, all breathless with awe. 'Our visitors must be famished,' she said. 'Look sharp, my daughters. Let's prepare our princes a feast fit for warriors.'

One moment the room was packed. The next, Fámorótì realised that he was suddenly all alone, by himself; even Fúyẹ́ was nowhere to be found. And then he saw, standing in the shadows, outside the reach of the flickering radiance of the crackling firewood lamp, the most fetching maiden he had ever set eyes on.

'You must thank Aya'ba Ọyátómi for me,' said Oyíndàmọ́lá, stepping into the light. 'Since my mother left for the land of the ancestors, Aya'ba Ọyátómi has been my mother and father. Tell me,' she said, 'how did my father die? What happened during the last moments of his life?'

'After the cowardly blow that felled him,' he told her, 'your father tarried only long enough to speak about you. This is what he said. That you were a child that must not be touched by dew. That you were the light with which he found his way on difficult journeys and in seasons of doubt. This is what he didn't say – and I wish he had, I wish he had. That your smile rises like the sun on the misty wilderness of a warrior's life. That your smile is like the dawn gone poaching in the dark orchard of this warrior's sleep. That the stars, melted together and cooled in the sea, and cut into a stone brighter than the sun, are bright, but not half as bright as the radiance of your smile. Your feet are set deep in the sea, home of Yemoja, who when she wakes up in time present, her eyes lidded with dream, shakes her head crowned with a nest of birds baited into her trap with promise of fish; escaping one at a time, the birds carry between their beaks greetings, hope, regrets, and dreams from time past to time hereafter. I am that bird of passage, Oyíndà. I have burrowed my past, a bloodstained bundle wrapped in seaweed, into the cleansing seawater vaults of the sea goddess. I wear time present like a charm for luck. And the future that I soar into is you, Oyíndà. I have come to your feet, set deep in the sea, the livelong home of Yemoja, night and day, who alone knows the path that leads into this world and the road that guides us out of it. Give me your ear, Oyíndà, I have but one thing to say to you: be with me.'

'My lord,' she said, 'I do not know the secret of the sea, where it goes or from where it sets or if its fish are thought made flesh. But I know this for I've seen it with my eyes: that from it the sun rises in the morning and into it, it plunges at night. I do not know the secret of rain, how it shelters from the sun. Or whether its mistress is the ocean. But I know this for I've seen it with my eyes: rain is the beard of God, rinsed in milk, the flag of being. No barber on earth possesses the blade to shave it off. I do not know the secret of the mirror, whether it sees the world or sees illusions. Or whether it sees a world filled with illusions. But I know this for I've seen it with my eyes: from this day till I'm ninety-nine or more, or till I die before making ninety-nine, I shall do up my hair in the mirror of your eyes. Be with me, Akogun Fámorótì.'

The high-flown poetry of these mating calls could have come straight out of the talking drums of Gbèdurèmí and Àyángbèmí. The travelling minstrels' vast body of work was, in truth, the mainstay of inspiration for many a courting couple, even if the lovebirds themselves often didn't realise that the lofty platitudes in which they were investing so much passion and sincerity had found their way to their lips from a skit poking gentle fun at a couple like them. Neither Fámorótì nor Oyíndàmọ́lá had ever witnessed a performance by the blind minstrels; and so, when they serenaded each other with these orotund verses, they were echoing lovers who may have been echoing lovers who may or may not have heard it directly from the talking drums of the travelling minstrels.

Talk of this exchange, which took place late in the evening, spread beyond the confines of Aya'ba Ọyátómi's house and into the town at a speed that was known to exist only in the realms of the metaphysical. When Fámorótì arrived at the palace the following morning, the talking drums were breathless with speculation about a young warrior who had come home to see his king and now was leaving with a dazzlingly fetching maiden by his side.

Fourteen

It was pouring heavily with rain the following evening when Fámorótì and Fúyẹ́ arrived back at Aya'ba Ọyátómi's house.

'This way, please,' said the housekeeper who met them at the door. A servant steered Fúyẹ́ in one direction while the housekeeper guided Fámorótì through a warren of rooms to a different wing.

If it had been a crowded house last night, tonight it was the arena for a feast.

The housekeeper showed him into a room towards the back of the house and immediately retreated.

Aya'ba Ọyátómi was standing by the window. A flash of lightning lit her face, briefly, and the house rumbled with thunder.

Fámorótì knew why he'd been sent for.

'I hope you don't mind the suddenness of it all,' he said.

'Affairs of the heart are never too sudden,' she replied. 'Make yourself comfortable.'

It didn't sound like an instruction, but it was. A carved wooden stool sat in the middle of the room. He reached for it and sat down.

'That girl is my daughter,' she said; her voice was firm, her face soft.

'I know,' he said.

'I'm the only mother she has.'

'I know,' he said.

'Of all the women of our bounteous town, Akọgun Fámorótì,' she said, 'from those that live in the gaze of the palace to those that dwell in the shade of the hills, the wives-to-be and the newly married brides. The maids with burnished marks on their cheeks, those cara-mel stripes that enhance their beauty still. The ones with radiant gaps in their teeth: an emblem of beauty, gifted by the gods. The elegant ones, the ones for whom a prince may lust, the ones for whom a slave revolt. The ones with childbearing hips. The ones with hips that spark unrest in the loins of happily married men. The ones that glow like the pearls on their neck. The ones with the grace of a lounging cat. Take them one and all together, ask them all bar none together, and you'll find, Akọgun Fámorótì, that none is as happy as my daugh-ter is tonight. And fewer, even still, as happy as I am for both of you.'

'Thank you, Aya'ba. My happiness knows no bounds.'

'I do not question your honour.'

'I'm sure, Aya'ba Ọyátómi.'

'Nor would I for a moment doubt your word.'

Fámorótì's smile faltered. 'I'm sure, Aya'ba.'

'I am merely a woman who likes to speak her mind. I know that many a time, on your numerous campaigns, in the course of your distinguished career, you have deflected from your side the arrow tipped with pestilent poison; the spear that quarters an elephant's flesh; the white man's brutal burning beans that spread like smallpox through the air.'

'The òrìṣà have favoured me, Aya'ba Ọyátómi.'

'May they continue to favour you, Akọgun Fámorótì.'

'Àṣẹ.'

'Àṣẹ. But all those scourges will be nothing – nothing! – com-pared to the boundless bane of my bitterness should you ever break my daughter's heart. You would wake up on that day and find that your dreams have turned into a rising pillar of dust. Do we understand each other?'

'We do,' Fámorótì mumbled.

'Good,' she said, laughing. 'I'm glad we've got that out of the way. We can now go back and join the others. We must discuss the wedding.'

He paused, then he said, 'Now?'

'Now,' she said. 'It would be a shame if all the troubles I went through this past week – the rams I bought for the occasion, the game, the wine, the yam, the fish – went to waste. Not to mention the musicians. I hired quite a few.'

'Wait, wait,' he said. 'You – what did you just say? What have you been preparing for a week?'

'The wedding.'

'Whose wedding?' Fámorótì found he was sweating.

'Your wedding,' she calmly informed him. 'I hope you don't mind.'

'I don't understand any of this, Aya'ba Ọyátómi. Your daughter and I met only two days ago. You said a week. You said you'd been planning for a week.'

'When word reached us weeks ago that your father, and her father, had both fallen on the field of battle, I knew at once that it was only a matter of time before you showed your face in Òṣogùn. So I began to plan a wedding feast for my daughter.' She laughed loudly, heartily. 'Upon my honour, Akọgun Fámorótì, Oyíndà knew nothing of my designs.'

Suspiciously – all too casually – he asked, 'Have you set the date?'

'You're free tonight, aren't you?' she said.

'Yes . . .' he began. Then he stopped and said, 'Tonight? This very night?'

'This very night.'

'But there's—' He tried to think. 'There's protocol, Aya'ba Oyátómi. I have to inform the king.'

'Which king would you be referring to?' she asked, patiently. 'I'm all ears. Tell me.' She waited. When he didn't respond, she said, 'We no longer have a king in this town. What we have in this town is a man who once was drunk with power and now is simply drunk, day and night. You've been trying to see him since you stepped foot on this soil several days ago. I'm sure you know why you haven't succeeded. He's in a stupor, that's why. He's always in a stupor. That's why you haven't been able to see him. He's outlived all his rivals — you've got to give him credit for longevity. But it isn't all that hard to outlive anyone if, first, you had them killed; a fail-proof formula for longevity Kábíyèsí used to swear by. Anyone he found threatening, he killed or drove them into exile. That's why your father left and never returned; you must know that. Only the sycophants flourished. The most shameless of them is Òrombó. He's the king of them all. I need not warn you to be cautious around that man. The only pleasant thing I can say about him is that when he strikes with his dagger he never strikes from behind.' And now, without warning, she changed topic. 'Is it true what we hear, about the Malian slave raiders? That they might be coming for us. Is it true? Is that why you've been trying to see the king?' Again she continued before he could respond. 'I'll tell you what you must do tomorrow morning. Don't waste your time going to the palace. I'll call for a gathering in the town square. Everybody in town will be there, and you will talk to the people directly. You must tell them what you know about the Malians. And what we must do to stop them. Òrombó will scream high treason. But there's many a father in this town, and many a mother too, who have been biding their time, waiting to throttle that creature. The king himself will be in a state of torpor. He'll be too befuddled to know what hit him. Listen to me, Akọgun. You've come home for three reasons: to take your bride, to save Òṣogùn from the Malian slavers, and to lead. I know you'll deny it; you'll say it's not true. But I'm telling you, on the contrary, it is. You believe you've come home to bring a message to the king. You're wrong. It is the gods themselves who have brought you here, and they didn't bring you here to act as a messenger. They brought you here to fulfil your destiny and that is what you're going to do.'

It was at this moment, as Fámorótì sat speechless before Aya'ba Ọyátómi, that Slow, Painful Death burst in, pursued by two irate housekeepers.

Fifteen

Slow, Painful Death was soaked to the skin and cold to the bone, but that didn't stop him from rising to his full height and puffing out his chest.

'Good evening, Aya'ba Ọyátómi,' he said officiously. 'I bring a message for your daughter, Oyíndàmọ́lá.'

'Give it to me,' she said. 'Tell it me. I'll pass it on.'

'Aya'ba Ọyátómi.' He said her name as if her name was a rebuke to good taste. 'Aya'ba Ọyátómi,' he repeated. 'It is a matter strictly between the palace and the princess.'

'In that case,' she told him, 'go back and tell the palace that I swept away your feet from the threshold of my house. Tell the palace that I used a broom. If I see you here again, it will be a búlàlà on your back.'

'Cane me?' Slow, Painful Death barked. 'You threaten to cane me?' His eyes were blazing with genuine astonishment. 'Do you know who I am?'

Aya'ba Ọyátómi turned to Fámorótì.

'The poor man doesn't know who he is,' she said. 'Can you help him?'

'I am a servant of the king,' yelled Slow, Painful Death. 'A servant of the king!'

She turned to Fámorótì again.

74

'We have before us a servant of the king. He's a servant of the king.'

Slow, Painful Death lowered his voice.

'I'm only doing my job, Aya'ba Ọyátómi,' he pleaded. 'You know I bear you no ill will.'

'I suppose I should be grateful for that,' she conceded, before adding, 'Now, leave.'

Slow, Painful Death turned to Fámoróti for help.

'Help me beg her,' he pleaded. 'Aya'ba Ọyátómi, you know what will happen to me if I go back to the palace without delivering this errand.'

'I have no pity to waste on you,' she told him. 'You have no manners.'

'They'd kill me, Aya'ba Ọyátómi, you know they'd kill me! I beg of you, Aya'ba Ọyátómi, let me see the princess.'

'You are beginning to try my patience. Leave my house.'

Slow, Painful Death sighed.

'You did not hear it from me,' he said, his voice reduced to barely a whisper. 'Kábíyèsí – long may he reign – tonight has seen it fit to honour your daughter.'

'Has he?' she asked coldly. 'How has he seen it fit to honour my daughter?'

'The usual way, Aya'ba Ọyátómi: by sending for her.'

Fámoróti looked, baffled, at Aya'ba Ọyátómi.

'Leave this to me,' she told him. 'O servant of the king,' she said to Slow, Painful Death. 'Why are you so drenched?'

'It's raining,' he responded, not sure whether to be confused or irritated by the question. 'You can see that it's raining.'

'Hear me out, servant of our king,' she told him. 'Was it raining when you left the palace?'

'No,' he said. 'It wasn't raining. But as I stepped outside the court-yard a great wind struck me in the face. I looked up into the sky and saw a flaming brand with dark wisps high above the towering cliffs of cloud. Flashes of lightning gave way to booming thunder. Ahead of me the earth shook with shrieking sounds. The wind collided with whirling dust. They heaved and twisted like wrestlers. The storm came swiftly. The rain, roaring like a great beast, began to pour. I was frightened, Aya'ba Ọyátómi. I'm not ashamed to admit to you that I was frightened. Out there, as we speak, Aya'ba Ọyátómi, the wells are filled to the brim, the creeks are overflowing, valleys are welling with water, trees felled by the wind, thickets squashed. I saw an entire compound bounding away on a rush of floodwater, like a boat caught in roiling rapids. The world is a frightening place tonight, Aya'ba Ọyátómi, people are dying out there.'

Aya'ba Ọyátómi let him finish, before she asked, 'Have you wife or child?'

He said, 'None,' looking pained.

'Good,' she said. He began to explain why he had neither wife nor child. She stopped him. 'The matter between us is simple. You want to keep your head and body together. I want to keep the king away from my daughter.'

The king's servant threw himself, face down, at her feet.

'Aya'ba Ọyátómi,' he said, his voice quaking with fear.

'Hear me out,' she told him. 'Get up. You say that you bear no ill thoughts towards me. I wish you no evil either. This is what I propose we do: you will shelter here tonight or until the storm abates. I shall arrange for you to be ferried out of town and on to someplace else where you can settle down, with five bags of cowries to your name, and start anew your life.'

'But Aya'ba Ọyátómi! Kábíyèsí will declare a bounty on my head.'

'He will do no such thing,' she assured him. 'How is he to know that you were not swept away by that great storm out there?'

'Very well, Aya'ba Ọyátómi,' he said, crestfallen, clearly not convinced. 'I shall do as you say.'

'Follow your right hand,' she instructed him. 'Our treasurer lives there.'

'I know, Aya'ba Ọyátómi.'

'Tell her I sent you.'

'I will, Aya'ba Ọyátómi,' he said. He walked a few feet, then he turned around. 'Aya'ba Ọyátómi,' he said, forgetting his manners. 'Did you say "bags"?'

'I did.'

He paused, thoughtfully. 'Did you say "cowries"?'

'I did.'

'Did you say "bags" and "cowries" together?'

'I did.'

'Did you say "five"?'

'I did.'

'Did you say "five bags of cowries"?'

'Yes,' she said. 'But, of course, if that's not enough?'

'Not enough?' He looked shocked at the suggestion. 'It's more than enough, Aya'ba Ọyátómi. It's more than enough.'

As he headed out, he could be heard murmuring to himself, 'I'm rich. I'm rich. God bless you, Aya'ba Ọyátómi.'

He was back a minute later, looking lost.

'I said follow your right hand,' Aya'ba Ọyátómi reminded him. 'Your right hand is the other way.' She leaned towards the door. 'Máyọ̀wá,' she called out.

Máyọ̀wá was standing by the door almost before the last syllable of her name rolled off her mistress's lips.

'Show the king's servant to the treasurer's house,' Aya'ba Ọyátómi told her.

'Right away, Mother.' Máyọ̀wá curtseyed.

'I'm rich. I'm rich,' he kept muttering as Máyọ̀wá led him away. 'God bless you, Aya'ba Ọyátómi. The world is a wonderful place.'

'Come on, my king-in-waiting,' Aya'ba Ọyátómi said to Fámorótì as she glided out of the room. 'This storm is a gift from the gods. It buys us time, but there's no time to waste. Every moment wasted is another arrow added to Òròmbó's quiver.'

Fámorótì hastened after her.

Sixteen

The guests held their breath. The drummers ceased playing. Even the rain seemed to stop on cue as Fámorótì lifted the blazing torch by its handle and presented it to Oyíndàmọ́lá.

'Take this flame,' he said to her. 'I will marry you. If anyone objects, burn their house.'

The sharp, percussive roar of the drums sailed far into the night, pealing across the towering trees of the forest, as if bestriding the land from a great height the thunder god himself had rumbled his approval.

Oyíndàmọ́lá waited until the uproar had died down.

'Those standing – let them stand well,' she said to the guests. 'Those kneeling – let them kneel well. Those sitting outside – let them receive our thanks. Those who could not join us tonight – we thank you for the priceless gift of goodwill. You the elders, who have braved the storm, I thank you for honouring this day.'

She passed the torch to a maiden who passed it on to another maiden, until the torch, passing from one hand to the next, had done a relay in the gathering.

'I pounded yam softly and offered it to destiny's gatekeeper Èṣù himself,' Oyíndàmọ́lá said. 'Èṣù refused to eat. Then I asked him: "Will you stay indoors or outside?"'

'Outside,' answered the guests.

'When Death comes looking for me,' she said.

'It will meet Èṣù outside,' they chorused.

'When illness comes looking for me.'

'It will meet Èṣù outside.'

'When poverty comes looking for me.'

'It will meet Èṣù outside.'

'When evil comes looking for me.'

'It will meet Èṣù outside.'

'What if a child comes looking for me?'

'Èṣù will bring him into your room.'

'And if laughter comes looking for me?'

'Èṣù will show him in.'

'And if good fortune comes looking for me?'

'Èṣù will tell her to knock on your door.'

The drummers affirmed her prayers with an invocation on wood and hide.

'When I left my house,' she said, moving, in rhapsody, to the gbèdu, 'my mother told me not to go through the market. I said—'

'But why?' they joined her in asking. 'Are you in debt? Do you owe the fishmonger?'

'When I left my house my mother told me not to go through the market. I said—'

'But why?' they asked. 'Are you in debt? Do you owe the salt seller?'

'Some people wanted to lead me to my husband's house, like a sheep to the market. But my mother said I should be escorted through the streets, like a freeborn child. You people of the world help me to thank my mother, for she decked me out in clothes rich enough to make a goddess envious. Let everybody thank my mother: she did not allow me to borrow dresses from those who would turn around and insult me. She dressed me in clothes so rich, I could confuse a god. And you my parent, Aya'ba Ọyátómi. When you don't see me any more, will you forget me? Is it not you who decides when a child is old enough to have a quiver? Is it not you who decides when a child is old enough to have an arrow? It was you who decided that I was old enough to move to another house. Mother, don't leave me alone in that place. I look right, and left, I look behind and in front of me, but I do not see my other parents, the ones who birthed me. What kind of god created me in a world of sickness to make my mother die like rotten yam? What kind of òrìṣà created me in a violent world to make my father die in war? If my head is not against me, I shall have them back with me in my husband's house. If my head is not against me, they shall re-enter the world through me. My head – which is wearing a bright scarf today – will surely give me male children and female children. My people; mothers, and fathers: today is a glorious day!'

Up in the sky outside, in a blinding shock wave of radiant light that exploded into the harsh, deep-belly laughter of the thunder god himself, a bolt of lightning formed a fiery arch that straddled the cloudy heavens above and the flooded earth of the forest canopy below.

It was a sign, all agreed, that the union had found favour with Ṣàngó.

Seventeen

It was at this moment, back at the palace, that Òrombó was informed for the third time that evening, after the heavy downpour, that there was still no sign of Slow, Painful Death. Òrombó had decided to spend the night at the palace so that he could be on hand to welcome the king's new bride.

'Perhaps it's the storm,' suggested Red, Dark Death, chief of the royal guard, knowing full well that this was unlikely to be the reason. 'Perhaps he stopped for shelter.'

'Perhaps,' said Òrombó, his eyes cold yet jaunty with malice. 'But he would not do that. He knows not to do that. I observed him carefully when he left. He had the look of a man with burning ambitions to live long enough to see tomorrow.'

They were inside the drummers' courtyard, in the house used by Red, Dark Death and his cohort of royal guard as a sheltering place, a home away from home. Every one of the senior guards had a colourful appellation, such as Slow, Painful Death and Red, Dark Death. The architect of this naming protocol was none other than Òrombó. He often said the idea came to him while he was suffering from a hangover, but he was only being modest. It actually came to him during a state of drunken stupefaction; on the morning it happened, when inspiration struck him, he hadn't yet stopped drinking from the night before. It hit him with such force, he passed out and it was true that when he came to, he was suffering from the mother and father of all hangovers, but the idea came to him much earlier, before the hangover.

The guards hated their new names; it earned them nothing but ridicule from the public who took to addressing them by inane variations on the theme, such as Utterly, Pointless Death and Stupid, Useless Death. On the other hand, the king loved the naming convention so much he rewarded Òrombó with yet another freshly cooked-up chieftaincy title. Not surprisingly, Òrombó took great pride in his invention. He seized on every opportunity to call the guards by their new names; no excuse was too flimsy. Tonight, however, he did it for a sound reason; he did it for reasons of state security.

'Swift, Violent Death, warrior!' he bellowed.

Swift, Violent Death stepped out, rubbing his eyes.

'Sly, Sudden Death, warrior!'

Sly, Sudden Death stepped out, rubbing his eyes.

'Savage, Brutal Death, warrior!'

Savage, Brutal Death stepped out, rubbing his eyes.

'Blue, Numbing Death, warrior!'

There was no sign of Blue, Numbing Death.

'Blue, Numbing Death, warrior!'

'Blue, Numbing Death's off sick today, Olóyè Òrombó,' Red, Dark Death informed him.

'Down with the fever, I believe,' Savage, Brutal Death told him.

Òrombó left the palace with these senior guards together with fifty lesser mortals whose singular mark of obscurity resided in the fact that they were not named for any manner of death whatsoever.

Eighteen

Òrombó shut down the merriment by the simple expedient of plunging his dagger into the lead drummer's gbẹ̀du.

He'd arrived at the wedding with a radiant but utterly chilling smile beaming from his face. It was a smile he'd cultivated over many years and weaponised, through trial and error, to induce utter panic.

'I see you're already celebrating ahead of the glad tidings,' he noted, treating the gathering to the full benefit of the smile. Its effect was instantaneous. Gloom gave way to despair; despair, in turn, gave way to foreboding on every face in the room.

Òrombó held out his hand. A gold embroidered gèlè from the trembling hands of an orderly came to rest in it.

Òrombó walked up to the bride and delicately placed the headwrap on her shoulder. She shrugged it off her shoulder. Fámoróti's hand immediately reached for his sword. Fúyẹ́ reached out and stayed his master's hand.

Aya'ba Ọyátómi stepped forward, discreetly inserting herself between the enraged groom and the taunting courtier.

'May I congratulate you, Princess Oyíndàmọ́lá,' Òrombó beamed, 'on this most delightful occasion of your coronation as Kábíyèsí's hundred and fifty-eighth consort. I tell a lie. You will, as a matter of fact, rejoice in being Kábíyèsí's hundred and fifty-seventh consort.

We had one only the other day who brought shame on her family name when she let her father, my very own chronicler, Ládèjọ, go about proclaiming her purity while she was in fact heavy with child. The task fell on me, as her father's bosom friend, to go and deal with the pauper who ruined his daughter. I tell a lie. As you all know, Ládèjọ comes from a long line of men and women who wouldn't know good sense if it ran into them in broad daylight and slapped them in the face. And so, it came as no surprise to me when I heard that Ládèjọ harboured the curious idea that since his daughter claimed to be fond of this young man she'd allowed to defile her, he would allow him to take her as his wife. I hear they do that in Ẹ̀gbá. That's not the way we do things here. It's a foreign idea. It's a barbaric idea. Anyone who wants to do that sort of thing should move to Ẹ̀gbá. When I heard about Tàmèdò's poor judgement from none other than Ládèjọ himself, I told him I would be paying him a visit to meet his new son-in-law. I think he knew exactly what I meant when I said that to him —' as he said this, he patted the dagger hanging down his kèmbẹ̀ '— and I did pay him a visit the following morning. Do you know what I found when I got to his compound? I found it deserted. There was no sign of Ládèjọ, no sign of his daughter, no sign of his son-in-law, no sign of any member of his family; no sign, even, of his livestock. I went over to his neighbour's house to ask what had happened to my chronicler. And his neighbour said, they left town last night, they said they were going to join his wife's relatives in her hometown in Ẹ̀gbá.' Òròmbó's chubby face rolled and swelled and a chortling sound erupted from his neckless throat. 'Anyone who wants to desecrate our culture should follow Ládèjọ and move to Ẹ̀gbá.'

A chilly silence descended on the gathering.

'Welcome to my home,' Aya'ba Ọyátómi said to the courtier.

'Make yourself comfortable. We have palm wine. There is ògùrọ̀. As you can see, we are celebrating a great and joyous occasion – the coming together in anointed matrimony of our prince and his princess. We had it in mind to invite Kábíyèsí. We had it in mind to invite you too. But what with the storm, and youthful impatience – and who can blame them – we were unable to do so. As you can see – and we all of us here can testify – they are now man and wife.'

'Let me stop you before you go any further,' Òrombó declared. 'He may be her man and she may be his maiden, but they are not man and wife. No man takes a maiden for his wife in this town without the king's say-so. It is the law of the land, passed on to us by our fathers.'

'That is a lie, Olóyè Òrombó. You know it's a lie.'

'It is in my nature to lie, Aya'ba Ọyátómi. It comes with the office. But I lie, remember, on the king's behalf. And the king does not lie. The king cannot lie. It is theologically impossible for the king to lie. Therefore, in my capacity as special envoy to the king – or, if you like, the king's chief liar – and for the reasons stated above, et cetera, et cetera, I declare this marriage illegitimate and void.'

'But you can't!' cried Oyíndàmọ́lá.

'O yes I can, my dear princess. Watch me, I'm a wizard. On a good day I can even predict that tomorrow will surely follow from today. Usually, I'm right. When you're ready, the king's bedroom awaits your sumptuous presence.'

'I'll kill him!' Fámorótì said. 'I'll kill him!'

It took several men to restrain him.

'You're a warrior, Akọgun Fámorótì,' Òrombó said. 'It is in your nature to kill. I sympathise with you. But I am the king's slave, and there's the rub: unless Kábíyèsí decrees to the contrary, my neck and body remain together. There's nothing I can do about it, I'm afraid. It's the law of the land.'

'Tell the king who sent you here,' Aya'ba Ọyàtómi said to him, 'that the sky will light up with stars once more. Tell him that soon, on a night like this, a million fireflies will be seen, and the luminous half-disc of the moon will be sent by God to watch over us.

'Tell him that the sun will spread across the land that has been laid dank by the floods.

'Tell him that the farms will suffer no more and crops now drowning will be nursed back to life.

'Tell him that rocks of mist will rise from the ground and the glut of water that has surged into many homes and taken many lives will be scooped up by the sun and poured back into the sky.

'Tell him that among the creatures that have survived the flood there will be mothers in milk. Tell the king who sent you here that prayer is the bounty of God and that the king, like God, must know this truth: that life is a whip that strikes the strong and the weak alike. Tell him that life is a journey. And that no matter how large a forest may be, there is a town at the end of it. And if there's not town, there's the sea. And if there's not sea, there's the desert. And no matter how large that desert may be, there's a town at the end of it.'

'I love it when you're angry, Aya'ba Ọyàtómi, you speak such cultivated nonsense,' said Òròmbó, quaking with laughter. He stopped to catch his breath. 'Pity you're not my wife. I'd knock that rubbish right out of your head with an onslaught of semen that'd hit you like a wild storm.'

Aya'ba Ọyàtómi smiled pitifully at him. 'You're out of breath,' she observed. 'And you haven't so much as lifted a finger.'

The crowd tittered. Òròmbó joined them in laughing at himself.

'My òrìṣà is thirsty,' he informed them, casually reaching for his dagger. 'He has not had a drop to drink in three long days.'

As his words travelled through the crowd, the laughter slowly died.

Aya'ba Oyátómì quietly conferred with Fámorótì and her daughter.

Òrombó pricked up his ears. 'You're talking about me, Aya'ba Oyátómì. I can always tell when someone is talking about me. What are you saying about me, Aya'ba Oyátómì?'

'I was telling the akògun,' she replied, 'that you come from a distinguished pedigree of hyenas.' Ignoring Òrombó's malicious smile, she inched closer to Fámorótì and said quietly, 'I can't wait to wipe that smirk off his face, but this is not the time. For now, let your bride go with them. I know these men he has brought from the palace with him. They are decent men all. I know how much they loathe him but tonight they are here on an errand for the king. They will come around to your side when they hear what you have to say tomorrow morning at the square. That is when the whole town will pay the palace a visit, every one of us, after you have spoken. And that is when you will have your day. And I promise you, my lord, you will have your day.' She patted him on the shoulder and then said, raising her voice, 'Go with them, my daughter. The king is a neutered dog on heat. I should apologise to dogs on heat. He's impotent. You have nothing to fear from him.'

'The king is the king, Aya'ba Oyátómì,' Òrombó declared, raising a warning finger at her. 'If you say that again, I shall be very angry with you.'

'I said the king cannot perform. Is that another theological impossibility?'

'Keep theology out of this,' Òrombó said. 'The king is well equipped.'

He now poured himself a calabash of palm wine and emptied it down his throat.

'Very good indeed,' he said. He helped himself to a second help-ing. 'This is the best palm wine I have tasted in a long time, Aya'ba Ọyátómi. My son is taking a second wife next month. I must ask you to lend me your tapper for the occasion.' He belched in appreciation and wiped the froth on his lips with the back of his hand. Then, turn-ing to Oyíndàmọlá, he declared, 'After you, our esteemed queen. Your groom eagerly awaits you at the palace. You'll have to excuse us, fellow citizens, good people. Duty calls. Let the feast continue, indulge yourselves on the king's behalf.'

Then, with the bride wailing inconsolably as she was yanked away from her husband's arms, Òrombó stormed out of the wedding.

Nineteen

The royal bathroom was lit with palm-oil lamps held aloft by a phalanx of torchbearers. Kábíyèsí was in the bath, stripped down to his testicles, a deliriously deranged glint in his dewy, pepper-red eyes. The torchbearers barely encroached on His Majesty's consciousness and he seemed perfectly unaware of the dozen eunuchs attending to his toilette, even as they scrubbed his buttocks, which looked like shrunken, dry banana leaves, and poured gourd upon gourd of warm water on him.

Kábíyèsí's single greatest achievement on the throne was the unbridled proliferation of his genes. He'd lost tally of the number of children he had sired, just as he'd long lost count of the number of maidens housed in the royal wives' quarters.

The maiden now kneeling before His Majesty – the newest addition to his harem, although he didn't know it yet – waited in trepidation.

'Our fathers say that anyone who shakes a tree trunk succeeds only in shaking himself.' Oyíndàmọ́lá's voice quavered as she spoke.

Gloriously pickled on Portuguese spirits and the finest ògùrọ̀ in town, His Majesty stared dimly at the maiden, wondering who on earth she was and why was she weeping, this pretty lovely gorgeous pretty lovely gorgeous pretty gorgeous lovely thing kneeling before him?

He blinked and immediately realised that if she was anywhere near his divinely royal presence, which she clearly was, it could only mean one thing: that she was a most fortunate maiden indeed! It was, after all, no mean feat for a maiden to be afforded the privilege of supping in the regal chamber.

His Majesty shrugged off the hands kneading his back and reached for a mirror from a mirror-eunuch. An apparition stared back at him. Bleakly, and most decidedly defiantly, he returned the stare.

'You're blind in one eye, deaf in one ear, and you're losing your looks,' he mocked the apparition, who was clearly someone other than himself, and felt rather proud of himself for speaking truth to power. 'But,' he sternly added, 'you're the king. And you must never forget that.' And with this pearl of wisdom dispensed to a monarch clearly riddled with self-doubt, he tossed the mirror on the floor, where it lay shattered.

As attendants scurried to clear up the mess, the apparition leapt out of the smashed mirror back into the bath and slid, through the monarch's left nostril, into the delirium-possessed body of the monarch in the bath, who was soused to the eyeballs, unlike the apparition, who was stone-cold sober. Now inhabited by the apparition, who was as pished as the inebriated body he was inhabiting, which meant that His Majesty embodied two drunks instead of one, the king snatched yet another mirror from the attendants.

He held it close to his nose and studied the ravaged, gin-soaked faces that petulantly stared back at him. 'You're the kings,' he barked at the crabby old dogs scowling at him, two faces falling in and out of focus. 'You must never forget that.'

The attendants were ready this time when His Majesty and his alter ego tossed the mirror aside and the apparition leapt out of His Majesty's right nostril and followed the mirror.

To the king's genuine consternation, his guest was still weeping.

'I do not resist you, my king,' she cried. 'The seeds of ayò do not complain about being shoved about.'

'Why do you cry, my pretty maiden? Why does she cry? Shush. Let the maiden speak for herself.'

'We've been taught, Kábíyèsí,' Oyíndàmólá responded, 'that you're like the ripe coconut that falls on a child at night.'

Kábíyèsí sighed. It was a profoundly sincere sigh, a sigh that conveyed the full depth of his compassion. Poor, poor thing. Now he understood the poor thing.

'You will not come to a sad end,' he assured her. 'Perish the thought. Wipe those tears from your face at once, pretty maiden.'

But the maiden knew she could not perish the thought. It would be folly to perish the thought.

'If a man greets you, there is trouble,' she mused. 'If a man forgets to greet you, there is trouble.'

'That is quite true.' His Majesty nodded sagely. 'Quite true indeed.'

The maiden had unwittingly unleashed a giddying onrush of self-reverence in the monarch.

'Fighting a battle to the right,' she said, 'you mark out the next battlefield to the left.'

'That is true,' gushed His Majesty. 'Quite true. We can be quite fearsome. But not with you, comely maiden, not with you. We'll be gentle with you.'

'You kill your enemies gently like the leopard,' Oyíndàmólá said. 'When it kills, its tail rests gently on the ground. Do not smile at me, Kábíyèsí, your smile frightens me.'

The old monarch pealed with laughter.

'Enough of that,' he said. 'Take off that lovely dress and join us in here.'

'I have something to tell you, Kábíyèsí,' Oyíndàmọ́lá said.

'Yes?' he responded.

'I'm married.'

The fog swiftly lifted from his eyes. Now it all came rushing back to him. Now he remembered who she was.

'So am I,' he growled. 'I've been told that you like to say no,' he cackled. 'I, on the other hand, have always been deaf to the sound of "no". It's a congenital affliction, you see: "no" always sounds like "yes" to my ears. I tend to take a "no" and "yes" it up. Come, lovely maiden, don't begrudge an old man those ripe, delectable bosoms.'

If the old man gave a sign, Oyíndàmọ́lá did not see it; she suddenly found herself up in the air, her legs flailing under her, in the iron grip of powerful hands depositing her into the arms of the monarch.

'Consider this to be a sacrifice to save your husband's life,' he purred as he peeled off her clothes, his arthritic hands trembling, unwrapping them like the leaves of a steaming, delectable tranche of moimoi. 'It's your very own plaything tonight,' he counselled, placing her hand between his legs.

'I don't think it wants to be disturbed,' she informed him.

'Only a shut-eye,' he assured her. 'Only a short nap. Perhaps it sulks. Let us see what happens when you bid it good evening.'

He shoved her head between his thighs. She remained there for several seconds before coming up for air. Once again, His Majesty shoved her down. She began to choke, to gasp for breath. Through the corner of her eyes she saw something on the floor: she reached for it; it tore through her hand.

93

She plunged it down. The eunuchs gasped. The blood drained from Kábíyèsí's face. He rushed to get up, to get away, but his legs betrayed him.

'Hang the witch!' screamed the king. 'Hang her.'

He noticed a strange but somewhat vaguely familiar object in the trembling hands of the head eunuch. The object, which the eunuch had picked off the floor, was covered in blood.

'What's that?' growled the king.

His Majesty followed the eunuch's frozen gaze and stared between his thighs and fainted.

Twenty

Every year just before the rains, a trader from Kano, the famed market city on the southern shores of the Sahara Desert, turned up in the town centre of Òşogùn and set up shop there. The man, whose slaves and servants called him the Sheikh, travelled with his own private army, a band of mercenaries who protected him and his merchandise from bandits and other opportunist wayfarers on his whistle-stop tours of the Yorùbá country.

Nobody knew whether the Sheikh's name was a title or whether it was his actual name. Not that they cared. The Sheikh was an Arab, and because he was white, everybody called him Òyìnbó, which was what they called the white European tribesmen whose wanderlust occasionally brought them this way.

The Sheikh's trade was in fine morocco, which he brought from Kano, whose tanneries he swore were the best in the world. He sold the fine goatskin leather in exchange for young boys and teenage girls whom he took back with him to the slave markets of the Sahel. There he sold them for a handsome profit to fellow Arab merchants who sailed with them in camel fleets across the sand-dune ocean of the Sahara, and to Arabia from there, the girls to be farmed into childbearing concubinage and servitude, the boys to be neutered – which was essential to prevent a kafir abeed, a heathen slave, from tainting the honour of his master's wives and daughters – and farmed into bondage.

Òrombó, the only merchant in Òṣogùn permitted to trade with the Sheikh and others like him, once explained to his òyìnbó friend, over a drink of honeyed shayi, how he came about this favour from the king. 'I put it down to one thing: loyalty,' he said, sipping the tea, although he'd much rather it was rum. 'His Majesty has rewarded my enduring loyalty by granting me exclusive licence to administer the royal supply of abeeds. That means I sell them on his behalf: I do all the work, he takes eighty per cent of the proceeds. And why shouldn't he, Òyìnbó? I am, by definition, his abeed as well – and everybody's happy. Except of course for the abeeds themselves. Excellent shayi.'

The time-honoured way of procuring the royal supply of slaves was to descend in righteous anger upon one's enemies; to lay siege on their towns and starve them into submission. But these were treacherous times. The last time the king had sent his chief of warriors on one such mission, the warrior-chief had accomplished the task apportioned to him but, instead of heading back home with the bounty, made for the coast, towards Abomey in the kingdom of Dahomí and was never seen again. That was several years ago; it was the last time Òṣogùn had gone to war for pillage.

But the Arab didn't cease coming to Òṣogùn even when he could no longer rely on her for his supplies of saleable assets. He had found the town to be something of a safe haven in this kafir empire; in the heart of a rainforest rife with perfidy and bristling with menace, it was nothing short of an oasis. He took root there whenever he was in this corner of the Yorùbá country; it was the caravanserai from which he set out and to which he returned during the long months when he painstakingly combed the neighbouring towns and villages for merchandise. In return for their hospitality, the Sheikh paid his hosts a handsome consideration, of course, always on his last day in the town, just before setting out on the arduous journey back to Kano, where he lived.

On this latest sojourn in Òsogùn, on his last night there, the Sheikh, having turned in early, slept through the worst of the storm. He was fast asleep, inside his ridge-top tent next to the tented barracoon holding the fifty or so abeeds he had acquired on the expedition, when he heard in his dream a familiar voice speaking to him.

'Òyìnbó,' said the voice. 'Consider yourself fortunate that I decided to commute your sentence to this.'

In his dream, he couldn't see the speaker, but the voice was unmistakable; he recognised it at once. It was the voice of Òrombó, purring with malice.

Alarmed, even though he was aware it was a dream, the Sheikh woke up in a blind panic. His panic gave way to a foul mood when he realised that it wasn't at all a dream, that Òrombó was in fact standing outside his tent, talking to someone.

The Sheikh slid into his pyjamas and lit a lantern. The guards standing outside his bedroom with their shotguns and pistols hurried after him as he stepped out of the tent.

He found Òrombó outside, surrounded by his usual retinue of royal guards, talking to a young maiden, who looked fairly bruised.

'You didn't know that I had it in me to be this caring, did you?' Òrombó was saying to her. 'Well, I am that sort of man. Hard on the surface, soft as a whispered sigh on the inside.'

Turning to the Sheikh, Òrombó said, 'Òyìnbó.' Without uttering another word, he stepped away from the girl and watched, with evident satisfaction, the white man's eyes greedily undress her.

The Sheikh knew, the minute he set eyes on her, that she would fetch a fortune at auction in Agadez. In all the years he'd been coming to the Yorùbá country, he'd yet to set eyes on a more beautifully endowed creature, and he'd seen them all, which was why he now turned to Òrombó, dismissively, and said, 'Is this why you had to disturb my sleep?'

His studied nonchalance was undermined by his protuberant Adam's apple which pulsed with each word he uttered and appeared ready to spring out of his scrawny neck.

This was exactly the response Òrombó was hoping for. It told him at once that the Sheikh was drooling with appreciation. But he played along with the Sheikh's charade of indifference.

'She's an acquired taste, I must admit,' he said in a suitably apologetic tone. 'I had to bring her at once. The king wanted her dead. And you're leaving at cockcrow.'

'How much?'

'You are sweating, my friend,' Òrombó slyly observed. 'Is it because of the rain? From you, I'll take the usual.'

The Sheikh would have paid four times the usual for her. And so, he said, as Òrombó knew he would, 'Out of the question.'

'Less five per cent,' Òrombó said.

'She's all swollen.'

'The king said, hang her. "She's a witch, hang the witch." Those were his exact words. So the boys got a bit excited and roughed her up a bit,' Òrombó explained, allowing a lavish hint of regret to coat his voice. 'I put a stop to it at once, of course. I said to myself, just in case. Just in case my good friend, Òyìnbó . . . And so on and so forth.'

'She hardly can walk.'

'Less ten per cent. That's the best I can do.' It was plain that, far from being the best he could do, this was merely his starting point.

'She looks half-dead,' observed the Arab.

'I'll accept twenty,' Òròmbó offered. 'That's a loss to me of a small fortune. But what's a small fortune between friends? Less twenty per cent.'

'And five. Twenty and five.'

'Done,' said Òròmbó. He eyed his ware with the proud, exacting gaze of a connoisseur. 'She's pure,' he declared, forestalling the Sheikh's next question. 'She's fresh, pure and untainted, just the way you like them, Òyìnbó. Judge for yourself. Have you ever seen the like of this gorgeous thing standing before you? Even I was tempted, let me confess. O yes. I was sorely tempted. And how could I not be tempted, Òyìnbó, faced cheek by jowl as I was by such unspeakable exquisiteness? Only a man who is not a man will see this vision and not be tempted. I was tempted but I said to myself, I said no, no, no. Three times, my friend; I said no three times. I said, just in case my good friend, Òyìnbó, and so on and so forth. You get my meaning. I refuse to be vulgar. It is unbecoming. Kola nut?'

He split open a kola nut, pushed half of it into the Sheikh's hand and sank his teeth into the other half.

'She was an enchanting destination and I sorely wanted to traverse those shores,' he confessed, crunching the kola nut between his teeth. 'But I said to myself, just in case my good friend, Òyìnbó, et cetera, et cetera. Therefore, I said to myself, you must not go there.'

The Sheikh was no longer listening to his good friend. Now he had eyes only for his new possession. He looked heavenwards as if for divine inspiration, then he shut his eyes briefly; when he opened them again, it was clear his prayer had been answered. 'Zainab,' he said.

'Sàìnóbù?' Òròmbó was momentarily lost. Then his eyes lit up. 'Of course,' he said. 'I understand. Sàìnóbù.'

'Zainab.'

Turning to Oyíndàmọ́lá, he said, 'That's you. You are Sàìnọ̀bù. That's a beautiful name, Òyìnbó. What does Sàìnọ̀bù mean?'

The Sheikh answered in Awúsá. 'It means "fragrant flower",' he said.

'Fragrant flower,' Òrombó repeated, clearly impressed. He turned to Oyíndàmọ́lá and told her, 'It means "smelly leaf".'

Oyíndàmọ́lá was quiet. She was no longer weeping.

'That means he likes you,' Òrombó explained. 'They are obsessed with smelly leaves, the whites. Their depravity knows no bounds.'

'Do as the king commanded,' Oyíndàmọ́lá told him. 'Kill me.'

Òrombó turned to the Sheikh and said, 'Kábíyèsí was involved in a ghastly accident tonight. We have our best herbalists looking after him but the prognosis isn't looking good. If he passes, and I'm saddened to say he will, I intend to be first in line for that lovely little trophy that's called the throne. In order to do so as smoothly as possible, I intend to round up a certain undesirable element and all his partisans, a dangerous character who will stop at nothing now he cannot have his wicked way with this gentle, beautiful damsel whom he would like to claim for his wife.'

'I don't quite catch your drift,' said the Sheikh.

'What I'm saying, Òyìnbó, is that there are a lot more waiting where this maiden came from. What I'm saying, Òyìnbó, is that you can have them all on the house. They will be my gift to you. As a matter of fact, did we say less five and twenty per cent for Sàìnọ̀bù? I reject that offer. I reject it as if it was an insult. Not an insult to me or an insult to you but an insult to the sanctity of our abiding friendship. From now on, your money is no good in this town. Yes, Òyìnbó, Sàìnọ̀bù is all yours and I shan't accept a single cowrie from you, not one kobo. All I ask of you is that you help me bring one or two upstarts to heel. Scratch my back, I scratch yours; I'm that sort of man.'

'Jingling horseman, fast traveller who settles his quarrels with a spear,' Oyíndàmọ́lá intoned. 'The road is clouded in dust when you pursue your enemy.'

'What's she saying?' the Sheikh asked.

'Don't mind her,' Òrombó replied. 'She's praying to Ṣọ̀pọ̀ná.'

The Sheikh leapt back. 'Has she the plague?'

'Come, come, Òyìnbó,' Òrombó snapped. 'Would I have her around me if she had smallpox? She hasn't the plague. She's merely praying for something like it to take her life.'

Òrombó noticed the flush of embarrassment on the Arab's face and decided it was best he allowed him a minute to save face.

'Why don't you and your men retire indoors to discuss my little proposal? Let me have a word with Sàìnọ́bù.'

'Wait here,' the Arab barked, before heading back into the tent.

'Jingling horseman in a cloud of sand,' Oyíndàmọ́lá chanted. 'Spare me, O horseman, and spare my household too. But if you must carry my load, horseman. If my time has come to go, horseman. Let me follow you to your home, horseman. Lead the way, horseman, take me with you. Take me home, my ancestor. Take me home to my ancestors.'

With the back of his hand, Òrombó struck her in the face, hard.

'It's fine by me if you want to kill yourself,' he said. 'But have the decency to wait until the white man has paid for you.'

Oyíndàmọ́lá continued to chant.

Twenty-one

Fámórótì and Fúyẹ́ came prepared.

They arrived at the hilltop caravanserai not long after the Sheikh bestowed the name Zainab upon his latest acquisition. They were accompanied by a band of warriors, many of whom had earlier that night been Aya'ba Ọyátómi's guests at her daughter's wedding. Some of them came as they were, in the ceremonial accoutrements they'd worn to the wedding; others had first to go home to fetch their beaded hunters' tunics: tunics embedded with amulets, totems, mascots, and other sacred icons and sacramental ornaments, without which a warrior would be wise to think twice before stepping on the battlefield. They brought with them machetes and crossbows and arrows; they brought single-edged swords and two-edged swords; they brought spears and lances, and wooden clubs, and iron clubs. All manner of knives and daggers girded their loincloths.

Fámórótì arrived at the Arab slaver's camp feeling utterly wracked with guilt. He was sore with himself for not having followed Oyíndàmọ́lá to the palace when, under his very nose, Òròmbó had abducted her. It made little difference that he certainly would have gone with her if his mother-in-law hadn't forbidden it. Aya'ba Ọyátómi had insisted she had to send people who knew the lie of the land, people who were intimately versed in palace intrigue and the devious cunning of its denizens. Her only concession to Fámórótì, to put his mind at rest, was to allow Fúyẹ́ to accompany her emissaries to the palace, but she would not hear of Fámórótì going himself, knowing, as she kept reminding him, that Òrómbó's father's father's father was remembered till this day only for the lies that came pouring out of his mouth and that his mother's mother's mother was remembered till this day for her treachery, and although these qualities hadn't skipped any generation in Òrómbó's lineage, they shone through so uncommonly clearly in him it was futile to expect anything from him other than treachery bundled with lies; it was as futile, and might she add, as stupid, as to expect anything other than venom from a scorpion even when it swears on its mother's grave that its days of stinging the world are well and truly behind it.

No sooner had Fúyẹ́ left Aya'ba Ọyátómi's compound with her emissaries than he returned, seething, from the palace.

The mood was contagious. 'What happened?' Fámórótì snapped at him.

'We followed them to the palace,' Fúyẹ́ answered. 'But the guards would not let us in.'

'Did they give a reason?'

'The same as always: "His Majesty is indisposed. Come back tomorrow."'

'Even with Ìyá Onídìrí and Ìyá Èjìrẹ́ and the others there with you?'

'That is what they said to Ìyá Onídìrí and Ìyá Èjìrẹ́ and the others. They refused to speak to me.'

'Nothing at all? They said nothing to you?'

'I might as well not have been there, for all the attention they paid to me. Ìyá Onídìrí and Ìyá Èjìrẹ́ are still there arguing with the fools.

I realised nothing would sway them, so I left immediately to tell you. We have no time to waste.'

'Òrombó was right,' Fámorótì declared. 'He said I had no business doing what I did tonight without the king's permission. He was right. It was rash of me. He was right and I was wrong. It was foolish of me. I blame myself for allowing Aya'ba Ọyátómi to talk me into it. You, Fúyẹ́, you should have advised me against it.'

Mildly, Fúyẹ́ pointed out that he did caution him against a hasty wedding. 'You instructed me to share my counsel with the wind.'

'You should have tried harder.'

'Indeed, my chief. I should have. I failed.'

'I'd had too much to drink.'

'I shall try harder next time, my chief.'

It was at this moment that Aya'ba Ọyátómi came to inform them that Ìyá Onídìrí and Ìyá Èjìrẹ́ had sent word that the king had decreed Oyíndàmọ́lá should die.

Fámorótì eyed her warily.

'Why would the king do such a thing?'

'I shall tell you on the way to the palace,' she said. 'Outside we have a group of well-wishers waiting for you to lead them there.'

The well-wishers were some of the most experienced warriors in the land, all of them long united in a feeling of deep unease with the daily excesses of the crown. What happened at the wedding that night was the final straw. They'd had enough. They'd had enough of His Majesty and his system of governance by phallic brigandage. They'd had enough of Òrombó's impunity and the king's complicity in it.

They found the palace, when they arrived there, cloaked in mourning; His Majesty, they were told, had succumbed to his injuries.

When they demanded to see Oyíndàmọ́lá, the guards told them, 'She's not here.'

'Where is she?' Aya'ba Ọyátómi demanded.

'Chief Òrombó took her away,' they answered.

'Where did Chief Òrombó take her?'

'He took her home,' said one of the guards.

'I heard him talking to Red, Dark Death,' said another guard. 'They were taking her to the hills.'

With a sharp intake of breath, Aya'ba Ọyátómi turned to Fámorótì and said, 'That spawn of a scorpion has gone to sell my daughter to his white master.'

They headed at once for the hills.

Twenty-two

On the hilltop, outside the Arab slaver's tented serai, Òròmbó was addressing his men, his mighty jaws gnarled and misaligned, his face grimly contorted, a vivid rendering in lurid caricature of the bad blood, no less deep-seated for being freshly manufactured, that now existed – now and forever more! et cetera, et cetera! – between him and the Sheikh. It was clear that he wanted the whole world, including the Arab – particularly the Arab, who could hear every word of the rant from his tent – to hear it all.

It was not enough that Òròmbó unleash a tirade, he had to proclaim it at the top of his lungs. Angry words covered in warm spittle and finely chewed kola nut flew out of his mouth.

'You all heard what the white man said.' His arms flailed in the air. 'He does not want to get involved. That's all the thanks I get for all the years of friendship and honest trade with him. He does not want to get involved. All I asked of him was a few men with those nifty fire-spitting metals that go ṣakabùlà! at a man and instantly it's hail and farewell for him. That was all I asked. But what does he say? He does not want to get involved, that's what he says. You all know what that means, don't you? It means that we're in the grandmother and great-grandfather of all trouble if His Majesty departs for the other world. It means that we're in hot pepper with that sorceress Oyátómi and her evil-twin Fámorótì. If His Majesty harkens to the call of the ancestors and departs, those two will use our scalps to drink palm wine.'

A hushed silence descended on the royal guards as Òrombó held forth. But the silence deepened, and the men became increasingly agitated, and, finally, deathly quiet as he continued to vent his spleen. At first, he thought it was the dire consequences awaiting them that had them benumbed, then he realised it had to be something else, something far more immediate. He could see it in their eyes, in the way they appeared to look through him to a spectre looming just behind him.

Slowly, deliberately, he shifted weight across his colossal frame, shoving heft from one side of his body to the other, so that his neck-less head and his commodious stomach tilting as one swung like a skewed pendulum and, turning, brought him face to face with the cause, standing behind him, of the overwhelming terror on the faces of the guards. He found himself staring into the eyes of Fámorótì, which were deathly cold and staring right through him, and into his very spirit, he could have sworn it.

'Where's my wife?' Fámorótì's voice was surprisingly calm, devoid of rancour.

Aya'ba Oyátómi was no less calm when she spoke, but she was pointed and direct.

'What have you done with my daughter, Òrombó?'

The only giveaway that she was seething inside was the thin smile on her face; it dangled on her lips but was completely absent from her eyes.

Her eyes simmered with fear and loathing.

It was a look that Òrombó had never seen before on her, and for a moment it baffled him, until it occurred to him that she did possibly have good reason to be fearful.

He swallowed hard and muttered, 'She's gone.'

'What did you say?' This time, Fámorótì's voice was thick with fury.

'Where has she gone?' Aya'ba Oyátómi leaned forward. 'Did you say she's gone?'

'She's gone,' he repeated.

Aya'ba Oyátómi could no longer keep up the pretence of smiling. 'What have you done to my daughter, Òrombó?'

She stared deeply into his eyes. He stared right back at her.

'I didn't do anything to her,' Òrombó replied. She almost believed him, until he added, smoothly, 'I didn't so much as lay a finger on her.' Aya'ba Oyátómi knew at once that he had done vile, unspeakable things to her daughter.

'May the ancestors spurn that usurper who decreed that my daughter be put to death,' she said. Her fear, which was mixed with hope, had turned to acrid fury. 'May he seek the welcoming arms of the ancestors tonight and not know where to look for them. May our mothers and fathers turn their backs on him. Where is my daughter?'

'Kábíyèsí is dead?' Òrombó gasped. His voice was painfully bereaved; so bereaved, it moved him to tears.

'The king is not dead, you scavenger,' Fúyẹ́ told him. 'You stand before the king.'

'Of course,' Òrombó said, uncharacteristically meekly. Meekly, he paid obeisance to Fámorótì. 'Long may you reign, my king.' The tears streamed down his face in perfectly formed rivulets of sorrow. 'I tried all I could for the princess. Believe me, I did. Every single thing. There was nothing I didn't do. But it was all to no avail.' He turned to the guards. 'You were all there. You all saw me pleading with her, you saw me begging her. You saw it all. I tried everything. Did I not?'

'No, you didn't, Chief Òrombó,' said a tiny voice, timid but unhesitant, from the back. 'You did nothing of the kind.'

For a moment Òrombó was stupefied into silence. Murder flashed through his eyes as he took in the fool who had dared to contradict him. He swiped off the tears and glared at the culprit.

'Sly, Sudden Death,' he said. 'You're right. I mocked her. But I did so only to discourage her. I egged her on. But I did so only to dissuade her. I may have nudged her a bit. But I did so only so she would stop.'

'I'm going to give you one more chance to answer the question,' Fámorótì told him. 'I won't ask you a second time. Where is Oyíndàmólá?'

'Tell them yourself,' said Sly, Sudden Death. 'Tell them.'

'He has sold her. It's obvious,' said Aya'ba Oyátómi. 'Why else would he bring her here? Where's the Arab? Tell the Arab to bring out my daughter before I go into those tents and fetch her myself.'

'She's not with Òyìnbó,' said Sly, Sudden Death, his eyes heavy with sorrow. 'Tell them, Chief Òrombó. Tell them what you did to the princess.'

Òrombó was left with no choice: 'She was swept away,' he said. 'She leapt into the river.'

'That's a lie, Chief Òrombó,' Sly, Sudden Death piped up again. 'The princess did not leap. You pushed her. You pushed her into the depths, and she was swept away.'

Fúyé unsheathed his hunting knife, his knife hand moistening with sweat. All he needed was the word from Fámorótì. All he needed was a signal. The execution would be swift. He waited, but, instead, Fámorótì said, quietly, 'Stand aside, Fúyé. This is a task I cannot ask you to do for me.'

Fúyé began to argue.

'I have to do this myself, Fúyẹ́.' Fámorótì's voice would brook no argument.

With utmost reluctance, Fúyẹ́ returned his knife to its sheath.

'You will die tonight,' Fámorótì assured Òrombó. 'But between us it's not over.'

He meant that he had a score to settle with him, and that one day, in this life or in the hereafter, or in another life, they would meet again to settle it.

'Thank you, Káṣìmawò,' Aya'ba Ọyátómi said to Sly, Sudden Death, calling him by his real name. 'Now you must go home,' she said to him. 'Go home.' She turned to the other guards. 'Go home,' she said to them. 'Go home to your wives and children.'

Òrombó waited until the last guard had melted into the night before turning to Fámorótì.

'You'll be pleased to know,' he said, with a baiting leer on his face, 'that your bride didn't die untouched. I saw to it.'

Fámorótì did not rise to the bait.

Fúyẹ́ did.

Fúyẹ́ charged.

Twenty-three

It was as if Fúyẹ́'s long torso had fused with the hunter's knife in his hand as he charged at Òrombó.

Òrombó was paralysed with fear, but also with astonishment. In his much-storied life of hard graft and unrelieved infamy, never had he come across a sight as accursedly confounding as this: a mere mortal who had turned himself into a spear.

Fúyẹ́'s body, in flight, appeared to take the shape of a spear, the knife the gleaming tip of its shaft.

There was no doubt whatsoever in Òrombó's petrified mind that this masterstroke of the esoteric arts was the handiwork of a powerful new oracle, an oracle he sorely wished he'd had the good fortune of knowing.

It wasn't just Òrombó who was dazzled by Fúyẹ́. The warriors gasped at the sight. Even Fámorótì, who had before witnessed Fúyẹ́ enact this feat on the battlefield, and who knew it owed everything to Fúyẹ́'s punishingly rigorous regimen of practice, over many years, was as wonderstruck as Aya'ba Ọyátómi who stared, speechless, at the spectacle.

It made no difference whether Òrombó fled or whether he stayed put; the wholesale scale of his bulk and the bounteous stretch of his body made the outcome a foregone conclusion: it was inevitable that the self-propelled spear hurtling towards him would make contact with his body and plunge into his insides.

The onlookers watched with bated breath.

But as Fúyẹ́ approached Òròmbó, as the knife firmly bolted to his hands set to impale Òròmbó against the tall mahogany tree behind him, the life suddenly and completely drained out of Fúyẹ́.

His poise unravelled, his trajectory faltered, and he dropped like a sack of yams.

Some said that he was already dead when he hit the ground; not only was he dead, they said, the blood that trickled from the countless wounds on his body came out congealed.

'I changed my mind.' It was the Sheikh. He was standing outside his tent, savouring the deep puzzlement, the unspeakable fear on the faces now turned to look at him. His men, nowhere to be seen a moment ago, now were everywhere – by his side, up the hill, and down the slope – their flintlock muskets squarely aimed, first, though unseen, at Fúyẹ́ – they were his executioners – and now at the warriors.

The warriors had heard of this new-fangled white man's wizardry, which they called ṣakabùlà from the sound it made, which possessed the ability to spit death at men, but few of them had seen it in the flesh, let alone at work. Until they saw it spit death into Fúyẹ́ that night, many of them had refused to believe it existed.

The manner of Fúyẹ́'s death shocked them to the marrow. Some likened it to the improbable sight of a swarm of fireflies colliding with an elephant and bringing it down.

The oracle who did this was not to be toyed with.

Even Òròmbó was shaken. Even though he was aware, more than anyone else there that night, of the killing power of ṣakabùlà – a prolific killing power unmatched by anything he knew, except,

perhaps, the lightning bolts of the thunder god – he, too, was profoundly shaken.

His shock was compounded by the fact that in those moments
when he watched certain death sail towards him in the shape of a
human spear, he had lost control of his sphincter muscle. The moist
evidence was concealed between his thighs and under his bulgy trousers but the rich odour could not be hidden.

'I will have Zainab,' the Sheikh announced. 'Where's my Zainab?'

Òrombó, stinking from head to toe, beamed from ear to ear.

'Sàìnóbù had to leave in a hurry,' he informed the Sheikh. 'She
had to leave, and, alas, she will not be coming back. Not tonight, at
any rate.'

'Where has she gone?'

'Let us just say, my dear friend, were she to come back tonight, it
will be another nine months before she emerges from her mother's
womb.'

'You reek of fear, my friend, and you make no sense.'

'Reincarnation is, I believe, what you call it.'

The Sheikh paused to take this in.

'Zainab is dead?'

'Dead?' Òrombó feigned confusion. 'Sàìnóbù has gone to deliver
a message to the ancestors, that's all. She'll be back, just not quite
yet. As a token of my apology for Sàìnóbù's inability to join us quite
yet, and so on and so forth, and to thank you for changing your mind
with such perfect timing, I gift you him,' Òrombó gestured at
Fámorótì, 'I gift her to you,' he gestured at Aya'ba Oyátómi, 'I gift
them to you,' he gestured at the warriors. 'I gift you every one of
them. They are all yours. Take them with you.'

Two warriors charged Òrombó. They were roasted to death
with gunpowder.

'How did Zainab die?' the Sheikh wanted to know.

'Between friends, there cannot be lies,' Òrombó declared, switching to Awúsá. 'I will tell you the truth, my dear friend. This is what happened. Once you turned down my offer, Sàìnóbù was of no use to me, so I encouraged her to take a swim.'

The Sheikh had come to know his friend quite well.

'You pushed her into the water?'

Òrombó bristled at the accusation, even though that was exactly what happened.

'I nudged her,' he said. He had the air of a man greatly wronged. He seemed on the verge of tears. 'I asked her gently, but she refused.' He used the edge of his gown to wipe non-existent tears off his cheeks. 'I sent a slave to my father last week,' he added, cryptically, by way of explanation.

The Sheikh understood at once.

'Any word from him?'

'From my father or the slave?' Òrombó asked.

'From your father or the slave.'

'Not a sigh from my father,' Òrombó declared, morosely. 'And not a pip from the slave I sent to him.'

'So you sent Zainab after the slave you'd sent to your father?'

Òrombó was grateful that his friend understood.

'That is more or less what happened,' he said.

'That's a pity,' said the Arab. 'I was going to keep her for myself.'

'Next time, my friend. Next time. There's a lot more Sàìnóbù where Sàìnóbù came from.'

The thought of all the Sàìnóbùs he would now be in a position to sell did wonders for Òrombó's spirits. It transformed his bleak mood into one of radiance. He felt radiant with smugness. The first object of his smugness was Fúyé.

He towered over the young warrior's dead body and wagged a reproachful finger in his face.

'I told you to know your place, but you said I had a smelly mouth,' he said. 'I said it was wise to respect your betters, but you said I had bad breath. Not that I blame you. How could I? I blame your parents. If your parents had brought you up well, you would in all likelihood still be lying here tonight, dead, but you wouldn't have had the bad manners to open your mouth and insult me.' He rose to his full height and declared, loudly, for the benefit of those who had ears: 'Let that be a lesson to you all.'

He paused, briefly, to watch the Sheikh's servants as they briskly set about casting the captives in iron neck rings and anklets of chains.

His attention swiftly shifted back to the dead man.

'You tried to kill me but all you succeeded in doing was to make me soil myself,' he informed Fúyẹ, towering over his body. 'But I must thank you for that because for a whole week now I haven't been able to relieve myself. There was nothing I didn't try, no concoction my wives didn't force on me, all to no avail. Every time I entered the forest and squatted and attempted to do my business, I would grunt and grunt. If you'd heard me grunting, you'd have thought it a new bride having her first child, but the constipation was all for nothing, nothing came of it. It was as if I had swallowed a rock. I suffered! O how I suffered. But now I'm purged. Now I feel like the fresh evening breeze after the first rains. And it's all thanks to you.'

He began to walk away from Fúyẹ. But then, suddenly, he stopped in his tracks. He turned around, as if some lowly commoner had dared to tap him, quite rudely, on the shoulder. But there was no one tapping him on the shoulder. He walked away. He had scarcely taken more than a couple of steps when quite suddenly, again, he swung around. He grabbed hold of his gown, firmly, by the shoulder and yanked at it, as if it were being pulled away, forcibly, from him.

'Let go of my gown!' he hissed at his invisible assailant.

'Say something!' he bellowed. 'Let go of my gown and say something!'

'Speak up!' he shouted.

'The white man merely killed you,' he yelled. 'He did not make you dumb on top of that!'

He cupped his hand to his ear and leaned forward, the better to hear Fúyẹ́'s spirit, for it could only be Fúyẹ́'s spirit he was talking to.

He listened and instantly reeled back.

'That is childish,' he fumed. 'Childish and immature.'

Then, glaring at the dead man lying before him, he hissed, 'And your mother too!' before stalking off.

Fámorótì, in chains, roared. He did not cease to roar until the Arab slaver's servants knocked him out.

Òrombó ignored him and sidled up to Aya'ba Ọyátómi. He leaned close to her, leering at her, breathing heavily into her face, his face vaguely terror-stricken, for he was still afraid of her, even though his old nemesis now stood before him in shackles.

His face was pugnacious; his eyes were divested of all trace of fellow feeling: they were the unseeing eyes of a heat-seeking two-headed viper poised to strike at itself.

'I told you,' he hissed at her. 'I told you.'

Then he stalked off.

Aya'ba Ọyátómi stood, her legs encased in leaden chains, and watched him walk away.

'Don't flatter yourself, Òrombó,' she called after him. 'You're a rancid human being, but that doesn't make you unique. Our land has been awash with vermin like you ever since the white man came, from the ocean and from the desert. It's the sign of the times, I suppose. It's every man for himself and the gods against us all.'

Little has come down to us about what happened afterwards to Aya'ba Ọyátómi and Fámorótì and all the other men and women who were that night betrayed by Òrombó, except that the Arab slaver to whom he sold them traded them a few weeks later, fed up, he said, with their never-ending troublemaking.

Fámorótì and Aya'ba Ọyátómi ended up in the hold of a Portuguese slaver in Lagos sailing to Rio. Their descendants today live in Brazil, and Cuba, and Trinidad, Jamaica, Haiti, Colombia, and in the United States of America.

Òrombó went back to the palace that night, and covertly installed himself as king after secretly interring the king's remains. He kept knowledge of the self-coronation to a select few sycophants and fellow conspirators, waiting for the perfect moment to share the glad tidings with his subjects, the people of Òṣogùn. In the days that followed, anyone outside this circle of perfidy who knew that the king had died, that an imposter had ascended the throne, was put to the sword.

Today, two hundred years later, Òrombó is considered to be the patron saint of African leaders; his spiritual scions continue to sell their people to the highest bidder.

Òrombó was still biding his time, still harbouring his bloodstained secrets, when the Malian cavalry came bursting through the city gates.

PART THREE

1821

The Madman

Twenty-four

Vultures hovered above the rising clouds of white smoke, beady-eyed and jaunty, as the raging fires engulfing the town began gradually to die down, revealing charred coal and brittle ash, and every so often, a sumptuous meal for the vultures where once stood wide adobe houses.

Since his capture, Àjàyí already had gone through the hands of two sets of Malians. Ìjí was no longer with him. When last he saw Ìjí, his friend was staring, forlorn, at the chains clamped on his feet; he was caged, together with a thousand others, in a thatched palm enclosure planted that morning on the hill by the invaders. The barracoon stood at exactly the same spot where only a week before had stood the tents of the Arab slave trader known to all of Òṣogùn as Òyìnbó.

Àjàyí's second owner, who had traded a horse for him, took him to another barracoon, this one standing outside the burned and blackened remains of the house Àjàyí had left that morning, the house he had known his whole life as home.

His mother was there – Ìyá's joy was beyond measure when she saw him, but it took him a moment to understand her first question.

'Where's your sister?'

He looked at her in consternation because, surely, she couldn't possibly be asking him about Bọ́lá.

'Where's Bọ́lá?' she asked again.

Clearly she was. He looked around him. He looked, first, at the glowing-faced Malians and their blood-soaked cowhide switches; then he looked at the wailing crush of people – all of them his neighbours, some of them his relatives; all of them his friends, or his sisters' friends, or his parents' friends – all cooped up with him and his mother and his sisters in the bamboo barrack. He looked at them, but what he was doing was looking for Bọ́lá.

'I'm talking to you, Àjàyí. Where's your sister? We haven't seen her since you left home together this morning.'

His eyes scanned each misery-filled face around him, locking in on each face before slowly moving on to the next.

He saw the face of Àjíkẹ́ the dyer.

He saw the face of Tọ́yèjẹ the hunter.

He saw the face of Táíwò the midwife.

He saw the face of Ódéléògún the blacksmith.

He saw the face of Kalẹ̀jayé the tailor.

He saw the face of Dégẹṣin the iron-smelter.

He saw the face of Bọ́sẹ̀dé the nut-oil maker.

He saw the face of Adesọji the tapper.

He saw the face of Ọbasá the roofer.

He saw the face of Adélabú the calabash-carver.

He saw the face of Àyánwándé the drummer.

He saw the face of Fágbémiró the soap-maker.

He saw the face of Ọláwálé the sword-maker.

He saw the face of Bankọ́lé the basket-weaver.

He saw the face of Bọ́lánlé the weaver of words.

He saw the face of Olúdọtun the woodworker.

He saw the face of Olúmidé the axe-maker.

He saw the face of Babalóṣà the herbalist.

He saw the face of Kíkẹ́lọmọ the mat-maker.

He saw the face of Fámúrewá the tanner.

He saw the face of Ládéjọbí the shaver of heads.

He saw the face of Bàbá Oníṣọ̀nà the carver.

He saw the face of Fáladé the potter.

He saw the face of Dérìn the hatter.

He saw the face of Fáṣọlá the rain-maker.

He saw the face of Lánlókè the fishmonger.

He saw the face of Adékọ̀yà the sculptor.

He saw the face of Ṣówọ̀ who made the finest knives, razors, bill-hooks and arrowheads in all the land.

He saw these faces and many more, but he didn't see Bọ́lá.

He didn't see Bọ́lá's face.

'Where's Bọ́lá?'

His mother's voice came as from afar.

Bọ́lá was nowhere to be seen.

'You left the house together this morning.'

He scanned the faces again, carefully, convinced he'd missed out a face the first time around. He scanned them carefully. He was certain Bọ́lá was there somewhere.

But she wasn't. He turned to his mother and said, 'Bọ́lá is not here, Mother. I don't know where she is.'

'We haven't seen your father either.'

She sounded calm, but her eyes were wild with worry.

Àjàyí looked carefully at the faces around them, the same faces he had twice already studied in great detail. He started the process all over again, gazing deeply into each face before moving on to the next. This time he searched for two faces; he searched for his sister and he searched for their father.

Neither of them was there.

Nothing daunted, convinced he'd somehow missed them, that they were there – he had only to pay attention – he started all over again.

He was halfway through the gallery of abject and terrified faces, and not any of them Bọ́lá or his father, when he heard his mother's voice calling.

'Àjàyí,' she said. 'What are you saying, Àjàyí?'

His lips were moving, furiously, passionately, but his mouth was soundless. He knew he was speaking, that there were words scrambling to get out of his head – clear, logical and intelligible words gushing out of his mind – but when they reached his lips, the words arrived with the sound cut off, so that even though his lips were speaking, his voice was not; his voice was silent.

His younger siblings saw the fear on their mother's face and the blank terror in his eyes and burst into tears.

He took a long, deep breath and started scanning the faces all over again.

His lips started moving again. Once again there was no sound coming out of his mouth. But in his head this time, he could hear himself; quite clearly he could hear himself. As his eyes settled on each face, his lips would move, and he would utter a name. His mouth was silent, but his voice was not; in his head, clearly, he could hear his voice chanting out the names.

Twenty-five

Ìjí, Àjàyí's friend, died that afternoon. He died while fleeing the barracoon.

His death was grisly, but saying that wasn't saying much; that final day in the legends of Òṣogùn's existence was nothing if not a catalogue of grisly deaths.

Àjàyí had no inkling about it; it happened while he was being goat-herded with his mother and his sisters and his nephew by the Malians. It happened while he was quietly sobbing as it became clear that he might never see them again; not just his missing older sister and their father but his entire family. He was sobbing, and his sisters were sobbing, and little Àlàdé too, because Àjàyí had been lotted up as the possession of a Malian chieftain who was said to be domiciled in Ìṣẹ́yìn, while Ìyá and the girls had been parcelled over to a chieftain who was headed with them to an unknown destination in the opposite direction.

Àjàyí would hear nothing about Ìjí's death until months later, in Ìṣẹ́yìn, which now was home, and where his path would cross with that of a man called the madman – Asínwín – because he was a madman.

It was from the madman that he found out what happened to Ìjí.

Ìṣẹ́yìn was a mere day's trek from the ash-strewn ruins of Àjàyí's hometown, but it might as well have been separated from Òṣogùn

BIYI BÁNDÉLÉ

by the mighty ocean itself. In Ìsẹ̀yìn, Àjàyí was known, euphemistic-ally, as Sárákí's houseboy. No one but his master and mistress knew his name, but even they rarely called him Àjàyí. As they were devout Malians, they deemed it only proper that he should go by a Malian name, but they never could quite make up their minds whether he should answer to the Malian name of Súnmóílà, or Mùráínà, or Bùráímọ̀. His mistress called him Súnmóílà, his master Mùráínà, and their children called him Bùráímọ̀. Sometimes they misplaced those names and instead called him Dísù, which was a diminutive of Ìdrísù, which was derived from Idris; all of which names at one point or the other they made him answer to.

To everyone else, he was Sárákí's houseboy. He was known as Sárákí's houseboy because his master's name was Sárákí. The neighbours who called him Sárákí's houseboy knew perfectly well that he was Sárákí's slave and not his houseboy; all houseboys were the property of their master, having been bought and paid for by him.

Before Àjàyí became known as Sárákí's houseboy, though, he was known, albeit briefly, as Jìnádù's houseboy. This was because he had been the property of a man named Jìnádù before he became Sárákí's property.

Before he became known as Jìnádù's houseboy, however, he was known, albeit briefly, as Sárákí's houseboy, because the self-same Sárákí, who became his master after Jìnádù, had been his master before Jìnádù.

The explanation for this was simple: Àjàyí became Sárákí's prop-erty by virtue of being given to Sárákí from a lot divvied up from the spoils of the Òṣogùn expedition. This division of spoils by the Malians took place even as Òṣogùn was burning around them. Min-utes after taking possession of the boy as his slave, Sárákí spotted his fellow war chieftain, Jìnádù, approaching on his splendid stallion and immediately traded Àjàyí for the horse.

After keeping Jìnádù's horse for two months, and possibly because the horse clearly despised him and bucked whenever he saddled the beast to ride, Sárákí came to the conclusion that his decision to acquire the horse had been rash, and if he had to choose between the horse and the slave he knew which he would rather own and it wasn't the cantankerous horse.

Sárákí was a native of Ìlọrin, as was Jìnádù, and they kept their wives and children there, but he kept a home as well as a second family in Ìsẹ́yìn, as did Jìnádù; and as they had both repaired to Ìsẹ́yìn, after the expedition, to see their families, and since they also happened to be neighbours, when Sárákí decided the horse had to go, it was simply a matter of going next door to return it to its owner.

Jìnádù took his horse back and returned Sárákí's property – namely, Àjàyí – without much of a fuss. It wouldn't have crossed his mind to make a fuss; Sárákí was an old friend. Although he did grumble a bit, under his breath, about being short-changed, he was secretly glad to be rid of Àjàyí. His plan to bulk him up and take him to the coast and sell him for a tidy profit had come to nothing: if Àjàyí was gaunt when he entered Jìnádù's house, he was little more than a scarecrow when he left two months later. He hadn't been starved: it was mainly because he was inconsolable with grief and unable to keep down anything he ate; and he was suffering from the ravages of ibà.

Àjàyí's departure from Jìnádù's house came as a relief not only to Jìnádù but to Àjàyí as well; if Sárákí had treated Jìnádù's horse with suspicion and not a little trepidation, Jìnádù had treated Àjàyí and his constantly being sick with suspicion and not a little fear; he was fully convinced that Àjàyí was hell-bent on picking his pocket by dying on him. And so, although he wasn't an exceptionally cruel master, he was cruel. Àjàyí's departure from his home brought him considerable joy. He threw a feast, ostensibly to welcome his horse back home but really to bid Àjàyí good riddance and to thank God for sparing him from the dire consequences of a thoughtless investment.

In Sárákí's house, life was considerably less desolate for Àjàyí. And he made a friend in Asínwín, the madman who came in from time to time to carry out household chores in return for scraps from the family table. The madman was the only houseboy in the whole of Ìséyìn who wasn't owned by his employer, and because he wasn't a slave, he didn't quite merit the title of houseboy.

The townspeople chose, instead, to call him Asínwín, the madman, and since he happened to be a madman, he did not mind at all.

It was from the madman that Àjàyí got the gruesome details of the last hour of his friend Ìjí's last day on earth.

Twenty-six

There was no getting around the fact that Asínwín was truly mad.

The most frequently touted account of the origins of his madness had it that many moons ago he got home one day to find his wife and children gone.

Together with his mother and father, and his mother's younger sister with her husband and children, and his father's older brother with his wife and children, his wife and five children had disappeared without trace.

They were the victims of the only game in town, the pestilence raging through the land: the slave trade. But the slavers responsible for the disappearance of Asínwín's family were not Malians; they did not wage war with predatory armies or lay waste to cities in the name of God. These men were a different kind of slaver; they belonged to an esoteric ring of people-snatchers known to deploy stealth rather than violence, to lay siege with spells rather than swords; ensnaring their quarry with incantations, they lured them away from home, farm and market with intoxicating wordplay laced with giddy-making epigrams imbued with hauntingly seductive rhythm, and in this way abducted them without the use of force.

That was how Asínwín lost his family, and he hadn't been the same since.

The chant-churning slavers' way of acquisition was bloodless, but it was no less devastating than the gore-soaked formula of the Malians.

This was the tale Àjàyí heard, and he had no reason to doubt it, even though when once he summoned the courage to ask the madman to comment on it, Asínwín simply carried on with the task at hand: namely, chopping a log of camwood timber into firewood.

He did not utter so much as a grunt in response.

Asínwín was by far the best-known person in Ìsẹ́yìn; countless were the number of times when total strangers arriving at one of the tollgates at the entrance to the town were heard to announce, 'I have come to see Kùsẹ́yìn, whose oldest daughter, Ọláòtán, was born the year the madman's kindred were taken from him.' Or they might declare, 'I am looking for Lábísí, whose smoked-fish stall stands at the spot in the market where the madman first arrayed himself in the clothes of nakedness,' or they might say, 'Take me to Kúdírá, who used to brew beer to sell, not far from the renowned madman's well-known place of abode.'

The renowned madman's well-known place of abode was a threadbare mat spread out on the bare earth right behind the rubbish dump at Ìsẹ́yìn market.

As if such enduring fame were not enough, Asínwín's immortal name was assured when poets took to singing verses about him. Of Asínwín's hair, one poet observed that it looked as if it had never knowingly come into contact with a comb. This was not poetic licence; it was true: when Asínwín stood still for any length of time, passers-by soon gathered to marvel at the shaggy thicket on his head, as if they fully expected a nestling to burrow its way out of this wilderness and take to the sky. More than one person had been heard to observe that the hair on Asínwín's head had much in common with the naturally matted coiffure of dàda, those children who are known to spring out of their mother's womb with the wildly knotted and impossibly entangled hair on their head exuberantly lush and fully formed.

Such was the hair on Asínwín's head. But Asínwín was no dàda. He was a madman.

On most days, when he stalked the market hunting for vultures, as he often did, he had a certain glint in his eyes; a glint the size of a distant star. It burned with the fierceness of a million wildfires. On such days, when passers-by hailed him, Asínwín ignored them, betraying not the slightest sign of recognition, not even of those whom he'd known all his life.

On such days, Asínwín looked thoroughly, and unconditionally, rabidly and unapproachably mad.

And yet Asínwín was not a full-time madman. This is not to say that he was only half-mad or that he wasn't completely mad. He was unutterably mad; that much was certain. But there were days — admittedly, not often — when his madness took leave of him and he became utterly and completely sane.

You might think he would be grateful for this rare gift of sanity. Not so; not Asínwín. Asínwín hated such days with every bone in his body.

It was said that he almost took his own life the first time he experienced this unannounced visitation of stone-cold tranquillity. He couldn't remember the last time he got up in the morning of sound and sober mind and body, and, really, he didn't want to. It was a feeling, he declared, that he wouldn't wish on his worst enemy.

He suspected he might have caught the affliction from a curse sprinkled into something he had eaten; perhaps it was the sumptuous meal he'd made of the bird of carrion he'd brought home the previous day. As a past master in hunting the bigger birds of the marketplace, it was his wont to every so often make himself a tasty bird stew, seasoned with just the slightest pinch of salt — salt was a vanishingly rare luxury — garnished with dollops of irú.

He was quite aware the vultures detested him. He could see it in their beady eyes and in the way they cocked their bald pates to the side to lower at him whenever he chanced to walk past when they gathered by the abattoir for their morning repast. He wouldn't put it past them to have had a hand in this vile irruption of inexplicable sanity that had taken possession of him.

'Fortunately,' reported the madman, gravely, to Àjàyí, 'the first time it happened, it lasted less than half a day. It started at cockcrow and by morning meal, it was gone, thank God.'

But that was only the beginning, he told Àjàyí; it only got worse. Now, there were whole days — sometimes many, many whole days — when he was afflicted with this shamelessly opportunistic malady called sanity.

'How does it feel for a madman to be afflicted by sanity?' Àjàyí asked him.

Asínwín glared at Àjàyí with a mad glint in his eyes, but he knew it was a serious question.

'That's like asking a dead man what it feels like to be alive.'

Àjàyí immediately sat up, genuinely startled at how suddenly the conversation had veered from madmen to dead men.

It didn't help that he was already in the grips of a virulent attack of ibà; that he was in the throes of a vicious episode that left him in a semi-permanent state of groggy befuddlement. He was constantly on the verge of passing out.

He felt like passing out, but it would be bad manners to do so while talking to the madman, so he fought off the dizziness by striking a pose of grave and earnest curiosity while listening to the madman with a carefully composed expression of rapt concentration.

To the madman, though, he simply looked mad.

'You look the way I like to feel,' Asínwín observed, peering closely into Àjàyí's burning eyes.

Àjàyí sensed himself keeling over. He realised this as it was happening and willed his mind to break the fall. His mind did its best, but its best wasn't good enough. Àjàyí toppled over.

A spark of recognition flared in the madman's eye. Now he knew what was wrong with Àjàyí.

'You are not mad,' he said, breaking Àjàyí's fall with his outstretched hands. 'Your madness is the madness of ibà.' He went quiet, briefly, and stared thoughtfully into the distance. Then, finally, he grudgingly conceded, 'It is madness. It's just not proper madness.'

Àjàyí was shivering, even though it was a hot, sunny day. His teeth were clattering; his eyes burning in their sockets.

He felt rotten from head to toe, but he didn't want the madman to stop talking.

'What happened the first time you woke up sane?' he asked the madman. 'What did you do to make it go away?'

'Why,' said Asínwín, 'I worked. I worked myself to oblivion.'

Work was the perfect antidote to those nauseous bouts of sanity. He found he could survive any onslaught of the affliction, no matter how severe it might be, if he occupied himself with a task that was physically all-consuming. And so, whenever he felt threatened by the spectre of sanity, he went to work.

It was on such days that he turned up at Àjàyí's master's compound, spruced up in his bedraggled but clean, wide-bottom kèmbè trousers and dàṣíkí top, his body freshly dipped in river water and thoroughly bathed, his unruly hair freshly washed with Ọṣẹ dúdú. Anybody now chancing on the madman who didn't know him would be forgiven for thinking he was but an indigent but respectable citizen on his way to a feast.

Of course, some rolled their eyes when they saw him. That this was how he would turn up to chop firewood – dressed up as for a bride-taking – was proof, they said, that he was a madman even on those days when his madness was at bay.

It pleased him no end when people said that.

Thus was he dressed on the day he told Àjàyí the story of Ìjí's death.

The lord of the house and his lady were out, with the children, gone to the mosque. Asínwín had finished his allotted tasks for the day.

He reached for his ikòko, his pipe, and filled it with fresh tabà. Then he made an announcement that came without warning.

'I shall now tell you what happened to your friend Ìjí,' he told Àjàyí.

The malaria fog engulfing Àjàyí's brain lifted.

'Ìjí?' he said, stupefied. 'How come you know Ìjí?'

Asínwín tamped down the tabà with his thumb.

'I was there when they killed him,' he informed Àjàyí. 'The Malians killed him. A man called Núrùdín struck the first blow. The Devil's Dín, they call him, because he's spawn of the devil. Núrùdín struck the first blow, but Sáráki was there too, and he, too, struck a blow.'

At the mention of his master's name, fear surged through Àjàyí. He stared at the madman's pipe. He cast an anxious look around.

'Why are you talking this way?' he asked angrily. 'Why are you saying these things?'

Unperturbed, Asínwín fired up his ikòko.

'I shall tell you what happened to Ìjí,' he said.

He pulled deeply on the ikòko.

Twenty-seven

The madman paused and looked off into the distance. He pulled deeply on his pipe and exhaled quietly; his fiery, bloodshot eyes unblinking but not harsh.

'It's a mystery,' he said, 'how Ìjí managed to slip out of the barracoon.'

And he did it, too, right under the noses of the eagle-eyed Malians standing sentinel with their bloodied knives and bludgeons. It was an even greater mystery how he managed to slip off the iron fetters locked to his feet and the metal ring shackling him by the neck, like a goat in a herd, to the others penned up with him.

He had gone past all the guards and was already approaching the great forest at the bottom of the hill when he walked straight into one of the very same Malian soldiers — the one afflicted in the foot with a jiga infestation — who earlier that day had captured him and Àjàyí in the palm grove.

If Ìjí had stepped aside for Jiga Foot and kept going, perhaps he would have pulled off his escape without incident. He did step aside but he made the mistake of apologising as he did so. He mumbled the apology in the best Awúsá he could muster, which was next to none at all, but he compensated for his poor vocabulary by saying it in his best imitation of a native Awúsá speaker. To Awúsá ears, of course, what he said was utter gibberish. It was utter gibberish uttered with an unmistakably Yorùbá cadence.

Jiga Foot's ears seemed to rise, like the eyes of a snail, out of his head. He came to a halt and, slowly, as if he was suffering from a stiff neck, turned and stared at Ìjí.

'You,' he said in Awúsá. 'Turn around. Let's see your face.'

Ìjí knew better than to obey him. He did the wise thing and he took off instead. He took off at a pace that fell short of a full-on race only because he was by nature an exceptionally poor runner.

Barely able to walk because of the suppurating weals on his feet, let alone run after the fleeing captive, the Malian fighter turned to a tall man with a dour face standing close by.

'Núrùdín,' he yelled. 'Are you just going to stand there picking your teeth?'

Núrùdín wasn't picking his teeth, but from the way he watched Ìjí run past without even bothering to give chase, he might as well have been standing there wielding a toothpick instead of the bow and arrows he had in his hands.

'You're still standing there picking your teeth.' Jiga Foot was now beside himself with rage. 'Which is why you didn't notice the Bayarabe when he breezed right past you in the first instance.'

Bayarabe was Awúsá for Yorùbá; with the Malians it was a synonym for slave.

'Stop fretting, Badaru,' Núrùdín said. 'Look at the boy. He runs like a monkey. He's going nowhere.'

'I don't care if he runs like your pregnant mother,' Badaru retorted. 'Get him now.'

In spite of his fury, though, Jiga Foot had to concede that Núrùdín was right. Ìjí's ungainly running posture and the erratic and convulsive movement of his body did bring to mind an aged monkey at full pelt.

If Ìjí possessed the gangly build of a superannuated monkey, Núrùdín had the legs of a duiker. And when he finally decided to give chase, his long legs combined with his natural facility for speed covered as much distance in one step as Ìjí could manage in ten.

Ìjí darted an anxious look over his shoulder and watched the tall Malian bound down on him.

Ìjí tripped and fell flat on his face.

He knew it was over. He was certain it was over.

He was wrong. Instead of pouncing on him, Núrùdín stopped running. Not only did he stop running, he came to a halt.

He gave Ìjí time to catch his breath, to gather himself off the ground.

Those who knew Núrùdín knew he didn't do it out of the kindness of his heart. When they observed Núrùdín and his quarry, they saw a cat amusing itself by indulging the futile escape fantasies of the mouse it was about to have for supper. Núrùdín halted when the Yorùbá boy tripped only because he loved the thrill of the chase and he saw no reason to end it just yet.

Gingerly, Ìjí picked himself off the ground. Once he realised that the Malian had come to a halt and was making no attempt to apprehend him, he paused to weigh his options. There wasn't much to weigh, really. Either he stopped running and gave himself up or he continued running until the Malian caught him. It was grim either way; whatever happened, the Malians were certain to make an example of him.

He was standing at the edge of the forest now, under the shade of a tall àràbà tree. He knew the tree quite well. It was the tallest àràbà in the forest – so tall, from the top of it you could see beyond Ìséyìn and well into the nearest villages.

Several Malians had now gathered behind Núrùdín to stare at him. Ìjí ignored them. He cautiously walked away from the àràbà. He walked slowly, not wanting to spook his hunter into resuming the chase before he was fully ready for him. After a few paces he stopped and then, suddenly, he was off again, running like a monkey, only this time he made straight for the àràbà tree and its endlessly sprawling trunk. He ran straight up the tree. With a burst of speed that seemed hard to fathom on land, let alone on a tree, he ran all the way to the top of the tree; he ran up the tree with a facile agility that left Núrùdín and Badaru and all the other Malians speechless. He didn't pause, he didn't look left or right, as he ascended the tree. He stopped only when he could go no further, when he'd reached the topmost branch of the àràbà.

He looked down below and saw the cindered remains of Òṣogùn and wept.

If he squinted, which he didn't, he could see the big birds of carrion swooping down and sailing up as they gorged on the remains of Òrombó behind the palace where the Malians had dumped his body after they slaughtered him.

Directly below, at the foot of the tree, Núrùdín and Badaru were having a heated argument.

Ìjí looked beyond them, his eyes searching for the barracoon. The barracoon was high up, on the hilltop. He could see faces glued to cages staring up at him, looking sullen, and beaten, but he could feel the goodwill exuding from them.

From one of the cages, he heard a voice call out his name.

'Ìjímèrè!' the voice yelled.

Ìjí knew that voice well. It was the voice of his best friend. It was the voice of the boy who gave him the name Ìjí, when they were but little boys, the first time he'd climbed this same àràbà tree at a sprint, like the very monkeys born on its branches.

'Ìjímèrè!' he'd called him. And the name had stuck.

'Àjàyí!' he replied. And that was when the first arrow from

Núrùdín's bow came sailing up. It was followed by another. And another. Soon, not just Núrùdín but every single Malian nearby was shooting arrows at him. There were so many arrows raining up, it was as if Ìjí had been engulfed by a cloud of locusts.

'He was probably dead by the time Núrùdín's third arrow struck him,' said the madman. 'But he didn't fall from the tree. He did not fall. His body was impaled to the branch he was sitting on.'

Except for Àjàyí's teeth clattering from the extreme cold wracking his body on this muggy day, there was silence in the house. The madman pulled deeply on his pipe and smoked.

Then he cupped the pipe in his hand and said, 'But you were there when it happened, Àjàyí, were you not? You witnessed it all. You were there, chained to Ìjí by the neck when he escaped. You helped him escape. You watched him escape. You saw him slip past the guards. You saw him run into the Malian. You watched him run. You saw him killed. Why, now, do you lie and say you didn't know he was dead?'

Àjàyí didn't say a word. His teeth were clattering so badly, he couldn't speak.

It was true he was present at the killing of Ìjímèrè. He'd seen everything. He was a witness from start to finish. But he wasn't lying when he said he wasn't aware of it.

Àjàyí never lied.

His mind, to protect him, had wiped it from his memory.

His mind had taken to doing all sorts of things that constantly bewildered him.

It had, for instance, conjured up the madman from the deepest recesses of his being; the madman was very real, but he didn't exist in flesh and bone. The madman was an emissary sent by the ancestors to mend Àjàyí as he lay shivering from a phantom cold, covered in a steaming blanket of his own sweat.

Àjàyí did not know any of this; he was blissfully unaware of it all: his mind, besieged, had gone into a blind panic and cried out for help. Of its own volition and without so much as a by your leave, his mind had gone at full tilt to a conclave of the ancestors, crying, 'Your son, Àjàyí, is going off the deep end. His entire world has turned upside down. I know you know all this, that I don't need to tell you: Òşogùn, his hometown, has been invaded and destroyed by strangers who couldn't have done it without the assistance of our own people. Everything has been taken away from him. His mother and father, and his sisters, his entire family, have been taken away from him. And his bosom friend, who was like his very own brother, is dead. He has lost everything in one day. His heart is heavy. His heart is heavy, and I don't know what to do.'

And the ancestors, whose hearts, too, were heavy with sorrow, said, 'Who shall we send to mend Àjàyí?'

And Èşù, the trickster god, said, 'I saw the child just now. He's lost his mind. He's gone mad. Let us send a madman to him. Madness only can heal madness. Let us send his kin the madman.'

So they sent the madman who called himself Asínwín. And with stories he cured Àjàyí of his madness.

The madman was not himself an ancestor; he existed nowhere in Àjàyí's past nor in the past of anybody who had ever lived. He came from the distant future, a future far more distant from us now than the time that elapsed between Àjàyí and his great-great-great-granddaughter.

The madman was a spirit being who had journeyed back a long way to look after a boy-child who was his own ancestor.

The madman's name wasn't really the madman. He came from the land of the unborn, where they have no names.

PART FOUR

1880

A Compact Atlas of Paradise

Twenty-eight

They had begun the long trek back to Lagos on the coast, the morning, several months earlier, when the steamer ran aground at an island near the headwaters of the great river, and sank, and they were forced to abandon the expedition. There were over two hundred men in the caravan of shipwrecked landfarers. There were naval officers, sailors, merchants, together with a team of stokers, porters, interpreters, cooks and other assistants; there were medical doctors, naturalists and geologists; there were linguists and lexicographers, like the old man, and missionaries, like Dandeson. Many, like the old man, who was better known as a clergyman, wore more than one hat.

Weeks on the trek turned into months; four weeks became four months. Gently rising hills and tablelands gave way to steep, conical mountains towering over deep, serpentine ravines; meandering trails of mud-caked riverbeds sloped into miles, endless miles upon miles, of lush vegetation.

The old man was over seventy years old and didn't look a day younger; his soft, baby face looked every inch the soft, baby face of an old man, a baby-faced man in his seventies, but there were days during the long trek when Dandeson, in his thirties, who insisted on walking alongside the old man, and carrying the old man's battered goatskin shoulder bag, found himself having to work hard to keep up with him. The old man walked at a steady, unhurried pace – some would say slow, even – but it was resolute and unflagging; once he got going, it seemed perfectly conceivable that he could keep on walking forever.

They sent messengers ahead of them to the towns and villages along their path – heralds to announce their approach – so that their arrival would neither be cause for surprise to anyone nor the occasion for a precipitation of poisoned missiles being let loose on them. As in all the land, there was good reason for the deep suspicion of unannounced visitors in these parts: from hamlets on the Atlantic coast and villages and towns in the rainforests and the savannah and cities at the edge of the Sahara Desert, thousands – tens of thousands – had been abducted and sold into slavery by marauding squads of Filani soldiers, mercenaries whose most versatile weapon was stealth and surprise. In the early days, such raids had been carried out in the name of God, but the raiders themselves, most of whom were not yet born in those early days, had long ceased to use the pretext of jihad as justification. They were born into plunder as a way of life and bred with beggar-thy-neighbour as the first rule of survival, as were their fathers and their fathers before them. To these men, being a plunderer was a trade no different than being a weaver or a cattle-rearer; it was just a lot more rewarding. Those of their targets who could do so robustly defended themselves, but most were no match for the fighting prowess of the raiders.

In pockets of the vast swathes of the lands stretching along the banks of the mighty rivers, the soldiers now ran a protection racket, a monthly communal toll where the people were made to pool together their ladan aiki – the fruits of their labour – to pay off the soldiers. Failure to do so meant that a village had to surrender a number of its inhabitants to the soldiers to be sold. It was kidnapping for ransom in all but name: those sold in this manner could be bought back by their families if they could raise the ransom.

This could be fiendishly difficult. The story was told of the man who sold his land which was all he had to his name and then had to sell himself to raise the ransom for his family.

The voyagers certainly did not want to be mistaken by anyone for people-rustlers. And so, they sent the runners ahead to proclaim their good faith: 'We come to you in peace,' and also their pedigree: 'We come to you in the name of our Sarauniya, the Sarauniya of England, who is also the Sarauniya of the coast country.'

If the response was warm – if it was an invitation to sup with the chief, as was often the case – they stayed the night. It sometimes happened, too, that the response to their peace offering was an arrow within a hair's breadth of the messenger's feet, a warning shot. This seldom happened. Sarauniya Victoria was a byword for the pinnacle of imperial might and prestige; every monarch in these parts had had dealings with one or other of her messengers. Or with the missionaries who often had come calling on them long before either the imperial messengers or the merchants showed up. Sometimes, that missionary also happened to be part of an approaching contingent. Oftentimes, that missionary was the old man.

At the entrance to one such town, a town the old man first visited during another expedition some forty years earlier, he enquired of the emissary from the king who had come to bid them welcome, an elderly eunuch, whether the old king was alive or dead. The question seemed like a bolt of lightning charging through the courtier's veins; leaping out of the bamboo palanquin he had arrived in, he rose to his full height – his back, hunched with age, now ramrod straight; his eyelashes bristling, shimmering with kohl – and tersely informed the old man, 'The king never dies,' before sashaying back into his carriage and being lifted up and carried away by his four attendants.

At supper that night, in the caravanserai right next door to the king's palace where they were lodged as His Majesty's special guests, the visitors reflected on the eunuch's exquisitely regal and haughty departure. The following morning, they were invited to an audience with the king. His Highness looked immaculate and deathless in his emerald-green, elegantly tailored, pure-silk velvet gown. He couldn't have been a day more than twenty-one years old.

Twenty-nine

They spent a weekend waiting out an unseasonal storm in a cluster of twenty villages which all bore the same name. Fortunately for the visitors, other similarly perplexed guests before them had cracked the enigma: since each village had a headman, and each headman his own name, the trick was to ignore such utter frivolities as individual village names, especially since there were none, and instead navigate your way around guided by signposts that were far more specific, namely the names of the headmen, meaning, for instance, you would set out for Shewu, where the headman was Shewu, or pass through Bakudu, whose headman was Bakudu, on your way to Yerima, whose headman was Yerima. The locals, who were perfectly happy with the name of their villages and not in the least confused by it, found the visitors' navigation formula overly complicated and utterly bewildering.

On their first day there, Dandeson and the old man went for a walk in Bakudu and came across a crowd gathered under a giant kuka tree.

They saw, in the middle of the crowd, a small, bearded man in a threadbare jalabiya holding forth in a loud, ringing voice, his tone bellicose, his face bristling with disdain.

'Do you know this chap?' Dandeson asked the old man. Dandeson knew that the place didn't exist where the old man didn't know half the town and somebody who knew the other half.

As Dandeson knew he would, the old man nodded. 'His name is Mustafa mai Hankali.'

'Mustafa the what? I thought hankali meant "gentle".'

'It does.'

'His name – this man's name – is Mustafa the Gentle?'

The old man nodded again. 'That's his name. You don't sound convinced.'

'If this is him being gentle,' said Dandeson, 'I would hate to run into him when he isn't feeling so good-natured.'

'It has been said of Mustafa,' replied the old man, 'that the vitriol that spews from his lips is a raging benediction; an invocation so fiery it is indistinguishable from a hex.' He smiled. 'You could call him an old friend,' he told Dandeson. 'It's been years since our paths crossed, though. The last time was at a salt market near Katsina in '68. We had a rather lively theological discussion.'

'You locked horns.'

'Let us say we had a difference of opinion and leave it at that.'

'What did you have a difference of opinion about?'

'My dear friend Mustafa was of the staunch belief, which he stated as fact, that Allah had assigned to every breed of animal, and every type of reptile and insect, the ages they are destined to live.'

'Meaning?'

'Meaning, for instance, mules are destined to live for fifty years, black scorpions a thousand years, snakes a hundred years, monkeys eight hundred years, and vultures a mere seven hundred years.'

'And you told him he was a few bricks short of a load.'

'I told him I was perfectly happy to accept a thousand years for scorpions but couldn't in all conscience give credence to his hypothesis for monkeys. I said I strongly believed that he had understated the fated age of monkeys by at least two weeks. Needless to say,

Mustafa wasn't best pleased with, as he called it, "my tone". He practically accused me of heresy. "Heresy?" I said. "Heaven forbid!" Fortunately, I was communicating with him mostly through an interpreter. I told him my interpreter had misheard what I was trying to say and had misinterpreted me.'

'And if I may ask,' Dandeson said, holding his sides, 'what were you trying to say?'

'I was trying to say that the hypothesis, not Mustafa himself, was, as you say, a few bricks short of a load.'

'I take it he's a cleric?' Dandeson asked after he'd stopped laughing.

The old man nodded. 'An itinerant cleric. They say of men like him, ya sha yawon duniya.'

'Which means? I know duniya means "world".'

'"He's travelled the world."'

'Not nearly as much as you have.'

'That may or may not be true,' said the old man. 'But we are talking about Mustafa the Gentle, not about me.'

'Why is he called Mustafa the Gentle?'

Mustafa the Gentle got the name because his wa'azi, his sermons, which were often concocted to the pattering kalangu of the gnawing pangs in his hunger-besieged insides, were anything but gentle. They were known for their ripe petulance and lively venom. This was his trademark; it was what announced him to the world; the habit that endeared him to his followers.

But antagonists claimed he was nothing but a sojan gona, a charlatan. His filthy jalabiya was a mere affectation, they said, a lurid display of poverty that had nothing to do with poverty; not unless constituting yourself into an affront to society's nostrils now counted as a measure of poverty. Everyone knew, they said, that the loathsome odour that followed Mustafa everywhere he went could be traced directly to his well-known aversion to personal hygiene.

To his followers, however, Mustafa the Gentle was the genuine article. His followers were matalauci, the poorest of the poor, men forever doomed to roam the land, condemned to live out their days in penury by the Filani raiders who hounded them all the days of their lives and made it unsafe and impossible for them to stay long enough in any one place to plant roots or pursue a trade. Ill-used by men in high places, powerful people whose wealth often derived from the trade in human beings, these men on the run flocked to hear Mustafa the Gentle wherever he was because they knew he and they were one. And he never failed to deliver. It mattered little that he could neither read nor write; what he had in abundance was a way with words; his wa'azi often possessed a heady, intoxicating quality, a frenzied ecstasy that was familiar to those who had experienced ravening fasting or tasted the cutting whips of dizzying hunger, a daily fact of life for those who lived hand to mouth.

'Anasara! Anasara!' The calls rang out as Dandeson and the old man made their way towards the spot in the centre where Mustafa stood, arms akimbo one moment, hands slashing through the air the next, hectoring, cajoling and bullying the crowd.

'Anasara! Anasara!'

A term drafted into Hausa from the Arabic nazareen, meaning 'Christian', anasara was also deployed as a catch-all for Europeans and Arabs, and for Africans dressed as the old man and Dandeson were dressed, in European garments. Mostly, though, it was taken to mean 'Christian'.

'Anasara! Anasara!'

Dandeson ignored the callers. The old man's enthusiastic nods made it clear to them that he, on the other hand, couldn't get enough of it.

He stopped and shouted, 'Kirista!'

Dandeson's face creased into a frown. He didn't speak the language, but he'd spent enough time in the old man's company as he worked on his Hausa primer to pick up a few words. He knew, for instance, that Jesus Christ was Yesu Kiristi, and a follower of the Christian religion, known in Hausa as addinin Kirista, was a Kirista.

But surely, he said to the old man, calling a Kirista a Kirista to a people in whose holy book, the Koran, Yesu Kiristi was known not as Yesu Kiristi but as Annabi Isa could only cause confusion.

'It can lead to some head-scratching,' the old man cheerfully admitted, 'but mark my word, Dandeson, some of these people will one day profess the Christian religion and call themselves Kirista.'

They had now reached the middle, where Mustafa was holding court.

He stopped, mid-sentence, when he saw them. Ignoring Dandeson, his prowling, bloodshot eyes came to rest on the old man. The old man beamed; his hand raised in salutation. But there was no shift in Mustafa's expression, not a glimmer of warmth or the faintest sign of recognition in his eyes. His eyes now took in Dandeson, who evidently commanded his interest far less than the old man, who slowly lowered his hand, then his attention returned to the crowd.

'Twelve years is a long time,' Dandeson said. 'And you only met once. In a crowded marketplace.'

'I said we met in a market,' responded the old man. 'I didn't say it was crowded.'

'It is a known fact,' Mustafa announced, speaking slowly, his gaze suddenly swivelling back to the old man, the faintest dawning of a smile creeping into his eyes, 'a fact as indisputable as the ages of animals, and the lifespan of insects and plants as assigned by Allah, that Allah – all praise be to Him – showers his bounties in abundance on the devout man.' Now his eyes moved to Dandeson and, addressing Dandeson, he said, 'Ka gaya ma shi, tafinta, ban sha'afa da shi ba.'

Dandeson turned to the old man. 'What's he saying?'

'He thinks you're my interpreter. "Tell him, interpreter. Tell him I haven't forgotten him."'

'O, does he now.' Dandeson turned to Mustafa and said, 'Mr Mustafa, I'm not his interpreter. I could be, but I'm not. He speaks your language far better than I ever will. He speaks it very well.'

'It's good to meet you again, Mallam Mustafa,' the old man said to Mustafa, his eyes reciprocating the warm laughter on Mustafa's face. 'Dandeson here is not my interpreter. He is my son, my youngest-born. He has followed in his father's footsteps and become a limami.'

'Your Hausa is much improved since the last time we met, Limami Shammil,' Mustafa observed. 'You speak the language almost like one of us bahaushe.'

'Nonsense, Mallam Mustafa,' the old man said, obviously flattered by the observation. 'Hausa is such a magnificent language. I haven't even begun to scratch the surface of its magnificent depths.'

'I see you've lost none of your great modesty, Limami Shammil,' Mustafa said.

Dandeson didn't get the finer details of the exchange, but he got the essence of it.

'I couldn't agree with you more, Mallam Mustafa,' he said in English. 'It is true. Limami Shammil is far too modest for his own good.'

'Dandeson agrees with you,' the old man told the mallam. 'He thinks I'm too modest, but I don't think it's possible to be too modest, do you?'

Mallam Mustafa warmly agreed with the old man that modesty

was indeed in Allah's eyes and in the eyes of all pious mortals a desirable thing.

'It's like the air we breathe,' he informed Dandeson. 'There can't be too much of it.'

The two old friends exchanged a few more pleasantries, then Mustafa returned his attention to the crowd.

'Allah's favours are lavish and never-ending,' he told them. 'And he bestows them on he who lives his days according to the teachings handed down to us by the Prophet Muhammad – peace be upon him. Allah lavishes abundance upon him, not just in the course of his earthly existence, but also in Aljanna.'

Through the corners of his eyes, the old man saw the word take shape on Dandeson's lips: 'Aljanna'.

He heard him say it a few times, rolling it on his tongue, biting into it, subjecting it to the scrutiny of his taste buds.

'Aljanna. Aljanna.'

'I'll tell you what it means, Dandeson. All you need to do is ask.'

'What does it mean, Bàbá?'

' "Paradise". It means "Paradise".'

'As soon as the waliyyi enters the first gate of Aljanna,' Mustafa told the crowd, 'he will be met by a budurwa.'

Immediately he said this, a cry of 'Allahamdulillah!' swept through the crowd.

Dandeson swung round to the old man. 'What did he just say to make them so excited?'

'They are excited,' the old man explained, 'because they have just learnt from Mallam Mustafa that the saintly man of God will be ushered through the gates of Paradise by a virgin maiden.'

Dandeson's mouth snapped open and then clasped shut.

'Now,' said Mustafa. 'When the waliyyi meets the mouth-wateringly pleasing budurwa at the first gate of Aljanna he would be stung –' he paused, and looked gravely back at the eyes staring at him, waiting eagerly for him to continue, then slowly, he continued '– he would be stung, as by a kudan zuma, with yearning.'

'Subhanallahi!' cried the crowd.

'A kudan zuma is a honey fly,' the old man explained.

'As opposed to a bee?' Dandeson asked.

'You could call it a bee,' answered the old man.

'Subhanallahi,' said Mustafa. 'And she, the virgin, reading his mind, will tell him, "No, I am not your bride-to-be. I am merely a keeper of the gate. Proceed and you will find your bride." So, what does he do?'

'He proceeds to the next gate!' answered the crowd.

'That is correct,' said Mustafa. 'The saint proceeds to the next gate, whereupon he meets an even more delightful specimen of Allah's creation, and he thinks to himself, surely this is she – surely this is the bride Allah has assigned to be my companion in all the days of my life in Paradise. But she tells him, "No, I'm not the one. I am but a slave. Proceed and you will find your bride." So, what does he do?'

'He proceeds to the next gate!'

'That is right,' said Mustafa. 'He proceeds to the next gate. And now he arrives at a gate so wide, it would take a man on a galloping stallion five hundred years to complete the journey from one side of the gate to the other.'

'Five hundred years! Allahu Akbar!'

'Inside the gate,' Mustafa said, 'there is a city, and inside this city there's but one building – a mansion so vast it has a thousand rooms, and inside each room there are a thousand beds, and on each bed a thousand virgins.'

There and then, a young man in the crowd died and headed straight to Paradise. He was exceedingly upset when, a minute later, he found himself resuscitated and still very much alive. Glaring sourly at the man who brought him back from the abyss by emptying a full buta of ablution water on him, he muttered loudly, 'Allah preserve us from those who will not mind their own business.' Others in the crowd who had similarly held their breath now exhaled and proclaimed, at the top of their lungs, 'Allahu Akbar! Allahu Akbar! Allahu Akbar!'

As this melee unfolded before them, the old man turned to Dandeson and said something.

'What?' Dandeson cupped his hand to his ear. 'I can't hear a thing in this din. What did you say?'

'I said, shut your mouth,' the old man said. 'It was wide open. A passing fly could easily have mistaken it for the third gate of Paradise.'

'What? What?' yelled Dandeson. He still couldn't hear a word the old man said.

'It would be impious of me to dwell on the exquisite, divinely proportioned qualities of these virgins,' Mustafa declared. 'I shall mention only their eyes and the hair on their heads. Their eyes are like shining gold — they give light to the distance of seventy-four miles, no less. It has been measured with the latest measuring instruments. And such is the radiance of the hair on their head, if a single strand of it were to drop to the earth, it will be visible as the sun in every part of the world, and all the plants and all the trees in all the forests will be forever scorched. These virtuous virgins, my friends, are the saint's brides. And his bed? The saint's bed is self-moving; it floats into any part of the room he pleases. And if, after seeking companionship in each of the thousand beds in this one room, he desires to pay a visit on any one of the nine hundred and ninety-nine other rooms in this mansion, he has two hundred and fifty thousand servants waiting to carry him in his palanquin from room to room. This is a fact. What I'm telling you are facts. Facts!'

Once again, the crowd exhaled as one and as one began to chant, 'God is great! God is great! God is great!'

'Now,' said Mustafa, 'let me tell you how the man of virtue finds his way to Paradise. It is no easy task. It's not simply a matter of dying down here on earth and waking up there in Paradise. Any fool can die at any time. It's the easiest thing on earth to do.' From the crowd, the young man who had just failed at that very task stared glumly at him, his eyes dubious, filled with bitterness, his body coiled forward, set to contradict him. Mustafa read his thoughts and responded by giving him the full benefit of a pure, undiluted look of withering contempt. 'I said any fool,' he hissed. 'But you are not just any fool. You are shashasha, a monumental fool.' The young man's defiant gaze crumbled. 'And it's not simply a matter of living a life of virtue here on earth and being ushered into Paradise when you die. There is more to it than that. First, there is kiyama – the Day of Reckoning, the Last Day, the Day of Judgement. Even he who has lived a stainless life, a life untarnished by impiety, must face kiyama before he's even considered for acceptance into Paradise. And only after kiyama – after the extent has been measured to which a saintly man has lived his life of virtue; and after his failings and merits have been placed on a scale and carefully weighed side by side, with his virtues overwhelmingly tipping the balance of judgement in their favour – only then may he be considered for admittance into Paradise. Now, we know this for a fact, that between the place of judgement and Paradise there's a bridge as narrow as the edge of a razor, a bridge that stretches over a chasm that is as deep as a journey of a thousand years and twice as wide. We also know it for a fact, that the most virtuous saint will step across this bridge in a split second.' The crowd gave a wild roar. Mustafa's voice dropped to a whisper. 'And there, at the very first gate, he will be greeted by a maiden whose striking beauty would make his heart flutter like the wings of a malam buda mana littafi.'

'What does that mean?' Dandeson asked his father.

'"Please, sir, open the book,"' the old man explained.

'What in heaven's name is that?'

'A butterfly,' answered the old man.

'And he would be stung, as by a bee, with desire,' Mustafa intoned. His voice-lowering ploy had had the desired effect: total silence once again had taken hold of his audience. 'And she, reading his mind, will say to him, "I am but a gatekeeper. Proceed and you will find she who is worthy of being the consort of your saintly eminence."' And now, Mustafa's voice rose again. 'What does he do?'

'He proceeds to the next gate!' the crowd roared back.

'That is correct,' said Mustafa the Gentle. 'I knew I was standing not among fools but in the midst of wise men!'

Thirty

When they got back to their room, Dandeson let rip.

'There seems to be no end to the utter rot that Mr Gentle is capable of coming up with,' he fumed. 'What's even worse — those fools swallowed it hook, line and sinker. There seems to be a Mr Gentle in every market square, every village corner, in this country, all spewing out the same hogwash.'

'Dandeson,' the old man cautioned. 'A Muhammadan can never be brought round if all you do is quarrel with his religion; if all you do is insult it; if all you do is fling charges of fraud and falsehood at it.'

'But Bàbá!' Dandeson protested.

'Consider the success we've had with the Yorùbá Mission,' said the old man. 'Had we insisted on exposing their superstitions to public ridicule, we would have been long ago turned out of the Yorùbá country, permanently banished from it, our converts even put to death. But we chose not to ridicule their superstitions. We were prudent, we exercised caution. And the result?'

'The whole country is opened to us,' Dandeson grudgingly admitted.

'Churches are built,' the old man said. 'Congregations are collected, converts are in the hundreds. And we are weakening the power of their superstitions, quietly but surely; we are loosening its grip on them.'

'That is true, Father.'

'In generations to come, those delusions will die a death. In generations to come, they will look back at a dire superstition such as Èṣù and see it for what it really was – an evil monstrosity; they will look back at a fetish such as the so-called Obalúayé – Lord of the World – and they will see it for what it really was – a malign pathology. They will look back at all the graven images they worship now, and they will say to themselves, "If the all-powerful God was in those graven images, why didn't He stop the slave traders? Why didn't He help us?"'

Dandeson listened and did not say a word. It was futile to try to get a word in when the old man was in this mood.

'The Lord's time has come for this part of Africa, when every valley shall be filled and every mountain and hill shall be brought low,' the old man declared. 'And the crooked shall be made straight and the rough ways shall be made smooth, and when all flesh shall see the salvation of God.'

He continued in this evangelical vein for some time. Then he seemed to catch himself and suddenly stopped. 'I got carried away,' he said, a rueful smile playing on his lips. 'What were we talking about?'

Dandeson knew the old man hadn't forgotten what they were talking about.

'Muhammadanism, Bàbá,' he said with a smile. 'We were talking about Muhammadanism.'

'Yes, Dandeson, yes. We must tackle Muhammadan superstitions in exactly the same way. Always remember that. Exactly the same way.'

The old man intoned a prayer.

A log fire crackled agreeably all through the night, between the old man's bed and Dandeson's, keeping the room warm, and the soft breeze wafting in through the rafters kept it cosy, affording father and son the soundest night's sleep either of them had experienced in months.

Once they fell asleep, nothing could make them stir, and nothing did, until just before dawn when the loud, resonant and forceful voice of the ladani rang out, like a ten-foot kakaki trumpet, calling the faithful to prayer.

Thirty-one

They arrived at a market town where it was said that if you were looking for an item at the kasuwa – the market – what you were looking for simply didn't exist. If it did, it was yours for furfura, but if bartering – which is to say, furfura – wasn't how you liked to do business, you were welcome to pay in cowries or dollars, preferably cowries.

Unlike the coast, where dollars were increasingly becoming the only form of payment accepted, here in the interior cowries were the very definition of hard-earned money. Dollars were those new-fangled metal coins some people with more money than sense bought to melt into bracelets and rings, not exactly everybody's idea of a medium of exchange. Where on the coast your dollar might easily fetch you two strings of cowries – four thousand cowries – here, nobody would so much as touch your dollar; but if you insisted, if you swore in the name of your unborn grandchildren and their long-deceased great-grandmother that all the kudi you were carrying on you was dollars and nothing but dollars, then out of the kindness of their heart, and only out of the kindness of their heart, they might offer you a string to the dollar – one string of cowries for one dollar, maestro, take it or leave.

Fortunately for the old man and his fellow wayfarers, they were not short of cowries. They did have more dollars in their purse than cowries – it was simply far easier, and much less cumbersome, to travel with a lot of dollars on you than with several hundred head-loads of cowries – but wherever they'd stopped along the way they rarely had to pay for food or lodgings, thanks to the unrivalled hospitality of their hosts, and so they had in their treasury more than enough cowries to see them through to the coast.

It was here at this market that the old man's serenity, which was legendary, briefly deserted him. This happened when a slave trader, mistaking him for a dealer from the coast, tried to sell him a young woman and her infant child.

They had finished stocking up and were heading to the river to board the canoes that would take them to the opposite shore when the man came up to the old man and offered the mother and child.

'She's a hard worker,' the man said, 'and there's nothing wrong with her.' To prove his point, he spun the woman round. The baby strapped to her back did not stir.

'I'll accept thirty-five strings for her.'

'We do not buy people,' the old man said.

His voice was quiet, but Dandeson could hear the telltale tightening in his father's throat. Dandeson glared at the slave trader and said, 'Go away.'

'Thirty-five strings,' the slave trader said, ignoring Dandeson. 'I'll tell you what I'll do for you. But only because it's you. I'll throw in the baby. The baby is yours for free.'

The old man's face had suddenly lost all expression. He stared at the woman and the baby on her back.

She was about eighteen, the child a few months old.

'I have good news and bad news for you, my friend,' said the slave trader. 'The good news is I'll take thirty-four strings. I'll even take dollars. Make an offer. The bad news is if you make an offer, I may turn it down.'

The blood vessels on the old man's forehead swelled and visibly throbbed. 'Dandeson,' he muttered. He did not take his eyes off the woman and her child. 'My bag, Dandeson. Let me have my bag.'

Without saying a word, Dandeson handed over the goatskin bag. The old man reached into the bag and counted out thirty-five dollars.

He flung the money at the slave trader.

'Take this and leave,' he said. 'We do not buy or sell people.'

The slave trader opened his mouth to say something but changed his mind when he saw Dandeson's face.

'Leave!' Dandeson snapped.

The slave trader scrambled to pick up the coins. He melted into the crowd.

The old man reached into the bag and took out all the coins left in it. He placed the coins in the woman's hands. He asked her, 'Kina jin Hausa? Do you speak Hausa?' She stared at her feet and didn't respond. 'Me nene sunan ki? What's your name?'

Briefly she looked up. 'Zanna.' Her eyes were stricken with searing, unspeakable grief. Her voice was low, so low the old man didn't catch what she said. 'My name is Zanna,' she said in hesitant, heavily accented Hausa. Then she switched to another language, a language that sounded nothing like Hausa, a language she obviously lived, dreamt, laughed and cried in. The old man nodded as she spoke, as the words spilled out of her mouth. It was Nufi. He didn't understand what she was saying, but he knew it was in Nufi. And you could tell from the marks on her face that she was Nufi.

The old man turned his head and called over his shoulder. 'Ibrahima,' he said. 'Where's Zanna from in Nufi land? Ask Zanna where she hails from.'

Ibrahima was the Nufi interpreter.

Zanna hailed from a village a day's journey away. The old man knew the village. He recalled spending an afternoon there in '54. Back in those days, it was a buoyant farming community. It had since fallen on hard times, thanks in no small part to the depredations of the slave raiders. The village was one of those communities being forced to pay for protection from slave traders by slave raiders. Zanna and her infant son had ended up at the slave market because the village had of late been unable to come up with the extortion levy and had also refused to give up any of its members in lieu of the extortion tax. Instead, they took to fleeing; they took to playing a grim and deadly game of hide-and-seek with the horsemen.

A week ago, they were caught napping.

Zanna was trembling as she told the story, but when the old man told Ibrahima to tell her she was welcome to come with them to Ìlọrin or even all the way to Lagos, her eyes widened in their sockets.

She didn't want to go to Lagos, she said, before adding, quite indignantly, 'What about my husband?'

What about him indeed? It was the first time she had mentioned a husband.

'Where is your husband?' the old man asked her. He apologised for having forgotten to ask about her husband.

Why, she said, he's right here in the market! That very morning, she said, she had shared a barracoon with him right there. She would go look for him now; if she hurried, he might still be where she last saw him. She had the money the old man had given her; she would buy his freedom with it.

There was a pained, faraway look on the old man's face as he watched Zanna go in search of her husband; a sombre, misty-eyed look that stayed with him for the rest of the day, even during the crossing to the opposite shore.

Thirty-two

They walked down the vast thoroughfares of the city escorted by liveried horsemen and footmen in dogari uniform, courtiers the emir had sent to the city gates to bid his guests welcome. All around them, they could hear fragments of idle banter, and snatches of earnest wrangling, and snippets of intense conversation in Hausa, Yorùbá, Nufi and Filani, the chief languages of the mixed inhabitants of the flourishing metropolis. Word of their arrival had spread through the city on the wings of hearsay and by the time they reached the palace a large crowd trailed behind them as far as the eye could see. As they were led into the inner courtyard to meet the emir, greetings in Hausa and Yorùbá rang out from every corner.

'Barka da zuwa!'

'Ẹ káàbọ̀!'

'Barka da sauka!'

'Ẹ kú ewù ọ̀nà!'

King Aliyu was attired in long, billowing trousers of the latest Turkish style: fashionably scarlet, gathered at the ankles; over this, he wore a richly embroidered silk damask gown, the neckline sparkling with gold lace, and a glittering, purple-red cloak. The musky fragrance and floral aroma exuding from His Majesty were the hallmark of a brand of perfume that had travelled over the Blue Nile and along the White Nile, beyond the Sahara and across the Niger to reach the emir's palace in the city of Ìlọrin from the souks of Khartoum.

It fell to the old man to do the honours, to present his caravan of Babel to the emir, since he was the group's sarkin harshuna, its language king, fluent as he was in Yorùbá, English, Hausa, Ibo, German, Greek, Latin, Krio, Temne, and with more than a smattering of Arabic, Portuguese, Aramaic, Nufi and a few other tongues under his command.

'Ran sarki ya dade,' he said in Hausa, Long May His Majesty Live, when finally it was his turn to present himself. 'My name is Shammil. In Turanci, they call me Samuel. I am a messenger of Jesus Christ the Son of God and the Saviour of the World.'

Everyone sensed the old man had dropped a bombshell in his introduction, but no one quite knew what the bombshell was, or why it was a bombshell, and if it wasn't a bombshell, why in the name of the Prophet, sallallahu alaihi wasallam, they thought it was.

A hush descended on the courtyard.

Finally the king said, 'What exactly does that mean, Mallam Shammil?'

'I am a limami,' the old man hastened to explain in language that would be clear, and not lead to head-scratching. 'A Christian limami. I teach the addini of Christianity.'

This time everyone understood him. A Christian imam was certainly a person they'd heard of, although they couldn't think of a single reason why they would require the services of such a man – a man whose calling was to go around teaching the religion of Christianity – but they were glad to make his acquaintance.

Now he'd explained himself, they followed the king's example and beamed at the old man.

'Limami Shammil,' said the king. 'We have heard all manner of things about Christianity. But there's still a great deal we do not know. Who do you hold fast in your addini, the Prophet Muhammad or Annabi Isa?'

'Annabi Isa,' the old man replied.

'So we gather,' said the king. 'So we gather. You must tell us more about your addini. You must enlighten us. But tonight I won't detain you any further; you've had a long journey. Tomorrow is another day.'

But as they turned to take leave of the emir, a voice announced in Yorùbá, 'We hold the Prophet fast.' The voice was quiet, but the tone was unmistakably pugnacious. It was the voice of the emir's limami. The old man turned to face him. 'What does your Book say of the Prophet?' the limami asked him. It was clear from his belligerent tone that he knew the answer to his question. 'We understand that Moses, Noah, Solomon, Joseph, David, Gabriel, Jonah, even Lot's wife appear in your Book, but not the Prophet Muhammad. What have you got to say about that?'

'Nothing,' the old man replied. 'Nothing except to say that it's true our Bible is silent about the Prophet Muhammad, but the Bible does have a sound reason for being silent about the Prophet Muhammad: the Prophet did not establish his doctrine until six hundred and twenty-two years after the death of Christ.'

Dandeson watched the limami soak in this information. He could feel the jitters running through the audience. Clearly, the limami was a powerful man, a man whose opinion carried weight. Even the emir appeared to deem it prudent not to pre-empt his verdict on the old man's answer. Finally, he bestowed his seal of approval on it with the appearance of a thin smile on the edge of his lips; the old man's answer had passed muster. A murmur of relief swept through the courtyard: the limami was mollified.

The limami was mollified, but far from won over: he quickly reached for a dare dressed up as a harmless question and aimed it squarely between the old man's eyes.

'Limami,' he said, 'which is the fuller: your Book or the Holy Koran?'

The courtyard was now packed. Every single adviser of the king was there, every person of eminence was in attendance; every personality normally to be found in the corridors of power was present; and they were all keenly aware that the palace limami's question wasn't nearly as innocent as it sounded or quite as throwaway as it seemed. It was a bait; a trap calculated to ensnare the Christian limami into committing haram, into an utterance that might be deemed sacrilegious. They all waited, keenly, for the old man to respond.

He did so by reaching into his bag. 'I'm glad you asked,' he said.

He brought out several books, placing them side by side as he pulled each out of the bag. He brought out two copies of the Bible: one in English, the King James Version; the other, *Bibeli Mimọ*, the Yorùbá translation, a work-in-progress. He brought out the Book of Common Prayer and a selection of translations from it, *Ìwé Àdúà Yorùbá*; and finally, he brought out Samuel Johnson's *A Dictionary of the English Language* and the Reverend Samuel Crowther's *A Vocabulary of the Yorùbá Language*.

'*Bibeli Mimọ*,' he pointed at *Bibeli Mimọ*, 'is the Yorùbá translation of the scriptures, of this,' he pointed at the KJV. 'When I read a passage from the English Bible, which is also known as the King James Version, I can interpret what I've read into Yorùbá by reading the same passage here, in *Bibeli Mimọ*.'

The gathering listened in rapt, if slightly bemused, attention. They watched as he now picked up the KJV. 'Our Bible is very full,' he said to the limami. 'It contains many books from which certain subjects were picked out or touched upon in the Koran when it was composed.' He looked at the limami and paused. 'Even as we speak,' he continued when the limami did not respond, 'there are now in Stamboul, and in Mizra, and Smyrna, Christian missionaries spreading the truths of the Gospel, which are being examined and embraced by many members of your faith in those countries. Here, too, at Lagos, Abẹ́òkuta, Ibadan, Bonny, Brass, Nun, Onitsha and Lokoja, we have established schools to carry out Christ's exhortation in the Gospel of Matthew: Matthew chapter twenty-eight, verse nineteen.' He rustled through the leatherbound volume: '"Go ye therefore and teach all nations."' He picked up *Bibeli Mimọ* and read out the same passage.

Next, he read out the same passages, in English and Yorùbá, from the prayer book. As he was reading from *Ìwé Àdúà Yorùbá*, he read out a word which seemed to draw blank looks from his audience. He immediately paused and reached for the Yorùbá dictionary. He found the word and read out the definition.

A look of stupefied incredulity immediately gripped the limami's face. Without so much as a salaam alaikum, he plucked the Yorùbá prayer book from the old man's hands and proceeded to lift it up to the heavens, then he brought it back down to earth, lowering it so much he had to hunch down after it; he held it close to his nose, then away from it. He even shook it, as if by doing so he might dislodge the amulet he knew to be concealed within its pages; it would reveal itself by dropping out. When his detailed inspection failed to reveal a hidden charm, he finally deigned to leaf through the book and study it. He was a theological scholar, but his purview was Arabic; the Latin alphabet now staring back at him was an undecipherable mystery, but not the principle behind it. He understood the principle and now, finally, allowed himself to be overwhelmed with a combination of unabashed awe and a feeling of exhilaration that felt very much like panic, because it was panic.

'Limami Shammil,' he addressed the old man, talking to him as if they hadn't just met, as if they'd known each other all their lives. 'You mean to tell me, Limami Shammil, that you can just open this book and it will tell you the meaning of a word?'

'Not all words,' the old man replied, 'but that's the general idea. That's what a dictionary does.'

'Your Majesty, what a clever idea,' the limami gasped, turning to the king. 'What an utterly clever idea! Who composed this litaffi?'

'Well . . .' said the old man.

Dandeson pointed to the old man. 'He did. See that on the cover? That's the writer's name. Reverend Samuel Crowther. This is he. This is Samuel Crowther. He's no longer a reverend, though. He's now a bishop. He's been promoted. The translation you've heard from the Bible is also his work. My father began this work of translation a year before I was born. That's how long it's taken him, and there's still a few more Books to go.'

'How old are you?' someone asked.

'I'm thirty-six years old.'

'He's applied himself to this one task for thirty-seven years!'

'Allahu Akbar.'

'And the Book of Prayer?' enquired the limami. 'Limami Shammil, is that your handiwork as well?'

Dandeson was beginning to warm towards the fellow.

'I wasn't going to mention that,' Dandeson said. 'But since you did, limami. You're quite right. The translator of *Ìwé Àdúà Yorùbá* does indeed stand in our midst: Samuel Adjai Crowther.'

'Did he say Adjai?' someone muttered.

'He did.'

'He's speaking through his nose. That's how you say Àjàyí when you speak yenyenyen.'

'What's that?'

'Through your nose.'

'With a name like Àjàyí, he must be one of us.'

'Is he really? I thought he was one of those kiri yó people from Saliyo.'

The old man turned to the courtiers and said, 'I am one of you and I am from Sierra Leone.'

'See?' the courtier said. 'I told you he's from Saliyo.'

'Now we want to know more about you, Limami Shammil,' said the limami.

'Where are you from?' the king asked. 'How did you become so knowledgeable? You must tell us!'

With some reluctance, the old man agreed to tell them the story of his life, a story that began with the abduction of a young boy nearly sixty years earlier in a town called Òṣogùn.

PART FIVE

1880

The Talented Mr Crowther

Thirty-three

After some time, *the old man told the emir and his court*, my master
took me to Ìséyìn and sold me to a Mussulman woman. I lived with
her and her son, who was about the same age as I, for a few months
and then she, too, took me to a slave market and put me up for sale.
I walked with my new master for a few days and finally he brought
me to a slave market on the coast, on the bank of a large river. I had
never seen anything like it in my life and it filled my heart with fear.
Before the sun had set, I was bartered for tobacco and became
another owner's property. At once, my new master announced he
was taking me across the river, to the slave market on the island of
Èkó. Nothing terrified me more than the river and the thought of
going to Èkó because I knew – every one of us slaves knew, because
we'd heard our masters talk about it – that one part of the town was
occupied by white men, who had come to buy slaves to take to their
land far away; far, far, across the ocean. When I was told to enter
the river, to walk across the sandbank of the water to the canoe that
would take us to Èkó, I stood quivering on one spot. Night was
approaching, and the men had no time to spare; they picked me up
and carried me into the canoe and placed me among the corn bags.
I sat crouched; my whole body shook and then became stiff from
terror. My eyes were red and swollen from crying. I was still in this

same position when, several hours later – it was four o'clock in the morning – we reached Èkó.

In Èkó, I was allowed to go any way I pleased; there was no way to escape, it was an island, we were completely surrounded by water. Although I was there for more than three months, I didn't once set eyes on a white man – until one evening when not one but six white men – Spaniards and Portuguese – came walking down the street. Even then, I dared not look directly at them. I thought if I did, they would notice me, and I didn't want them to notice me. I suspected they'd come for me, so I cast my eyes down hoping that they wouldn't see me if I didn't see them. They did see me that day, but they weren't in the least interested in me. But they were back a few days later. This time, I was made the eighth in a number of slaves one of the white men bought.

I had by now become something of an old hand in servitude. I had lost all hope of ever seeing my country again and had learnt to be patient, and to take whatever came. But it was not without fear and trembling that I received, for the first time, the touch of a white man, who examined me to see whether I was a sound purchase or not.

We were herded together in a room with one door, which was locked as soon as we entered, with no passage for air other than the opening under the eaves. Men and boys were at first chained together; the chain thrust through an iron fetter on the neck of every individual and fastened at both ends with locks. It was torture for everyone, particularly so for us boys: the men sometimes, getting angry, would pull the chain so violently, it would cut into our bony little necks. It was worse at sleep time, when they drew the chain close to ease themselves of its weight so they could lie better. You had two choices: either to be strangled until you stopped breathing or to be gouged to death. When fights broke out at night between two or more men, as often happened, everybody suffered.

At last, as more men were added from the slave market to the drove, the boys had the joy of being separated from the men and corded together by themselves. Manacled together, we did everything together. We ate together, we washed together . . . The girls and the women fared no better.

We lived this way in Lagos, which was what the white men called Èkó, for four months.

This was in the year of our Lord 1822. At that time, fifty-eight years ago, in the United Kingdom, the slave trade had already been abolished; it was a crime to trade in human beings. It had been a crime for fifteen years. But only in the United Kingdom. Not so in some other places. Spaniard and Portuguese boats were still sailing the seas to these African shores to fill their cargo holds with slaves. So, the English Navy sent out boats to cruise the coasts off our shores looking for slavers. This was why we had to spend months in Lagos after we were sold to the white men, months after the Portuguese trader who bought me had acquired enough human cargo to fill his hold. It was because it was deemed too risky to take us to the ship. English Navy boats had been seen lurking on the waves.

At last, after four months of waiting, the coast was deemed clear, and one night we were bundled out of Lagos by canoe, nearly two hundred of us: boys and girls, men and women. Before dawn the next morning, we were on board the ship. We hadn't eaten the night before; the crew were too busy loading us into the canoes to give us our evening meal. And we didn't eat that morning, because they were too busy loading us on to the ship, which was waiting out at sea. Not that we were, any of us, in any fit state to hold down a morsel, let alone eat a meal. As the ship bobbed up the waves and down, the world spun before our eyes from an illness they called seasickness.

That same evening, we were accosted by two English warships, and we found ourselves in the hands of a new band of conquerors, fearsome men armed with long swords.

Our chains were cast off and our owner and his men suddenly found themselves in shackles. Only the cook was left unshackled, and only because he was preparing our morning meal. We were hungry and hunger made us bold. We took the liberty of ranging about the vessel in search of fruits and plunder of every kind. We quickly sobered up when, after breakfast, we were divided into several of the vessels around us. We did not know where they were taking us or whether our misery would end. By now we had all become one big family and as each batch entered a vessel to depart, we took affectionate leave of them, not knowing what would become of them or what would happen to us. Six of us, brothers in affliction, kept very close so that we might be carried away at the same time, and soon we were conveyed into a man-of-war, the HMS *Myrmidon*. After nearly two months' sailing, we landed in Freetown, over a thousand miles from Lagos.

In Sierra Leone, I was put under the care of the Church Missionary Society. And being convinced that I was a sinner, and desiring to obtain pardon through Jesus Christ, I became a Christian, and was baptised Samuel Crowther, casting aside the name Àjàyí.

I also joined the mission school.

Thirty-four

I was a quick learner. Within six months of reaching Freetown, I could read and write. I thirsted for knowledge. I read everything. I read the Bible. I read the Old Testament, all of it, and the New Testament. I read everything I could lay hands on. The teachers all took notice of me. Young Mr Crowther, they called me. At Sunday worship, I became the reader. At school, I was made the monitor of class. When Father Joyce was laid low with malaria – he was our class teacher – it was my responsibility as monitor to take his place at the front and teach my fellow pupils. And that's what I did. I picked up a chalk and went straight to the blackboard and taught. It all came quite naturally to me. It was as if I'd done it all my life. It was clear to me – there was no doubt in my mind – that my life in bondage had been the Lord's will. The Lord had put me in bondage to bring me to the light and to use me as a vessel for bringing others to the light.

I was not the only pupil who showed promise. There was another pupil, a young girl, who was even more zealous than I in her quest for knowledge. Her name was Hassana, a Muslim girl from Ìlọrin. Hassana applied herself to learning with all her heart. We were the same age and had arrived on the shores of Freetown on the same day, on the same boat. We were even baptised on the same day. She was baptised Susanna.

As well as being clever, Susanna was blessed with a kind heart and a warm, caring character. She was fond of me, and I was quite fond of her.

A knowing, teasing smile sneaked into the limami's eyes.

I take it, *he said to the old man*, that by that you mean she desired you, and you desired her.

The old man broke into a warm, gentle smile. He did not mind being teased.

If you put it that way, *he replied*, Susanna and I have been man and wife for over fifty years. Meeting her is the happiest thing that's ever happened to me. I have lived a life full of blessings – our children; my work as a teacher; my mission as a fisher of men, leading souls to salvation – but only the day many years later when I was reunited in Abẹòkuta with my mother compares to meeting Susanna.

It was nothing short of a miracle. I had just arrived in the Ẹgbá city from Freetown to start a mission there. And because it was less than a day's trek from my hometown, the first thing I did when I arrived in Abẹòkuta was to embark on a thorough search for my mother and sister and other members of my family, even though it was nearly a quarter of a century since I last laid eyes on them.

Abẹòkuta was a new town, founded by refugees fleeing the Yorùbá wars; it came into existence a decade after Òṣogùn was destroyed. In the decades previous to its founding, its forest-dwelling Ẹgbá founders had seen over a hundred and fifty of their towns and villages besieged – one town after another, one village after the other – and razed to the ground, its inhabitants captured, barracooned and sold into slavery, just as had happened to Òṣogùn and hundreds of other towns in the Yorùbá country.

Pursued by all the peoples in the countries surrounding their forest homeland, the Ẹgbá had fled, hunted down like the wild beasts of the primeval forests they once called home, until they arrived at a sweltering, fiendishly humid labyrinth at the top of a mountain awash with vipers, toxic plants and death-dealing arachnids; its caves reeking with the pungent smell of bat guano and everywhere bathed in morning mist, the lulling decoy behind which the deadly heat of the blistering sun came sneaking on the unsuspecting wayfarer. And there, at last, the wild-eyed, matted-haired wanderers found their very own paradise; for the first time in living memory, they felt safe from their enemies, and there they settled, atop the rocks and inside the undulating valleys below. Long years of hiding in it, long years of deploying it to outwit and outrun those seeking to kill them, those seeking to capture and sell them, had left these vagabond forest people at one with nature in all its renegade, obscene and sublime ecstasy. In a hostile and pitiless world, it was their one abiding friend; a constant friend whose gruff embrace could be sanctuary or suffocation. They knew this rock-strewn landscape for what it was: a volatile, unforgiving ally, boundless in its munificence, indiscriminate in its ferocity. They were smitten; they couldn't have asked for a better place to call home.

Abẹ́òkuta embraced all comers. Thousands flocked to it from everywhere in a land riven with war, and within just a few years of its founding, it had become one of the most prosperous towns in Yorùbá.

I was convinced that if Ìyá were still alive and living in the Yorùbá country; if my sister Bọ́lá were still alive and still in Yorùbá; if they had somehow avoided being sold to the Europeans buying people to ship across the ocean, the only place where it seemed likely they would be found was Abẹ́òkuta.

But Ìyá and Bọ́lá were nowhere to be found in Abẹ́òkuta.

After a while, I stopped looking for them. I gave up all hope of finding them.

Soon after I gave up the search, Ìyá came looking for me.

It turned out she had been living in a village at nearby Porto Novo. Word had reached her there that a Sierra Leonean missionary answering to the name of Àjàyí had been going around looking for her. When she heard this, Ìyá knew at once that it was her son and immediately set out to meet him. And she did.

She came upon me in a marketplace where I was preaching the Gospel. I recognised her at once, even from afar. Age had slowed her down, her face was ridged and creased with the ravages of deep suffering; but the old woman shuffling towards me, one slow step after another, was still, if one looked closely enough, the woman from whose arms I had been torn away all those years ago in Òsogùn.

Ìyá stood trembling when she saw me. We grasped one another, looking at each other in stunned silence. Tears rolled down her emaciated cheeks. She shook as she held me by the hand, repeatedly calling my name. Beside her stood another woman who looked only slightly younger than my mother. It took me a few moments to recognise this old woman to be my sister, Bólá. She was crying uncontrollably, tears of joy.

A crowd gathered around and followed us as I took them home to meet my family. As we walked side by side through the town, we did not say much. We could not. After twenty-five years of being torn apart, there was too much to say and it all felt like pouring out of our lips, all at once.

It took many conversations over many months for me to get their story out of them. I found out that on the very day the slave raiders descended on Òsogùn, not long after I was separated from them, one of our relatives managed to steal Ìyá away from her capturers. To effect this, five heads of cowries were required to bribe the men who had been charged with keeping an eye on them. My sister was purchased for twenty-four heads of cowries which were borrowed, and she was put in pawn for it till the debt was paid. My father died in battle on the day we were captured.

Five years after our fateful reunion, Bọ́lá died, sadly, in childbirth. Ìyá is still with us. She has lived with me and my family for thirty-four years now.

PART SIX

1861

The Vicarage

Thirty-five

Reverend Crowther stepped out of the bedroom and hurried down the stairs, intoning the *Te Deum*. At the bottom of the stairs, he paused by the door of the study and listened to the two voices coming from within.

'Katanga,' said the first voice, the voice of a grown-up woman. 'What on earth is Katanga?'

'Katanga is Ọ̀yọ́,' replied a high-pitched voice, a teenager's voice. 'Katanga is the name often set down in the charts. The Yorùbá themselves call it Ọ̀yọ́.'

'Why is that?' asked the female voice. 'Why is Katanga put down in the charts?'

'European travellers obtained the name from Hausa traders,' replied the teenage voice. 'The Yorùbá themselves never call it Katanga. Yarriba is also set down in the charts instead of Yorùbá. Yarriba is a pronunciation European travellers obtained from Hausa traders.'

'So it is a Hausa word,' said the woman. 'Just like Katanga?'

'It is not,' replied the boy, emphatically. 'Yorùbá is what the Ọ̀yọ́ call themselves and their language. Yorùbá is a Yorùbá word, but the Hausa pronounce it Yarriba.'

Crowther gently, with a foot, pushed the door ajar and stuck in his head.

'Young man,' he said to the teenage boy at the writing desk, 'what brings you into my humble abode?'

Dandeson glanced over his shoulder and said, 'Good evening, Bàbá.' His forehead was furrowed, deep in thought, his fingers tapping on the desk. 'Màmá is helping me with an essay Mr Macaulay has asked us to write.'

'What's the subject matter? Let me hazard a guess: The History of Katanga? The Yarriba Nation? The Yarriba Country of Katanga?'

'Three good guesses, Reverend Crowther,' said Mrs Crowther. 'Very good guesses indeed, Reverend Crowther, but all wrong, sadly.'

'We've been asked to write about the kingdom of the Ọ̀yọ́,' Dandeson informed him.

'How clever of Mr Macaulay to ask you to write about Ọ̀yọ́,' said Crowther.

'He feels it's important that we also know about our history. He got the idea of teaching it, he said, from a conversation with you.'

That seemed to give Crowther pause for thought. 'Mr Macaulay said that?'

Dandeson nodded.

'Mr Macaulay is a rather thoughtful man, isn't he?' Crowther said. 'What brings you here, young man?'

Ignoring his question, Dandeson said, 'He said we come from royalty, that Grandma is a princess. Is that true?'

The mention of Grandma seemed to remind Crowther about something.

He turned to his wife to say something. Before he could speak, she said, 'Much better.'

He glared at her. 'What's much better?'

'Ìyá's leg is much better,' Susanna Crowther said. 'That was what you were about to ask me, wasn't it? The pain is all but vanished since she started taking the tincture Junior brought for her last time he came round.'

Samuel Jr was their eldest son. Everybody called him Junior.

'How did you know I was going to ask you about Ìyá's leg?'

She beamed at him. 'I know everything.'

'I pride myself on being impossible to read.'

Dandeson smiled indulgently at his father's evidently flawed self-assessment.

'Will you wipe the smile off your face, please.'

'I will, Bàbá,' Dandeson replied. 'Just as soon as you answer my question.'

'What is your question? I didn't realise you too were smiling.'

'Is it true Ìyá is a princess?'

'Young man,' Crowther said. 'Ìyá is upstairs in her room. Why don't you remove yourself upstairs and ask her?'

'Her father was Aláàfin Abíódún, King of Òyó,' Màmá told him. 'Ìyá is indeed a princess.'

'You still haven't told me what brings you home, Dandeson.' Crowther was trying to look stern, but his idea of stern didn't appear to have the desired effect on his son. Dandeson simply brushed it off, like a falling leaf from his shoulder, and returned to his schoolwork.

'I went and got him from school yesterday,' Mrs Crowther informed her husband. 'I told you I was going to.'

The ineffectual look of sternness on Crowther's face was now replaced by an even far less convincing look of outrage. 'Mrs Crowther!' he gasped. 'You mean to tell me this young man has been sleeping under my roof and I didn't even know about it?'

'Reverend Crowther,' said Mrs Crowther. 'You would have

known about it if you'd spent but a little more time under your own roof. You've hardly stepped foot in this house in two days. You've practically lived in the palace with Dòsùnmú and his ten thousand concubines.'

'Just like you to undercount the number of Kábíyèsí's consorts,' Crowther observed. 'Merely ten thousand? Pshaw!'

'Has he summoned you to the palace again tonight?' Susanna asked, clearly not happy with King Dòsùnmú for taking her husband away from home. 'The treaty has been signed. What now does he want from you?'

'That's for me to find out when I get to the palace,' Crowther said. 'When are you going back to school, young man?'

'He's going back first thing tomorrow morning,' Susanna told him.

'Good riddance,' Bàbá said. 'I mean – good.'

'And you are taking him back.'

'I didn't take him out,' he pointed out, taking his glasses off. 'Why should I be the one to take him back?'

'Reverend Crowther,' said Mrs Crowther rather sweetly.

He rubbed his eyes. He put the glasses back on. 'Yes, Mrs Crowther.'

'I should have thought the answer to your question was quite obvious.'

' "Màmá says so." Is that the answer?'

Dandeson, who didn't appear to be paying any attention to the conversation, nodded.

'What is wrong with the intruder's neck?' Crowther asked. 'But of course,' he said to Màmá with a long-suffering sigh. 'Bàbá must do as Màmá has said. The logic is unimpeachable.'

'I'm pleased we both agree on that, Reverend Crowther,' said Mrs Crowther.

Dandeson gave them a sideways glance.

'Don't think I didn't see that, young man.'

'What, sir?' Dandeson asked innocently.

'You were making a face at your parents.'

'You're mistaken, sir, I was wiping my nose,' Dandeson said, pointing at his ear.

'What Bàbá would like to know,' said Crowther, 'is why did Màmá insist on bringing this face-making interloper home in the first place? O, I do remember now. There were rumours of rumours of war.'

'The rumours did not lack credibility,' Susanna said, quite seriously. 'We heard Dòsùnmú was not going to sign the treaty.'

'But he did sign it.'

'He did sign it. But if he'd stuck to his guns and withheld his mark, as we'd been told he intended to, McCoskry was going to summon the *Prometheus*.'

'Rumours,' Crowther said. 'Rumours without substance. I did warn you not to pay attention to those idle stories.' He saw a figure slowly descending the stairs. 'Dandeson, go and give Ìyá a hand. How is your leg, Ìyá mi àtàtà, my dear mother?'

'The pain is all gone,' Ìyá said. 'Those òyìnbó herbs Junior gave me to take are working wonders.'

Dandeson ran up the stairs, towards his grandmother.

'Ìyá,' he called out. 'Tell me about your father. I want to know everything you know about him.'

Ìyá gave her grandson a swift, clear look. 'Your great-grandfather died a long time ago,' she told him. 'I was but a child when he died.'

'Your mother must have told you something about him. What did she tell you about him?'

'You are quite right,' Ìyá's eyes lit up, 'my mother did tell me many things about him. I will tell you everything she told me about him, everything I can remember.'

Màmá and Bàbá stood by the door listening as Ìyá began to tell her grandson about his great-grandfather, Abíódún, who was king of the empire called Òyó.

PART SEVEN

1851–1864

In Walked the Queen

Thirty-six

Crowther was fifty-two years old when King Dòsùnmú was cowed into ceding Lagos over to the British, making the island of Èkó the latest addition to Queen Victoria's burgeoning imperial possessions. Lagos was a key coastal city on whose soil the French, who had already one foot in Dahomey next door, were known to be keen to plant the tricolour flag; the carving up of Africa by the Great Powers was well under way. This was why Prime Minister Lord Palmerston was so utterly convinced that Lagos was in dire need of British protection, whether or not Lagos had asked for it. This wasn't the rationale given by Whitehall for the takeover, of course. Officially, the reason the *Prometheus* was summoned to Lagos lagoon, with its large gun turrets squarely set on King Dòsùnmú's palace, was not at all to compel the king to put his signature on the treaty, perish the thought; rather, it was to protect Lagos from a threatened attack from Dòsùnmú's arch-nemesis, the notorious Kòsókó, who had been sighted in Èpé thumbing his nose at an effigy of Dòsùnmú.

Less than three years after Lagos formally became a British protectorate, Reverend Crowther was summoned to London by his employers, the Church Missionary Society, for a meeting so urgent he wasn't allowed time to take a change of clothing with him when he set sail from Lagos. In England, at a consecration by the Archbishop of Canterbury, attended by the great and the good, he was

195

made a bishop of the Anglican Church. Canterbury Cathedral was packed to the rafters. The ordination would be seen by many to be the crowning glory of Crowther's inexorable rise to the top.

But becoming Bishop of the Church of England in the Niger was not the driving ambition of Crowther's life. He did not seek the position; far from it: when it was first offered to him, he turned it down. Many of his white cohorts in Lagos, Badagry and Abẹ́òkuta, who terribly hankered after the position and had painstakingly lobbied for it for themselves, would turn green with envy, some of them venomously so, one or two of them in language not only overflowing with racism but steeped in racialist entitlement of the first water, when word reached them that the episcopate had landed on Crowther's lap. But Crowther himself did not want it: it took much persuading to get him to accept it.

He would always remain at heart the humble schoolteacher who was plucked, aged thirty-two, from an obscure but quite fulfilled existence in the classrooms of Fourah Bay College, Freetown, and planted, a chaplain's assistant, on a fleet of steamers embarking on a grandiose scheme involving a voyage across the River Niger named the African Colonisation Expedition, being funded, lavishly so, by a London-based organisation with links to Queen Victoria's consort, Prince Albert, called the Society for the Extinction of the African Slave Trade and the Civilisation of Africa. What turned Crowther into a household name in London, Freetown and Lagos was a book he co-authored about the ill-fated expedition, brought out the following year by the London publisher Hatchards of Piccadilly.

The Reverend James Schön, a German, was the expedition's official chaplain. Schön, to whom Crowther was answerable on the expedition, and who became Crowther's mentor and an early supporter of the young Sierra Leonean schoolteacher's writings, was a highly regarded linguist whose speciality was Hausa. His seminal works, which included the first Hausa–English bilingual dictionary, would have a strong influence on Crowther's subsequent career as a linguist and translator. It was Schön's journals alone that Hatchards originally intended to publish. On Schön's recommendation, however, they decided to publish Crowther's own daily account of the expedition as well, bringing both diaries out in a single volume called *The Journals of the Rev. James Frederick Schön and Mr Samuel Crowther: who, with the sanction of Her Majesty's government, accompanied the expedition up the Niger, in 1841, in behalf of the Church Missionary Society.*

The book was a runaway success. It made Crowther famous.

Mr Samuel Crowther's travel writing introduced the reader to a humble, self-effacing and witty raconteur with an uncommon talent for evoking place and bringing his galleries of true-life characters fully, and exuberantly, to life; his way of seeing was compassionate but not at all sentimental.

Crowther was a man of earnest, unquestioning faith whose public and private lives were beyond reproach; he was a good son, a loving husband, a devoted father, a loyal friend and a visionary leader. These attributes, together with his singular talents as a writer, linguist and translator, stood him in good stead in the Church.

But what created his career in the first place was a little fly called the anopheles, the mosquito that transmits *Plasmodium falciparum*, the deadliest species of the parasite that causes malaria in human beings: of the one hundred and fifty Europeans who went on the Niger expedition in 1841, fifty-five succumbed to malaria almost immediately when they reached the anopheles-infested River Niger. The voyage was abruptly called off when it became clear that the rising death toll was set to continue. On the other hand, not a single

African who travelled on the expedition died from the illness. This was remarkable, given the fact that for each European on board the three steamers that embarked on the voyage, there were at least five Africans.

These numbers gave Crowther an idea which he described in an afterword to his half of the *Journals*: 'As regards Missionary labours on the banks of the Niger and in the Interior of Africa,' he wrote, 'very little can be done by European Missionaries, except by such as have, before ascending the river, become inured to the climate of Africa. I am reluctantly led to adopt the opinion that Africa can chiefly be benefited by her own Children. I have read, in Sir T. F. Buxton's work *The African Slave Trade and Its Remedy*, that some promising Youths among the Children of Africa should be sent to England for education, who would afterward hold situations in their countries, and whose conduct would have a beneficial influence upon their country-people. If such a plan be in contemplation for other employments, could it not be adopted for preparing Missionaries, too, from the Coast of Africa, who might become useful among their countrymen?'

The Church was more than happy to oblige and, although it was not at all his intention, Crowther himself became the poster child for the policy he was advocating. The schoolteacher was sent to the Church Missionary Society Training College in Islington, north London, where Anglican missionaries were prepared for work overseas; he returned to West Africa an ordained priest. His education in England would culminate in a Doctor of Divinity degree from the University of Oxford. His ordination as the first African bishop in the Church's 330-year history was a direct result of this policy of creating a cadre of Africans who were to work as missionaries and educationists in Africa. CMS Grammar School, the first secondary school in what would become known as Nigeria, was founded to train students for missionary work, an elite class whose reaches would eventually spread to all aspects of life in Lagos and beyond.

For nearly three decades, this policy was vigorously supported and enthusiastically championed by the Church, and Crowther, its creator, conferred with the status of a living saint. Then something happened that changed everything: quinine was found to be a cure and prophylactic for malaria; West Africa, known up till then as the white man's grave, was finally tamed. As soon as this happened, the Africanisation policy began to come unstuck. Its author had risen to a great height within the hierarchy of the Church, and from that precipitous height he was eventually nudged, ever so gently, over the precipice.

The heft Crowther possessed, while it lasted, was considerable. He used it to pursue the driving passion of his life, which was to end the slave trade, by any means necessary. In the course of his day job as an ecclesiastic, which saw him journey in Hausaland and Iboland and Yorùbáland, often by foot, and in all the contiguous territories that would eventually merge into a geographical entity named after the Niger, he encountered everywhere a predatory ruling class and venal potentates whose subjects lived desperate lives of serfdom and could be sold and often were. Crowther was convinced that the only way the trade in human flesh, as he called it, could be stopped, once and for all, was through the deposition of these aristocrats of misery.

There were two ways, he thought, to go about it.

The first was to create an educated class.

The other way was to emulate coastal Sierra Leone, his adopted home country, where there were no slaves because Sierra Leone was a British colony; the slave trade had long been outlawed in the colonies.

Crowther was in the vanguard of both solutions.

Aside from his dictionary of the Yorùbá language, he also worked on the first primer of the Ibo language and the first grammar and vocabulary of the Nupe language.

Long before the Scramble for Africa began in earnest, he once paid a visit to Windsor to see Queen Victoria and Prince Albert to make the case for making Abẹ̀òkuta a British protectorate.

Thirty-seven

It was a bone-chilling, nose-numbing day in August when Crowther went to Windsor to see the royals. In London, the day before, he'd had lunch with Sir Francis Baring, the First Lord of the Admiralty; and the Foreign Secretary, and future Prime Minister, Lord Palmerston. These engagements with some of the most powerful members of the establishment were among the perquisites of success that had come his way since his book was published, when he became not just a celebrity author but a man of the cloth.

Lord Wriothesley, Canon of the Ninth Stall of Windsor Chapel, met him outside the chapel, and took him straight to the palace. When they got there, they were informed by the servants-in-waiting that Prince Albert was not in.

The door opened while they were waiting for the Prince Consort in a drawing room. A magnificently dressed lady, with a long train, regally swept into the room. Crowther immediately got to his feet and made a deep obeisance. The lady bowed to them, picked up something from the chimneypiece and regally swept out.

'A lady-in-waiting,' Lord Wriothesley explained to the guest.

They were led to an upper drawing room where they met Prince Albert standing by a writing table with a large map open wide from that year's edition of the Blue Book, the annual accounts of revenues and expenditure, and civil establishment and various statistics from the colonies.

Formal introductions out of the way, the Prince Consort turned to the map and said to his guest, 'Can you find the place on the map?' The place he was anxious to find on the map was Abẹ̀òkuta.

Crowther could not find Abẹ̀òkuta on the large map spread out before them, but he had anticipated this; from his pocket, he brought out a small map: Samuel Jr, who was something of a dab hand at cartography, had made it, a map of all the slave markets in West Africa with all the towns and seaports.

On the smaller map, he was easily able to pick out Abẹ̀òkuta. As he was doing this a lady entered the room, simply dressed, a bit plump; she joined them at the table and listened as Crowther told Prince Albert about the war that had been waged against Abẹ̀òkuta by King Ghezo of Dahomey and his formidable army of female soldiers, the Amazons; how the Ẹ̀gbá finally repulsed the ferocious attack and sent the Dahomean army fleeing in retreat, with thousands of lives lost on both sides.

'It was Ghezo who attacked Abẹ̀òkuta,' Crowther explained. 'But it was his close friend, Kòsọ́kọ́, who encouraged him to wage war.'

Kòsọ́kọ́ was King of Lagos at this time. Akíntóyè, whom he had ousted, was living in exile in Badagry. Kòsọ́kọ́'s grouse against Abẹ̀òkuta was that the new town was trying to set itself up as a trading rival to Lagos, and that it had an open-door policy for European missionaries and those traders whose interest was in buying produce and not human beings. It welcomed Sierra Leonean recaptives, such as Crowther, a benighted class of people who had been told in no uncertain terms that they were not welcome in Lagos; the first batch who landed there had been robbed of all their belongings, some of them killed.

Kòsókó's Lagos was a slave emporium. All of the European traders living in Lagos during his reign were slave traders and none of them was happy that their business had been crippled by the Navy patrols that were to be found everywhere off the coast of the island. In Dahomey next door, Ghezo's slave-trading Portuguese and Brazilian patron-merchant friends were also beginning to feel the pinch, though not to the extent that the merchants did in Lagos, which was located within a British sphere of interest, but they knew it was only a matter of time before they too would have to contend with the ships of war.

Ghezo's raid on Abéòkuta, which involved sixteen thousand soldiers, was intended to serve two purposes: the bounty of human prisoners, which would have numbered in the tens of thousands, would have yielded enormous returns, the sort of returns that had seen dealers like Domingo Martínez accrue a fortune in the millions of dollars only a few years before. The other reason was to smother the legitimate trade that had dawned there. Legitimate trade, wherever it seemed to succeed, was bad news for an economy built on the slave trade.

'Ghezo and Kòsókó are of one mind about the raids on Abéòkuta,' Crowther told Prince Albert. 'They might as well have planned it all together. As long as the slave trade is allowed to continue in Lagos, Abéòkuta is in peril.'

The prince wanted to know where the reverend was born.

'I was born in a town called Òsogùn,' he told Prince Albert, 'which no longer exists.'

He told him the story of the day Òsogùn was destroyed and how he and his mother and sister were captured. The prince and the canon and the plump lady listened with breathless attention as he told them about how he finally arrived in Lagos and was sold there to a Portuguese man.

'Lagos,' muttered Prince Albert, 'ought to be knocked down by all means.'

He lit a lamp; it was getting dark: he wanted to identify the relative positions of the various places on the map where Yorùbá slaves were shipped. He returned to the Blue Book map and flicked a page open; it blew out the lamp, which caused some laughter. When the laughter finally died down, the prince turned to the lady and said, 'Will Your Majesty kindly bring us a candle from the mantelpiece?' Only now, on hearing this, did Crowther realise who she was. Trembling from head to toe, he completely forgot what he was about to say.

'Don't be frightened,' Prince Albert told him.

The queen returned from the fireplace with two lighted candles.

'What facility of trade,' she asked him with a warm, reassuring smile, 'would Lagos possess should the slave trade be abolished?'

'Your Majesty,' Crowther took a deep bow, 'Lord Palmerston and Sir Francis asked me the same question yesterday.' He launched into a detailed analysis of Lagos and her potential to become a major cotton and palm-oil producer.

The queen listened with rapt interest, and then she said, 'What did Lord Palmerston and Sir Francis say?'

'They expressed satisfaction at the information, Your Majesty.'

Lord Wriothesley now mentioned Crowther's Yorùbá translations.

'What's the sound of the language?' the queen asked.

Crowther obliged, to her obvious delight, by reciting the Lord's Prayer in Yorùbá.

'It is soft and melodious,' she observed. 'What language is it classified with?'

The conversation turned to a young girl called Sarah Forbes

Bonetta, who had been sent, aged four, by King Ghezo as a gift to the queen.

'Is Sally a princess?' the queen asked. 'Is she a relative of Ghezo?'

Crowther told the queen that Sarah, who also went by the diminutive of Sally, was not related to King Ghezo, as far as he could tell, though she might be related to some Yorùbá chiefs; she had been captured during one of Ghezo's perennial raids on Abẹ̀òkuta.

Sally would grow up to marry an Ẹ̀gbá industrialist and establish herself as a leading light of the Lagos upper class.

Thirty-eight

A few weeks after this most convivial afternoon at Windsor Castle, nearly five thousand miles away in Lagos, Her Britannic Majesty's Consul for the Bight of Benin, and Governor of Fernando Po, John Beecroft, paid a visit on King Kòsọ́kọ́ at the Iga Ìdúnganran.

Beecroft had come to the palace bearing a stark message from London.

'The British government is resolved to put an end to the African slave trade,' he informed the king. 'And has the means and power to do so.'

'Your man talks through the nose,' Kòsọ́kọ́ said to the interpreter. 'What is he trying to say?'

'He has been authorised by the queen's government to conclude a treaty for the abolition of the slave trade with you,' the interpreter told him.

'Has he now,' Kòsọ́kọ́ replied. 'We'll see about that. Tell him to go and tell his queen that I'll think about it.'

A few days later, when Kòsọ́kọ́ spotted Beecroft and his entourage approaching on the bar beach, he welcomed them with a barrage of gunfire. Beecroft was outgunned; several of his men were killed.

'There's my reply,' Kòsọ́kọ́ yelled. 'Go back and tell your queen.'

Beecroft fled with his tail between his teeth. He sent for the big guns of the Navy. The big guns left Lagos a smouldering ruin. Kòsọ́kọ́ fled to Èpé.

Crowther, freshly returned from England, was on the boat that brought the new king, Akíntóyè, back to Lagos from Badagry where he had lived in exile since he himself was deposed, six years earlier, by Kòsọ́kọ́, who was actually kin to him; Kòsọ́kọ́ was his uncle.

When Kòsọ́kọ́ overthrew him, he did so for the very simple reason that at the time the previous incumbent died, he, Kòsọ́kọ́, was the rightful heir, the next in line to succeed him as king. Akíntóyè got the job only because Kòsọ́kọ́, a wild man of the seas, who often disappeared for months at a time to unknown destinations on the water, could not be found when he was being sought to be proclaimed king. By the time the news found him, Akíntóyè, his nephew, who was next in line after him, had been tapped for the job.

Kòsọ́kọ́ came, all guns blazing, and shooed his urbane, mild-mannered nephew out of the Iga Ìdúnganran.

Akíntóyè got reinstated, not exactly because his claim on the throne enjoyed an iota more legitimacy than Kòsọ́kọ́'s but because he was a savvy politician: he was still in exile in Badagry when he asked for the abolition treaty to be brought to him *now, now! At once! At once!* for him to sign; and he signed it with a flourish. He didn't wait to be asked.

In actual fact, during his subsequent reign, the treaty he signed wasn't worth the paper it was written on, but it was evident to anyone who cared to look at the beautiful document that it had been signed not only with discernment but also with a certain *je ne sais quoi*.

Kòsọ́kọ́'s ouster was Crowther's first salvo of retribution — it certainly would not be the last — against the powerful clan of which both Kòsọ́kọ́ and Akíntóyè, uncle and nephew, were prominent scions;

the same fat-cat aristocracy to whom had accrued, thirty years before, the percentage tax payable on every transaction that took place at the barracoons on the island of Èkó where a thirteen-year-old boy from Òṣogùn called Àjàyí was traded and sold.

He would not be done with them, not until he'd wrested the entire town from their claws, not until every barracoon on the island had been torn down, every dugout canoe with a clandestine consignment of captives confiscated, its cargo set free, shorn of their chains.

He would not, God help him, he would not!

PART EIGHT

1855

The Death of Dr Irving

Thirty-nine

You will scarcely be prepared to receive the most painful tidings of the death of Dr Irving which took place on the 29th of April at the Church Mission House, Lagos, Crowther wrote in his private journals. *On Saturday March 31st he was long detained at the waterside, for several hours in the night, unable to cross from Ikorodu to Lagos, the market canoes not being ready to start. This exposure, with the exertions of travelling a great part of this way on foot, the road being bad for horses, tended to worsen his complaints of diarrhoea and gripes, from which he suffered during the journey. He arrived at the Mission House Sunday morning about 5 a.m., having been caught in a heavy shower of rain accompanied with a strong tornado that morning just before landing; however, some coffee and tea refreshed him. He was unable to attend service on account of the diarrhoea from which he was suffering.*

Forty

Monday April 2nd

Today he was feeling much better. After breakfast about 9 a.m. we rode out on a visit to King Dòsùnmú, but we could not speak with him as he had some trading matter to settle which took a long time; we were two full hours in the King's house, to whom he gave an umbrella for a present as we were leaving. From the King's we paid a visit to Mr Grotte of the House of Diedrickson, where we had some conversation about the interior and the state of trade; from there we went to the expelled Chief Mewu of Badagry, who was exceedingly glad to see the doctor; we then returned home about 7 p.m.

Forty-one

Tuesday April 3rd

From this day till the 17th when he was not able to leave his bed, the doctor was not able to go out of the house beyond the yard, but was always up in his dress, doing some little drawing, reading, or revising his papers; he continued to take medicines and macaroni, to support his wasting body.

Forty-two

Saturday April 21st

Dr Irving still confined in bed; he tried to get himself salivated, but he did not succeed although he took large doses of Calomel. He felt very weak although he had no actual pains to complain of. He could take nothing also, but weak tea and macaroni boiled plain.

Forty-three

Monday April 23rd

I got in early this morning to ask how he was. He had shifted from the bed to the sofa in the next room. He felt squeamish, could not stomach anything, neither tea nor macaroni; even the sight of water in the tumbler was sickening to him. He took hold of me by the hand and wept because he had become so helpless and could do nothing; he said, 'It is not often that I give way thus.'

I got some toast and water made for him and also some very weak plain chicken broth, which for the novelty of the change, he seemed to enjoy. He had expressed a wish sometime back to get some good port wine, but of all the merchants I made enquiry, none to be had. So, I wrote to Mr Sanderson to request, if he had none himself, to send to enquire on board the Observer *whether any could be got there, but there was no reply that day.*

Forty-four

Tuesday April 24th

Went in early to see how he was; he passed a restless night; he said, 'I cannot tell how I am, but I am in the hand of God.' We then had some talk about the certainty of our support when we place ourselves in the hand of the best of physicians. He took some more Calomel to effect salivation. I proposed for a little change if he should like to be carried in a chair for a short time carefully wrapped up, but he said he could not bear it, the least exposure to the wind gave him griping pain. He had all the glass windows darkened as he could not bear much light. He begged me not to allow any Naval officer who might come to the house, to come in, for they would urge him to go on board for a cruise which idea he detested, and neither did he wish anyone to write to Mrs Irving to say how ill he was, for they would surely say more than they ought. He felt very uneasy all day, took but very little tea and soup, but toast and water he continued to take largely.

Forty-five

Wednesday April 25th

The doctor passed another very bad night. I was up about 12 a.m. to help in his wants, again at 4 a.m., when he requested me to reach him the bottle of laudanum; he had taken some with water in a wine glass, all of which he had not drunk, so I gave him the remainder and put the bottle away; he slept for about two hours in the forenoon, and at 12.30 he took another dose of laudanum and about an hour later, according to his prescription, I mixed 4oz of powdered gum acacia in half a pint of water, but unfortunately, the gum being mouldy, it became good for nothing, he could not drink it. I made him a small teacup full of laudanum with half a glass of port wine which he took. His bowels continued in a bad state.

Forty-six

Thursday April 26th

The doctor was very weak today; he took no tea, nor broth, but toast and water and half a small teacup full of laudanum with port wine. He asked for a little pale ale, I gave him half a tumbler full but he could not keep it; sometime afterwards I made him some thin rice water with port wine which he drank: I perceived that he was going to take another dose of laudanum measured out to 50 drops, I advised him to stop from taking any more as he was weak and sleepy all day, speaking confusedly; he was feverish and had his hands and head bathed several times with cold water.

We have been on the lookout for the mail, he requested me to drop a few lines to Mrs Irving to say he was sorry he could not write; he was ill longer than he had expected.

Forty-seven

Friday April 27th

The doctor passed a very restless night; his mind continued to wander. Today Mr Swain, master of Her Majesty's Ship Pluto *off Lagos, called to know how the doctor was. He at first said he could not see Mr Swain, but after a little persuasion from me, he admitted him in; when he saw Mr Swain, he gave vent to his feelings by shedding tears and said he was very sick of dysentery, he was very much obliged to Mr Swain for calling, he could not speak much; after hasty enquiries of persons and ships Mr Swain left the room with a promise that the surgeon of the ship would call the next day to see the doctor. On the 6th hour when he was in want of good solid opium, ours on the shelf being beyond good for nothing, I sent on board HMS* Minx *for some. I told the doctor that I had desired the surgeon of the ship in my letter to pay him a visit, but he did not like it and expressed his regret that I had done so: however, and unfortunately, my letter which was entrusted to the gunner was lost by him, and I had to write another, so I omitted my request of the surgeon's visit, accordingly only the opium was sent. When Capt. Skene landed, the surgeon of the* Philomel *came first and paid the doctor a visit and brought some more solid opium; he afterwards accompanied Capt. Skene and the consul to the Mission House in the course of the day. The doctor's reluctance to see them was the cause of a drawback on my part to invite them frequently to visit him. In the course of the day, he expressed a wish to be shaved so I sent for a Hausa barber who commenced the operation with his own tool, but the doctor called for his razor and in an inclined position he managed to shave himself which he did not think he could have done: this was certainly encouraging because he was so weak yesterday that he could not hold a tumbler in his hand. In the afternoon a messenger brought some arrowroot and a bottle of port wine, the only one Mr Mazer had in store against the time of emergency, a bottle of cherry from Abeokuta: the arrowroot was a valuable present and a nice change, especially as my stock of opium began to get low and none to be obtained as far as I had asked at Lagos. I immediately made him some arrowroot which, for the novelty of the change, he seemed to enjoy — but he soon refused taking any more.*

Forty-eight

Saturday April 28th

Seeing he refused almost everything we had, I made him some macaroni broth, of which he was persuaded to take a cup; scarcely would he touch anything more the whole day, save some cold tea and toast and water. As he had taken no medicine since the morning, in the evening I gave him 8g of jalap powder in two doses, hoping this might relieve him a little and compose him to sleep, but to no purpose.

Forty-nine

Sunday April 29th

About 4 a.m., being very uneasy, I gave him 30 drops laudanum; the remainder left in the bottle, but he said it could do him no good. As soon as it was daylight, he got out of his bed and wanted to go out of the house; with some difficulty I got him back to his room. Just before service, he got out of his bed again and came into the parlour and wanted to go to the medicine shelves which I considered was not advisable, so I did not let him but told him that I would fetch any bottle he might name, which he did not: so with great efforts and with the assistance of Messrs Wright and Pearse and his two servants, I got him back into his room, and left Mr Wright to watch him in my absence during the service time. From this time his talk became more and more confused and unintelligible, he sat in an easy chair nearly all the service time quite insensible of what he talked, from this time he did not know me. In the afternoon Mr Campbell sent his desk to enquire how the doctor was, and to inform me that the surgeon of the Philomel *was unwell and therefore was unable to come yesterday as was intended: he kindly offered to send two more bottles of port wine for which I was very much obliged but did not need it. Before I left for the afternoon service, I left Mr Wright to take care of him. At my return I found him growing weaker; with our assistance, he put on his morning gown, shifted from his bed to the sofa in the next room which he never left and whereon he breathed his last at 11.48 p.m. when I closed his eyes.*

PART NINE

1861

In the Palace of the Kings

Fifty

The driver of the hansom cab nimbly tugged at the rawhide reins harnessed to the powerful, mottled stallion pulling them at a canter; he steered the cab out of the parsonage, past the chapel.

A lone, distinguished figure sat in the passenger compartment.

It was the Reverend Samuel Crowther.

At the intersection of Breadfruit and Broad Street, a pack of barouche carriages loped past; like sea waves chasing sea waves, luxury carriage bounded after luxury carriage across their path and the driver was compelled to bring the cab to a precipitate halt.

The high-society dandies jauntily installed in the plush double seats of the passing carriages were decked out in their sparkling fineries; they were boisterously merry on fine whisky and spicy conversation laden with double entendres. They had just left a carousal on the Marina at the house of Madam Pittuluga, the businesswoman known in her expatriate circles as 'that Aussie spinster', and were now on their way to the Five Cowrie Creek residence of the Sàró industrialist J. P. L. Davies and his wife Sarah Forbes Bonetta to enjoy a recital of Handel sonatas by S. O. Thomas, the renowned concert pianist Mrs Davies had brought down to Lagos all the way from Sierra Leone, would you believe it.

The pianist had sailed first class on the mail steamer *Ethiope* whose regular route from Liverpool took in Madeira, Tenerife,

Bathurst, Freetown, Cape Palmas, Cape Coast, Accra, Lagos, a few stops along the Benin River, and at Nun, Brass and Bonny. On board the steamship were industrial quantities of Manchester and Glasgow fabrics; goods from the brassfounders, gunsmiths, silversmiths and button makers of Birmingham; rolled tobacco and rum from Bahia; and package piled upon package of the highly sought-after blue shells of Zanzibar – the gold-ring cowrie, considered by connoisseurs of shell money to be the finest shell currency of them all. Also on board the *Ethiope* was a fifty-ton iron boat, built at Woolwich, disassembled and carried in separate parts on the deck, and a thirty-foot-long canoe, for service at Lagos and Badagry. The thirty-three passengers who were travelling in steerage, self-emancipated ex-slaves heading back to their Yorùbá roots, were listed on the manifest as 'Spanish negroes from Havana'.

Sarah Forbes Bonetta was famed for her great beauty, her uncommon intelligence and her magnificent banquets; on top of these, she was also known to be Queen Victoria's god-daughter. At her *soirée musicale* tonight, guests would be treated to port and champagne; mince pies and plum puddings would be served. Reverend Crowther's own daughter, the 25-year-old Abigail, and her husband, Babington Macaulay, were among the young, Islington, London and Fourah Bay, Freetown-educated Sierra Leonean elite, and the Brazilian *emancipado* who had been invited to grace the occasion with their presence.

Just last year, Babington had founded the first secondary school in Lagos, formed of the six brightest pupils he could gather together on the island: all were boarding students, living at Cotton House, the small, single-storey residential building on Broad Street which had been repurposed into the school's inaugural home. Babington's brother-in-law, Dandeson Coates Crowther, was the brightest light in the radiant galaxy of the foundation class of CMS Grammar School, just as his father, Babington's father-in-law, had been the first student admitted to Fourah Bay College, Freetown, the first Western-style university in black Africa, three decades earlier.

The cab turned right on the Marina, the wide promenade over-looking the lagoon. Groves of rose trees, and acacia trees, and tall, gangly palm trees, with their long, skinny fronds swaying languidly in the sea breeze, fringed the water. There, on the right, gliding away from them as they raced past the walls behind which it was enclosed, Madam Pittuluga's, an imposing cuboid edifice straddling an entire block planted between four streets; Madam Pittuluga lived on the top floor, her factory was on the ground floor; and there on the left, opposite the Pittuluga building, Madam Pittuluga's own private pier. And on the next block, also possessing its own private pier, stood the Sardinian merchant M. Carrena's grand building, painted chalk white and pale yellow; next to it, the Wesleyan Mission House. And there − that's the French Comptoir, walled in by a sprawling, sumptuous garden; and that was, of course, Mr Grotte's House of Diedrickson, opened back in 1852 by W. Oswald of Hamburg.

After spending nearly a decade in Lagos, the Sardinian business-man and diplomat Giambattista Scala had returned home two years ago, but his factory was still there on the Marina, standing pat, if not a little worse for wear; next door to it was Sandeman's, the eponym-ous store owned by an Englishman who was known to the islanders as òyìnbó onírun − hairy white man − for no reason other than the undisputable fact that he was an exceptionally hairy man; and over here, just past òyìnbó onírun's was the towering whitewash house with a slate roof that the acting consul, William McCoskry, another hairy òyìnbó, had built for himself. McCoskry, a Scotsman of Irish descent, was a redhead with a long, thick beard the colour of the shock of hair on his pate. Naturally, in all the aqua vitae dives on the island, and the houses of ill repute, and the markets, he was known as Redbeard – alágbọ̀n pípọ́n. Next to Redbeard's, there stood the Church Mission House, where the reverend and his family had lived until the parsonage at Breadfruit was completed a few years ago; right next to that stood the corrugated-iron curiosity that had for years served as the Ilé Ajélẹ̀, otherwise known as the British Consulate, where earlier that day, in the reverend's presence, the consul had appended his signature, King Dòsùnmú his thumbprint, to the treaty of cession.

Much of the cargo on the *Ethiope* and other trading vessels like her were destined for factories like Madam Pittuluga's and stores like Sandeman's on the Marina, and the bulk of the freight the mail steamer would haul back to Europe would come from them. Among the merchandise that would be brought to the *Ethiope* from the bar beach by Fàǹtí boatmen and loaded into its hold while it remained rocking offshore were some:

207 boxes of oranges
831 tusks
63 cases of ivory
2 bags of tortoiseshell
342 puncheons of palm oil
902 billets of camwood
64 bags of gum copal
73 bales of moss
27 bags of cochineal
47 packages of beeswax
2 casks of malagueta pepper
70 cases of cayenne

85 logs of teak timber
33 bags of coffee
46 cases of arrowroot
61 pipes of wine
89 packages of sundries and returnables.

More cargo, including 3,000 ounces of gold, would be added at Cape Coast and at each of the other stops along the way.

The reverend's shoulder bag was lying by his feet. He leaned forward and reached into the bag. He pulled out his journal. He was constantly on the move and because he was constantly on the move, he had become quite adept at writing on the move – the translations, the dictionaries, the letters (he wrote a prodigious number of letters), the sermons, and the daily journal he kept, in which he wrote down his thoughts, meticulously, often in great detail; it also served as a diary of incidents from his daily life.

He reached for his pen and edged closer to the hurricane lamp hanging by the carriage door.

Outside the carriage, nightlife and the streets hurtled past.

Fifty-one

There were sounds of revelry issuing from every corner of the island. It came from the seafront, from Broad Street and the Marina – the European District. And from Ìsàlẹ̀ Èkó, at the back of the town, where the Native Islanders had lived clustered around the Iga Ìdún-ganran, the king's palace, for generations. And it came from Pópó Àgùdà, at the back of the eastern end of the European District, home to at least a hundred and thirty families of Brazilian Africans of Ẹ̀gbá origin, highly skilled craftsmen and artisans, ex-slaves who had scrimped and saved to purchase their freedom and return to the land of their ancestors, and Cuban returnees like the ones on the *Ethiope*; and from Olówógbowó on the western edge of the island.

The name of the district, Olówógbowó ('the owner claims their money from the debtor'), was a withering put-down of indigence framed as a casual statement of observation. What it really meant was, pay up, just pay up; it's their money, shut up and pay up; a hymn to the dog-eat-dog hustle.

Olówógbowó was home to some of the wealthiest African deni-zens of Lagos, the Sàró émigrés who first moved there from Sierra Leone in the early forties; the clerks, teachers, nurses, traders; the merchants who purchased the hulks of decommissioned slavers and painstakingly refurbished them into seaworthy vehicles plying the Gulf of Guinea trading, among other things, in farm produce; if a clergyman in the Niger or the Delta or in Yorùbá was African, chances were he was Sàró. Of course, not all Sàrós lived in Olówóg-bowó. The most famous Sàró living in Lagos in the sixties, the Reverend Samuel Adjai Crowther, didn't live in Olówógbowó. He lived on Breadfruit Street, in the very heart of the European District.

'Reverend sir. We've arrived. We're at the Iga Ìdúnganran.'

Reverend Crowther stirred from the light slumber that had crept on him unawares. He looked up. It was the driver, speaking through the hatch. He pulled aside the lace curtain drawn over the glass window and looked outside. The driver had parked right in front of the black and white marble pavement leading into the main entrance of the palace. Reverend Crowther tugged at his collar and rearranged it. He stepped out of the hansom cab.

Fifty-two

In the depths of the iga, inside the small, rather claustrophobic room that served as the council chamber, Reverend Crowther sat surrounded by King Dòsùnmú's closest advisers. He sat facing the king himself. Crowther was sitting in the same carved mahogany chair he had been offered the last time he was summarily summoned to the palace, which was exactly twenty-four hours ago.

At around this time last night, and from this very same chair, his eyes had been locked in a stare with those of King Dòsùnmú. It was not a dare, not a provocation; it was just the way things were at an audience with King Dòsùnmú. Crowther had been summoned to the iga to offer to the crown the benefit of his advice, which was what he was in the midst of doing, and the king, leaning forward and perched at the edge of his own far more elaborately carved seat, was listening intently; he was listening keenly, and somewhat anxiously trying to detect and decipher the minutest variations in his visitor's facial expressions, especially those fleeting, almost imperceptible varieties that were local to the brow or specific to the eyes. It was the king's opinion that the kernel of an utterance could be gleaned only at the confluence of what the utterer was saying and what their naked eyes revealed they were in fact saying when they said it. What they said could well be a lie, or it could be the truth; it could be a truthful lie, or a barrage of outright lies garbed in the plain gown of unadorned truth; it was often impossible to tell. Not so with the eye, not so at all: even if we seldom let it tell the truth, the eye never lied.

'Look me in the eye,' King Dòsùnmú was often heard to say. 'I want you to look me in the eye.'

He did not say this to Crowther. He didn't need to. But the fact that he knew the reverend for a man of his word was also beside the point. In the king's line of trade, people often came to him with everything and anything but the truth; they would in fact look him in the eye and, without so much as a blink, proceed to feed him a confection of lies. He had come to appreciate that it wasn't personal, it was just the way of the world.

Once again, for the second time in two days, the reverend's eyes and those of the king were locked as in a tight but wary handshake. Last night, the king wore an anxious, tortured look. Tonight, he looked even more worried, far more tortured, and lurking in his sleep-bereft eyes there was a hint of paranoia. He looked furious and outraged; he looked quite close to panic.

King Dòsùnmú was known for his voracious appetites: he had over a hundred wives and kept a most magnificent table; champagne flowed like lagoon water at parties that sometimes went on for days. His flamboyant wardrobe was the stuff of legend. Of course, tonight, in consonance with his sombre mood, he was dressed down in a loose black robe; but his feet, sheathed in a pair of resplendent red silk slippers, were making no concessions to the downbeat mood; nor were his hands which, together with his wrists, were adorned with a dizzying array of gold, silver, brass and copper rings and bracelets; and clutched between the shimmering digits of his hands was an embossed parchment paper which he now placed before Crowther.

'You know that I am not a book man,' he said to the reverend.

'You know that none of us here are book people. You, on the other hand, are a book man, just like those òyìnbó people. That's why, last night, in this very room, I asked you to go through this document with a fine-tooth comb. And you did. And I asked you, not once, not twice but three times if you thought I should sign it. You said I should. You said it was the best we could get from them under the circumstances.'

Crowther nodded. 'Under the circumstances, it was,' he said.

'And this afternoon at Ilé Ajẹ̀lẹ̀, I put my mark on it. You were there when I put my mark on it.'

Again, Crowther nodded. He was present at the Consul House when the treaty was signed by the acting consul, William McCoskry, and Norman Bedingfeld, commander of the frigate *Prometheus*, whose 21-gun report during the ceremony, a salute to the queen, was said by some to be the very meaning of gunboat diplomacy. In other words, it was like holding the barrel of a gun to the king's head and giving him the treaty to sign.

Dòsùnmú clearly thought so too.

'I had no choice but to put my mark on it,' he said. 'You were there when McCoskry said the warship would blow up this town if I refused to put my mark on it. I'm not afraid to die but I do not want my country to be destroyed. But after putting my mark on it, I've shown the document to others who are book people like yourself. Do you know what they say? They say that all I've done by signing this treaty is to give my country away. Is that true? Read it out. Do me this favour and read it out. That's why I sent for you tonight. I want to hear it again, word for word, point by point. Read it out.'

Crowther reached across the table and picked up the embossed document. He knew everything in the document by heart – he had a photographic memory – but still he spent a long time running his eyes through it. He read the whole thing, every word in it, all over again, then he placed it back on the table and looked up at the king. 'It's exactly what I read out to you last night, in English and Yorùbá. Nothing in it has changed, not a word, not a syllable, not a single punctuation mark.'

'I know nothing in it has changed,' the king said. 'But I'd still like for you to read it to us again.'

'Just over ten years ago I came here to Lagos from Abẹ̀òkuta,' Crowther said. 'I had lived in the Ẹ̀gbá country since the mid-forties when the Church sent me there to minister. I was visiting Èkó by special invitation of your father, our most dearly departed King Akíntóyè. It was my first trip to Lagos in thirty years. The last time I was here Èkó was still no more than a collection of barracoons scattered all over a fishing village by a lagoon, it was little more than a slave market on a small island; I arrived at the slave market a commodity for sale and was forced out of it a commodity sold and bought on a cold day, loaded naked and in chains on to a Portuguese slaver bound for Brazil. And now, thirty years later, I am conveyed to this same place, now a fine metropolis thriving on legitimate trade – on a Brazilian merchant's boat, it so happens, Señor Maurício, a friend of the king's; and I'm lodged in a house inside the king's palace. What a contrast! When Señor Maurício dropped anchor that morning, it was opposite the very spot where I was shipped thirty years before. I pointed out the place to my fellow passengers; even three decades later, the day I was sold to the Portuguese man was fresh in my mind. I do not need to remind you, of course, that only a week before I boarded Señor Maurício's boat and came to Lagos to lodge with King Akíntóyè, the king would not have been in a position to invite me – together with my wife and children – to be his guest in Lagos as he was himself at the time still living in exile in

Badagry; the usurper Kòsọ́kọ́ was here in his place, having betrayed the king's trust and abused his generosity, as you all know, and installed himself on the throne. We all know that it was the British Navy that finally restored to the rightful king the throne that legitimately belonged to him, the throne from which he had been dislodged by Kòsọ́kọ́. We also know the reason why John Beecroft, Her Majesty's Consul for the Bight of Benin, aligned the interests of Great Britain with those of King Akíntóyè and summoned the British Navy to act on behalf of the king: it was because King Akíntóyè had fallen in step with the mood of the times and renounced the trade in human flesh. His rival Kòsọ́kọ́, on the other hand, refused to do so. It was as simple as that. If Kòsọ́kọ́ had agreed to append his seal on the document when he was approached by the consul, who had been instructed to ask him to sign a treaty for the abolition of the slave trade in Lagos, Kòsọ́kọ́ in all likelihood would still be the occupant of this royal house today. But he's not. And that's because he refused outright. Mr Beecroft approached him twice, and twice Kòsọ́kọ́ rebuffed the consul. The second time Mr Beecroft came to him, he was carrying with him another message from Her Majesty's government. This time, he was instructed to remind Kòsọ́kọ́ that Lagos is near the sea and that on the sea are the ships and cannon of England and that he, King Kòsọ́kọ́, did not hold his authority without a competitor. Still, Kòsọ́kọ́ would not turn his back on the trade in human flesh. And why would he? He was making a fortune from the trade. He absolutely would not put his stamp on the treaty. And so the gunboats were summoned, the palace suffered heavy bombardment, lives were lost, quite unnecessarily, but finally Kòsọ́kọ́'s forces were routed, and he fled to Porto Novo where to this day he remains banished.'

The reverend knew that nothing he'd said so far was news to

Dòsùnmú or anyone else in the room. He was aware that the king was listening out of politeness, his chiefs with him, because they knew he was working his way towards some other matter; they were not wrong.

'The Lagos that King Akíntóyè left when he was overthrown by Kòsókó was quite different from the Lagos waiting for him when he was reinstated to the throne,' he said. 'Except in one respect. Some of the most powerful persons on the island, the very people whose backing and goodwill he sorely needed to enjoy a successful reign, were still firmly caught up in the old ways. These people deeply yearned still for the glory days of their darling trade in human flesh and hoped secretly, some not so secretly, for its return under the king's resurgent power.'

When Crowther said this, lightning bolts of bitter hostility immediately assailed him from every corner of the room. Clearly, he had touched a raw nerve.

Fifty-three

But King Dòsùnmú hadn't invited the reverend over to the palace to make an enemy of him. If anything, it was quite to the contrary; not only was Crowther the only black man in Lagos who spoke Yorùbá as fluently as he spoke the king's all-powerful òyìnbó enemies' language, he was also the only black man they seemed to fully trust. It would be sheer folly to make an enemy of such a man. The king knew he had to take the edge off the hostility towards the clergyman at once.

He began by retiring his choice weapon of pre-emptive assailment: the artifice of ever so politely eyeballing a speaker until they became just a little uncomfortable; not so uncomfortable that they imagined any ill designs towards them, but uncomfortable enough to make them think he could read their minds, that he somehow knew their innermost secrets. When this 'look me in the eye' flim-flam worked, as all confidence tricks will when sprung upon the unsuspecting world perfumed in the pheromones of wealth and power, it had been known to transform cocky, belligerent swaggerers into servile, self-seeking flatterers. Never with Reverend Crowther, though. The king had long noticed that the reverend had a penchant for running off at the mouth and a habit of talking to his betters as if they, not he, were the ex-slave. That had not changed; it was never going to change.

And so the king deftly replaced the piercing stare of inquisition, the projectile with which he had tried without success to impale Crowther, with a look of mortified embarrassment. This change of weaponry was instantly telegraphed across the chamber and the bellicose snarls on some faces turned, without warning, into fawning solicitude.

The reverend took it all in with a slight, if gracious, smile that only served to further antagonise those chiefs who were not yet aware that peace had broken out. At least one of them was heard muttering under his breath that he would die a happy man if he could wipe the snooty smile off that Sàró man's face.

'I know what you are thinking,' Crowther said. 'You're thinking, how dare he! How dare he, a common ex-slave, come here to lecture us.'

This was exactly what was going through their minds, but they would sooner die than own up to it. Only an imbecile would own up to such a thing. It just so happened that among the chiefs was a man who, as a middleman for one of the Portuguese slave traders and from the ten per cent he earned on each transaction, had amassed great wealth during the heyday of the trade in human flesh. This man's imbecility was said to be as of the magnitude of his great wealth, so it didn't exactly come as a surprise to anyone when the man began to nod, quite enthusiastically, at the reverend's statement about impertinent ex-slaves. Olóyè Alábẹtútù only stopped nodding when he saw the king bearing down on him with a frosty look on his face.

'But I do completely understand Olóyè Alábẹtútù's feeling, Kábíyèsí,' Crowther hastened to assure the king. 'It's only natural to feel that way. There was a chief, during my stay here as a guest of the late king, a bosom friend of His Highness the king, your father, who turned up at the iga one day while His Highness was entertaining guests. I shall not mention the man by name – everyone in this room would know who I'm talking about, and that's not the point. The point is – I'll tell you what the point is in a moment. This man was a fine-looking person of about forty; he was wearing a black velvet silk covering, as I recall. The minute he noticed me and my wife and the other Sierra Leoneans in the gathering, he launched into a speech about the number of slaves he had sold and how many more he would sell. He asked us whether the people liberated in Sierra Leone did not tell us that he had sold them and that he would sell more of the Sierra Leonean people if he could come at them. He lavished praise on Domingo Martínez, the Brazilian slave trader who used to be a close ally of King Akíntóyè and whose career attained its greatest heights when he lived in Lagos, a trading partner of King Akíntóyè during the era of the king's first reign. Domingo is known to have accrued a fortune of close to two million dollars during King Akíntóyè's first reign. This chief talked at length about Domingo's four ships riding at anchor off Porto Novo, waiting to open the slave trade with the powerful people of Abéòkuta who would seize the opportunity of doing business with Domingo if Lagos was closed for business to him.'

Someone at the back of the room was gasping for breath. It was Olóyè Alábètútù. He had roared with gleeful laughter all through Crowther's speech.

'I know who you are talking about, slave boy!' yelled the retired ten-per-center. 'You are talking about that fat fool Ògúndìran.' His cheeks rolling with tears, he turned to the man sitting next to him. 'The slave boy is talking about your good-for-nothing Uncle Ògúndìran,' he said.

'Tútù!' the king snapped at him.

'Kábíyèsí!'

'Raise your hand, Tútù.'

Alábẹtútù found the very idea side-splittingly funny. 'I should raise my hand, Kábíyèsí?' When he finally stopped laughing, he raised his hand in mock obedience and informed the king, 'I have raised my hand, Kábíyèsí.'

'Good,' said the king. 'Now, cover your mouth with it and hold it there.'

Alábẹtútù's face darkened, then he realised it couldn't possibly be the king talking to him; he gave His Highness a knowing wink and asked, with a guffaw, 'Have you been drinking again, Your Highness? Champagne for breakfast. Have you been imbibing an early breakfast?'

A well-aimed nudge from his neighbour's elbow made sharp contact with Alábẹtútù's ribs and he doubled over in agony.

'Are you trying to kill me?' he yelped.

'Did I step on your foot?' the elbowing neighbour asked in apparent surprise. 'I'm so sorry.'

'You son of a concubine's slave!' Olóyè Alábẹtútù shouted at the man. 'Does my stomach look like a foot to you?'

The man who was called the son of a concubine's slave was indeed the son of a concubine's slave, and from these humble beginnings he had risen to become a stellar member of the ruling class. He now stamped on Alábẹtútù's foot, quite viciously, a move he would later put down to an 'absence of mind', meaning an accident, at a mediation hearing before a cohort of chiefs. The mediating chiefs, who had all witnessed the incident and who knew it couldn't possibly have been an accident, skewed their judgement in favour of the defendant when they unanimously agreed that it, in fact, couldn't possibly have been anything but the sort of unfortunate accident caused by an absence of mind. The plaintiff was therefore awarded an apology and a bullock, which was to be shot in the fields, instead of the apology, five bullocks and seventy heads of cowries Tútù, the prize fool, had asked for. Their message was easy to decipher: that it was one thing to be the son of a concubine's slave, quite another to be called one.

At the palace, on the night of the incident, Alábẹtútù sat in a heap, his enormous body, which was plump and rounded and extremely well fed, bent forward in a foetal position, moaning in pain.

'Kábíyèsí,' he cried to the king. 'These upstarts are trying to kill me, Kábíyèsí.'

'Nobody's trying to kill you, Tútù,' Kábíyèsí assured him.

'I'm about to die,' Alábẹtútù declared, his gin-soaked eyes swimming in their sockets. 'I'm in so much pain, I'm going to die.'

'You're not about to die, Alábẹtútù.' A note of exasperation had crept into Kábíyèsí's voice.

'I am, Kábíyèsí. I am,' Alábẹtútù insisted, clutching at his foot as searing pain shot through it.

'That is not the foot I stepped on,' noted the man who stepped on his foot.

Instantly, the tears rolling down Alábẹtútù's cheeks dried out. He shot the man a frosty look and snapped, 'That is where I'm feeling the pain,' before letting go of the foot he was holding and clutching at the other foot. 'I have one request to make, Your Highness,' he wailed at Kábíyèsí, 'before I go calling on my ancestors. One minor request.'

'You're not about to die, Tútù, but go ahead.'

'I request permission to seal my lips shut.'

The king waited for Alábẹtútù to go on, then he realised he wasn't going to go on because, 'That is your request?'

Alábẹtútù nodded, grimly. 'I insist, Your Highness.'

'What a thoroughly civilised idea,' said the king, slipping in the new buzzword, which meant that he thought Alábẹtútù was thoroughly mad. 'And I dare not turn down a man's last wishes. It would simply be wrong. You have my permission to seal your lips shut. But tell me, Tútù, how do you propose to do it?'

Alábẹtútù showed him. He did it, just as the king had earlier suggested, by raising his hand to his mouth and pinching his lips between his thumb and finger. After that, any time he felt the urge to speak, he clasped his lips between his thumb and finger and pinched them shut. It worked perfectly well.

Fifty-four

The schoolmasterly smile on the reverend's face appeared to vanish as the chiefly contretemps in the council chamber unfolded, but it was still there, if you looked carefully, concealed in the dark of his brown eyes.

'My father did turn his back on Señor Martínez,' the king brusquely informed him. 'After the treaty of abolition, Lagos was closed for business to Señor Martínez. And you well know that, Reverend Crowther.'

'I do indeed, Kábíyèsí,' the reverend nodded in agreement. 'And that was exactly the point I set out to make; it wasn't at all my intention to cast aspersions on King Akíntóyè. Quite the opposite. It was the very point I was trying to make, that once King Akíntóyè set his seal on the treaty abolishing the slave trade in Lagos, he kept his word.' He now rose, slowly, from his seat. 'I intend to copy his example and keep mine.'

'I don't get your meaning, Reverend,' the king said, giving him a quizzical look.

'Kábíyèsí,' said the reverend. 'I promised my wife that I would take Dandeson back to school first thing tomorrow morning.' He lifted his timepiece close to his eye. 'The time now is almost exactly tomorrow morning, Kábíyèsí.'

'If you must go, you must, of course,' the king said impatiently. 'But you haven't answered my question.'

Crowther's face lost all expression.

'What was the question, Your Highness? I beg your pardon.'

'Is it true what people are saying out there that I have given away my country by putting my mark on this confounded treaty with the white man?'

Crowther considered the question thoughtfully; then, looking him in the eye, he said, 'Your Highness, all I can say to you is, you've agreed to it, you've got to honour it.' He paused, then went on, 'Remember what I just said about your dear father?'

Drily, the king replied, 'You've said many things about my father tonight, Reverend, most of which won't bear repeating.'

'He kept his word, that's what I said. I'd advise you to take a leaf out of his book and do the same. King Akíntóyè signed a treaty and kept his word.' He gestured at the document on the table before them and said, 'You've signed this treaty. Keep your word.'

'I should keep my word,' the king said.

'That would be my advice, Your Highness. And with that, I bid you goodnight.'

'That's your advice?' The sheer fury loaded into the question stopped the reverend in his tracks.

King Dòsùnmú now launched a broadside against quislings and other traitors who hated their own country so much they would go out of their way to help outsiders destroy it.

Kábíyèsí was now yelling directly at him. 'Our country has been forcibly taken from us. And that's all you have to say?'

Crowther locked eyes with him. How dare you, his eyes said, how dare you! Then, refusing to concede so much as a blink, he walked towards Kábíyèsí; he headed directly towards him, as if the king were a wall in his path: a wall with an open, invisible door; a door which opened into and shut out of Kábíyèsí's chest, and he was going to walk through it. Since the king did not think of himself as a door and had never entertained the thought of anyone walking through him, what he saw when the reverend approached him with what appeared to be a defiant look on his face was that the priest was about to physically attack him. And because the man looked so conspicuously unthreatening, so peaceable and incapable of assaulting anything, not even a housefly, the king, frankly speaking, was completely unnerved; so unnerved he found himself glued to the spot, unable to move.

When Crowther reached the door, which was situated precisely where the king was standing, he came to a halt. He cut an arc around the door, and consequently around the king also, meaning that he sidestepped Kábíyèsí and walked past him. It was fortunate for him that he did so; Kábíyèsí's limbs had by now, of their own accord, shaken off their paralysis and were, quite independent of any such will to do so by Kábíyèsí, in fight or flight mode and they had chosen to stand their ground and fight.

If Crowther had known quite how close he'd come to being beaten up by His Royal Highness's limbs, he would have turned around and gone home at once, but he didn't, so he headed straight to the table on which the embossed document was lying and picked it up.

After having picked it up and looked at it, it would have been far better for him to put it right back where he found it and turn around and leave at once, but he didn't.

What he did instead was, he went and stood by a hurricane lantern, and read out the contents of the document.

The room listened in rapt attention.

'"Treaty between Norman B. Bedingfeld, Commander of Her Majesty's Ship *Prometheus*, and Senior Officer of the Bights Division, and William McCoskry Esquire, Her Britannic Majesty's Acting Consul, on the part of Her Majesty the Queen of Great Britain, and Dòsùnmú, King of Lagos, on the part of himself and chiefs."'

He adjusted his glasses and looked around the room. The king had gone deathly quiet; so had everyone else in the chamber, and their gaze was as one set on him. He repeated the passage he'd just read out but this time in Yorùbá. He translated it off the cuff.

He then returned to the document and read out the passage that followed.

'"Article One: in order that the Queen of England may be the better enabled to assist, defend and protect the inhabitants of Lagos, and to put an end to the slave trade in this and the neighbouring counties, and to prevent the destructive wars so frequently undertaken by Dahomey and others for the capture of the slaves, I, Dòsùnmú, do, with the consent and advice of my council, give, transfer, and by these presents grant and confirm unto the Queen of Great Britain, her heirs, and successors forever, the port and island of Lagos with all the rights, profits, territories and appurtenances whatsoever thereunto belonging, and as well the profits and revenue as the direct, full and absolute dominion and sovereignty of the said port, island and premises, with all royalties thereof, freely, fully and entirely and absolutely. I do also covenant and grant that the quiet and peaceable possession thereof shall, with all possible speed, be freely and effectually delivered to the Queen of Great Britain, or such person as Her Majesty shall thereunto appoint for her use in the performance of this grant; the inhabitants of said island and territories, as the queen's subjects, and under her sovereignty, crown, jurisdiction and government, being still suffered to live there."'

Some of the men in the room had a working knowledge of English and Portuguese; they could hold their own in any palaver in either tongue. At first, they listened with knitted brows and a sober face as the reverend read out the treaty to them, but they quickly began to get quite agitated.

When in the Yorùbá rendition he reached the passage where 'I, Dòsùnmú' gave and transferred ownership of the port and island of Lagos to the Queen of Great Britain and her heirs and successors in perpetuity, someone gave a long-drawn, shrill scream – King Dòsùnmú let out an anguished howl – but they all waited until Crowther had read out the last sentence before they erupted.

'Moò fi ìlú mi tọrẹ!' the king yelled. 'I did not give away my country.'

'Moò fi ìlú mi tọrẹ!' he repeated.

The intensity of his anger went up another notch each time he said it.

'We didn't give away our land!' The entire palace echoed him in word and fury. 'It's a lie! The òyìnbó lied!'

Everybody in the room seemed to be yelling at the same time. Even Alábẹtútù had broken off his vow of silence.

But it wasn't until someone took a swing at the reverend – fortunately they missed, but only by the skin of Crowther's teeth – that Crowther realised he had overstayed the welcome, that he should have gone home much earlier.

'I really must go now, Your Highness,' he said, backing slowly away. 'My son mustn't be late for school. His mother will not let me hear the end of it.'

'Where do you think you are going?' Kábíyèsí roared at him.

Was there a threat hidden somewhere in that statement? Crowther could not be sure. But when the king then said, 'Come back here, Àjàyí, let me chastise you!' Crowther knew, without a doubt, that he was being threatened in some shape or form by His Royal Highness the King. The clue was in 'chastise'! He wouldn't have used that word if all he planned to do was talk to him. He would have said, 'Let me talk to you!' But he didn't. He didn't want to talk, he wanted to chastise.

Through the corner of his eye, the reverend saw the person who took a swing at him coming towards him again, a murderous glint in his eye. Crowther now found himself backing away faster and faster; then he found himself running away but with his face squarely set in the direction he was running away from.

Luckily for him, the man so determined to strike him was Olóyè Alábẹtútù and the chief could barely walk, let alone run. He had suffered a badly sprained ankle from the foot-stamping attack and his damaged foot was in no condition to participate in ambulation of any sort – not a leisurely walk, let alone a chase.

But the reverend's life was far from being out of harm's way. He saw two wild-eyed beings bound past the hobbled Tútù. The two madmen were heading for him.

Get thee behind me, Panic, he prayed, as panic began to set in. And with this reverse invocation he was able to will himself to turn around, but he found out that turning around only served to give the rush of panic full and unfettered expression – meaning, instead of standing his ground as he'd planned to, he dived, like a startled duiker, into headlong flight.

Fifty-five

Reverend Crowther had good reason for fleeing: he feared for his life, as who would not when a murderously angry mob was hot on their heels.

'You jumped-up òyìnbó houseboy!' the king yelled. 'Let me chastise you!'

Surely, thought the reverend, that's incitement to murder.

He kept trying to run. But there was nowhere to run to; he was surrounded.

He stopped – he had no choice, really – and turned around to face the king.

Better die standing, yenyenyen.

As he was turning around, he remembered an incident which took place a decade earlier, in Abẹ́òkuta, an incident involving a female convert who had antagonised devotees of Òrìṣà Orò, who then decided to assail her with a siege.

One night when she was alone with her four little boys at home, the Òrìṣà devotees came calling on the convert, furiously howling their bullroarers on her roof until it shook. The four boys were overcome with fright; they clung to their mother. Terror-stricken, the woman sat her children down and asked them to sing their most recent lessons from the Mission School, which that week happened to be the Latin alphabet.

The devotees heard the strange noise coming from inside the house and stopped to listen; as soon as they heard the children's voices reciting the ABC, and imagining the woman and her children to be performing some book incantations against them, they fled.

The reverend decided to take his cue from this incident.

But instead of unleashing ABC on his assailants, or even 123, which he did consider, Reverend Crowther came swinging at them with a far more formidable weapon: he proceeded to belt out a plainsong chant from the Anglican hymnbook.

It worked like a charm.

When the palace crowd heard the terrifying eruption rumbling up the reverend's throat and out of his mouth, the noise sounded to them like the voice of an ancestral spirit boiling with fury, but since no one knew or had heard of this ancestor, they decided it was an invocation to some alien deity, a malicious deity unknown to them, and they turned around and fled.

A lapsed catechumen eventually brought some semblance of calm to the palace after alerting them to the reverend's ruse. 'It sounds like an invocation, but it's not an invocation,' he told them. 'He's just singing one of their songs. All their songs are miserable. Their songs are miserable to sing, and miserable to hear; their songs are made to make people miserable. That's one thing you should know about those church people. They and misery are like five and six. The only time they are happy is when they are miserable. That's why I left them.'

The real reason the man had had second thoughts about joining the church people was because of their unyielding insistence that in order for him to save his soul he also had to forfeit three of his four wives. He balked at the idea, he told his listeners, firstly because it wasn't right. These were women who had borne him children, women who had spent all their adult lives with him. If he divorced them, he said, where would they go?

But also, it just didn't seem normal. 'People wey normal for that church nuh reach two,' he said, switching to pidgin; by normal he meant people who were not fugitives or ex-slaves, people who were not estranged from the community; people who were not outcasts fleeing to the church for sanctuary.

'If you normal and you come go join those people,' he said bitterly, 'your name na Sorry, your bàbá name na Fool.'

By the time the former convert finished regaling the palace with his treasury of chilling stories from his utterly brief, utterly miserable life with the church people, Reverend Crowther had long made his getaway from the iga and was homeward bound. The reverend was inside the passenger compartment of a hansom cab, serenading the dawn with a Gregorian chant, drawing more than one raised eyebrow from the night owls and early risers who recognised the crooning tenor riding past them for the famous clergyman who lived on Breadfruit Street with his wife Susanna, the schoolteacher, and Dandeson, the youngest of their children, and his aged mother who was known to everybody as Ìyá, which means 'mother', because on the Marina, Ìyá was mother to all.

PART TEN

1892

Happy New Year, Bàbá

Fifty-six

After the bishop was struck with apoplexy, Dandeson took him from Bonny, where it happened, to be with Abigail who lived on the waterfront in Lagos, to recuperate.

The stroke left him paralysed on one side of his body, in the right hand and leg. He could barely move his facial muscles, let alone speak.

It came as a severe jolt to his children.

Abigail, whose youngest son, 27-year-old Herbert, was away in Plymouth studying to be a civil engineer, had never seen her father ill. Dandeson, her younger brother, who was for many years employed as the bishop's private secretary, travelling with him everywhere he went, had never seen him laid low, not even with a common cold. Not even Junior, their eldest, now in his sixties and a grandfather, had ever seen Bàbá unwell.

Crowther himself couldn't remember the last time he had been sick. He couldn't remember the last time he'd suffered an ailment that left him bedbound. At a push, he would say the last time this happened was when as a thirteen-year-old slave boy, Àjàyí, he had suffered a severe bout of fever that almost finished him.

He said he was eighty-two years old, but that was an estimation he had arrived at when, as the first student to be enrolled at Fourah Bay College, Freetown, where he later taught, he was required to put his date of birth on the admission form. More likely than not, he was a few years older.

For more than seventy of those tumultuous years, he had been blessed with unbroken health.

The breeze on the waterfront was good for him. After a few days with Abigail, he began to regain his speech, but with a slur that made his voice, which had always been soft, hard to make out. It took weeks for him to sit up in bed unaided. Even after he could sit up, he still required help to get out of bed. He would lean on Abigail and together they would make their way, one agonisingly slow step after the other, across the parlour and out on to the veranda where he liked to sit, not in the armchair that was there but in a straight-back chair she brought out from Babington's study.

'Who built this thing?' he asked her the first time she brought it out for him. 'The workmanship is tip-top.'

Abigail answered him with a strained smile. She knew her father was joking, that he was only trying to bring a smile to her face. He knew who built the chair. He built it.

Bàbá was a highly skilled woodworker. Long before he became a teacher in Sierra Leone, more than a decade before he harkened to the call of the priesthood, he had served an apprenticeship with a master carpenter. When he and Susanna as young parents were raising their children in Freetown, and later on in Abéòkuta, he had taken great pride in building every last piece of furniture in the house himself. Nothing was too big or too trivial; he would make time to build it. He had worked as a roofer on many of the churches he had built as a minister, often because he was the best carpenter on the construction site.

The chair from his son-in-law's study was a wedding present to the newly-wed couple.

The pained look in Abigail's eyes was because bringing out the chair brought it back to her that nobody had sat in it for thirteen years. That was how long ago it was since Babington had been gone. He had died, on his birthday, during a smallpox epidemic that had swept across the island.

Abigail was convinced her father wouldn't have suffered a stroke if he had been accorded a modicum of dignity at the Church meeting he was attending in Bonny when he collapsed. Salisbury Square, the Church's headquarters on London's Fleet Street, had sent two operatives, both in their mid-twenties, both freshly graduated from Cambridge, both ravenously ambitious and fragrant with righteousness, to talk down to him and humiliate him in order to elicit his resignation from the most important decision-making body in the Niger bishopric: his bishopric. They were assassins and, like all assassins on a mission from on high, they struck without remorse. Their mission was an unqualified success; he resigned from the chair and was instantly replaced in the post with a white man, their intention all along. It was the beginning of a wholesale cull of all traces of the African presence in positions of authority within the CMS in West Africa, a pointed reversal of a policy which had for decades actively promoted the involvement of 'the Natives' at the highest levels of their own affairs.

Dandeson had witnessed the public assassination of his father's name, through devoutly sanctimonious dog whistles and insidious semaphores of incompetence, which had begun years before the two enforcers arrived with the explicit mission of securing the bishop's signature on a letter of resignation. Their other mission was a zealously pious one, to bring the Light of Christ to the dark souls of the Native, a task they thought beyond the capabilities of any indigenous missionaries they had come across. The white man alone was sanctioned by God to do so.

They walked all over the bishop, and then, once their aim had been achieved, when once he had resigned the chair, there transpired a great deal of hand-wringing at Salisbury Square, and much soul-searching for the shameful way they had treated the African bishop.

The bishop himself was philosophical about it. Not so his son, the Archdeacon of the Niger; Dandeson would never forgive Salisbury Square for what they did to his father. He was appalled by it, but not entirely surprised. Years earlier, the ordination of Abigail's husband, Babington Macaulay, his headmaster at CMS Grammar School, almost didn't take place because Henry Townsend, one of the then Reverend Crowther's closest associates in the Abẹ́òkuta Mission, strongly objected to it.

'I have a great doubt of young black clergymen,' Reverend Townsend explained. 'They want years of experience to give stability to their characters; we would rather have them as schoolmasters and catechists.'

When word reached Townsend that Crowther had been invited to England to meet the queen and Townsend thought it was to talk about the matter of a black bishop which had been demanded by a powerful member of the CMS, he raised a petition against the notion of the appointment of a black bishop.

'Native teachers of whatever grade,' he cautioned, 'have been received and respected by the chiefs and people only as being the agents or servants of white men. As the Negro feels a great respect for a white man, God kindly gives a great talent to the white man in trust to be used for the Negro's good. Shall we shift the responsibility? Can we do it without sin?'

Within the Church, Townsend's not so peculiar way of seeing the world was for a long time banished to its eccentric fringes. It took decades for this way of thinking to come to represent the mainstream view at Salisbury Square; when this happened, it quickly became entrenched. Such that, for years after the Crowther prelacy, the very notion of another black bishop seemed so olde worlde, it simply didn't arise.

Fifty-seven

A stream of callers flocked to Mrs Macaulay's Marina veranda to pay homage to the ailing bishop. Visitors found him lost in thought, gazing across the lagoon, his tea barely touched. He responded to their attempts at conversation in barely audible, hardly intelligible monosyllables.

The bishop did have much on his mind.

His daughter wasn't alone in having lost her spouse. Crowther, too, had lost the love of his life, Abigail's mother, Susanna.

After the shipwreck that found him and Dandeson and the rest of the 1880 expedition trekking all the way back to Lagos from the headwaters of the Niger, he had returned home to Breadfruit Street to find Susanna at death's door.

They were married for fifty-two years; they'd known each other much longer. They were friends and had been at each other's side since the day they met, fresh off the slaver from which they'd both been rescued, in Freetown. And even though after the first twelve years of their marriage – the Sierra Leone years: when once they moved, first, to Abẹ́òkuta and then to Lagos; and especially after he became bishop – they were often apart, it remained always a close and deeply loving union.

She took her last breath with her head resting in his arms.

Ìyá died three years after Susanna.

She was ninety-seven years old. She had lived with him and his family during the forty years that had elapsed since her reunion in Abẹòkuta with her son.

When Ìyá fell ill in her granddaughter's house in Lagos, Crowther was on ecclesiastical duty in Onitsha. Abigail wanted to summon Bàbá back to Lagos to bid his mother farewell. Ìyá would not hear of it.

'Why would you do such a thing?' she said, quite cross with her granddaughter. 'Your father has not gone out to play. He has gone out to work. There will be time enough for you to tell him after I'm gone.'

Also gone was his friend and mentor Father Schön. The German priest, whose encouragement had started Crowther on the path to becoming a writer and a translator, was at home in Chatham, in Kent, correcting the galley proofs of his latest work, a Hausa translation of the Book of Common Prayer, when he slumped at his desk and could not be revived.

Fifty-eight

On New Year's Eve, the bishop woke up glowing with zest. Abigail, down the hallway in the kitchen making his tea, could hear it in his voice as he said his morning devotions, and afterwards as he sang a string of hymns to himself reading through the piles of letters from well-wishers that had continued to arrive since news of his illness spread abroad.

On Christmas Day, a week earlier, he had surprised Abigail by insisting he was well enough to attend morning service with her. Christ Church was only a short walk from her, less than a block away, but for an octogenarian who could hardly get out of bed unassisted, it was clearly delusional of him to think he could manage the walk. But all his life Crowther's gift had always been to be able to casually achieve the impossible. Not only did he get to the church with his daughter, he also stayed on after the service, shaking hands and trading pleasantries with parishioners.

They were ecstatic to see their beloved bishop, hovering at death's door only a few weeks ago, now standing in their midst and looking, if not exactly in rude health, at least well enough to be out and about enjoying the sea breeze with them.

On the last day of the year, as Abigail finished making his tea, she heard him calling her from his room.

'In a minute, Bàbá,' she shouted back. 'I'll be with you in one minute.'

When she entered the bedroom, he was waving a letter in the air.

'Read this to me, Abigail,' he said. He was lying on his back in the bed with his eyes shut.

After placing the wooden tea tray on the bedside table, Abigail took the letter from his hand and quickly ran her eyes through it. It was from Salisbury Square, from the Secretary of the Church Missionary Society, an earnest prayer for the dear bishop that the Lord would grant him full and speedy recovery.

She didn't bother concealing her reaction to it from her father: his eyes were still firmly shut. She rolled her eyes.

Instantly, without opening his eyes, he said, 'Is something wrong with your eyes, Abigail?'

'Bàbá,' she said wearily. 'I have read this letter to you several times.'

'I have read it too,' he said, not yielding an inch.

'After what they did to you, Father,' she sighed, 'why does a letter from these two-faced, back-stabbing people mean so much to you?'

He opened one eye then the other.

'Do not judge them ill, Abigail,' he said. 'They mean well. Remember the Gospel of Matthew: "But whosoever shall smite thee on thy right cheek, turn to him the other also."'

'If you want any more letters read to you, Bàbá,' she said, turning to leave, 'you'll have to wait for Dandeson; he should be here anytime soon, he will read them to you. I am going to be busy with your breakfast.'

Dandeson had had to rush back to Bonny immediately after bringing his father to Lagos following the stroke. He was now coming back to check in on him.

A few minutes later Dandeson arrived, straight from the boat that had brought him from Bonny. He took his time reading the letter. When he had finished, he folded it neatly and placed it on the bedside table.

Ominously, he said, 'Father.'

His father knew that tone. 'Yes, Dandeson,' the bishop said suspiciously.

'I have terminated all links with Salisbury Square.'

The room got deathly quiet.

'I'm not sure I understand what you mean, Dandeson,' the bishop said when he finally reached to the floor and picked up his jaw. 'What do you mean?'

'As Archdeacon of the Niger,' Dandeson patiently explained, 'I have removed all the churches within my jurisdiction in the Delta from the control of the Church Missionary Society. We're breaking away from Salisbury Square, from the mother Church; it will be a total and complete separation from her.'

'Is it legal? Can you do that?'

'We can and I have,' Dandeson replied.

'Do you know about this?' The bishop turned to Abigail who had chosen that moment to enter the room. 'Did your brother tell you he was going to do this?'

Abigail had no idea what she was being accused of having connived in.

But when her father asked Dandeson, 'When is this schism intended to take effect?' she knew what was going on.

'You're breaking away?' she asked her brother, trying to mirror the appalled look on their father's face but ending up looking anything but appalled.

Dandeson nodded. 'It has already taken effect.'

'When exactly did it take effect?' the bishop asked. 'A week ago? Three days ago? Today?'

'As of three days ago,' Dandeson said, 'all the churches in the archdeaconry of the Lower Niger which were previously known as

CMS churches have become members of a new communion called the Niger Delta Pastorate Church.'

'What denomination does this Niger Delta Pastorate Church belong to?'

'We're Anglicans. We remain within the Anglican Communion but we will be autonomous and self-sustaining.'

The bishop paused to take it all in. Then he said, 'Why?'

'I will have nothing to do,' Dandeson said, choosing his words carefully, 'with those who cannot see that all men are created equal before God. It's a sin.'

Dandeson Crowther's Niger Delta Pastorate Church was the first independent Church in West Africa.

Abigail gave her brother a hug.

'You've done the right thing, Dandeson,' she said, her eyes clouding with tears. 'Don't you think so, Father? Dandeson has done the right thing.'

The bishop slowly nodded. He stretched out his long, bony fingers and took hold of Dandeson's hand and held it tightly.

'God bless the Niger Delta Pastorate Church,' he said.

'Amen,' said Abigail.

'God give you the vision and the strength and the humility to lead wisely, Dandeson Crowther.'

'Amen,' said Abigail.

'Amen,' said Dandeson.

A coughing fit took hold of the bishop. It shook his entire body.

Dandeson leaned over and held him in close to his chest, gently rubbing his back.

'No pain,' Bàbá said, wheezing, his eyes watering from the stabbing pain.

Abigail ran out of the room and fetched some brandy. She gave him a tot mixed with water and sent for Doctor Baudle.

'No more talking, Father,' she instructed him. 'You must rest.'

'Yes, Ma,' he answered obediently.

Shortly after midnight, he came to and found Dandeson sitting by the bed.

'It's 1892, Bàbá,' Dandeson told him, beaming. 'We're now exactly a quarter of an hour into the new year. You slept through the New Year's Eve celebrations.'

Bàbá didn't appear to have heard anything Dandeson said. 'When are you going back to Bonny?' he asked. 'Where's Abigail? Where's your sister?'

'Happy New Year, Bàbá. I'm right here,' Abigail said. She was sat right next to Dandeson. 'It's time to take your medicine.'

He glowered at the bottle in her hand. She poured a measure of the tincture into a tablespoon and fed it to him.

'I hope this is the last dose,' he said with a grimace. He turned to Dandeson and asked him again, 'When are you going back to Bonny?'

'Monday,' Dandeson said.

'You're not going back on Monday,' Abigail told him. 'Tuesday or Wednesday, perhaps.'

Dandeson shot her a look, then he turned to their father and repeated, firmly, 'Monday.'

'Your grandson,' Abigail said to her father, 'is returning from England on Monday.'

'Herbert is returning on Monday?' Dandeson was grinning from ear to ear. 'Why didn't you say so?'

'I just did.'

'In the first place.'

'You didn't ask.'

'It's settled, then,' Dandeson said. 'Wednesday. I cannot leave Lagos without spending time with my favourite nephew.'

'Your favourite nephew is looking forward to spending time with his favourite uncle,' his sister told him.

'I shall leave on Wednesday, Bàbá,' he said. 'But I'll be back to see you in a few weeks.'

'There'll be no need for you to come all this way to see me,' Bàbá told him. 'We're travelling together on Wednesday. I'm going back to Bonny with you.'

Quietly, through the corner of her mouth, without looking at him, Abigail said, 'You're not going anywhere, Father.'

'There is unfinished work waiting for me in Bonny,' Bàbá pleaded.

'I'm not letting you leave this house until Doctor Baudle gives you a clean bill of health.'

Dandeson stood, arms folded, watching his father and sister battle it out in a decidedly unequal duel; then, turning to leave the bedroom, he paused at the door to offer the abject loser a word of advice: 'The sooner you're reconciled to the fact that you're going nowhere, Father, the better. Arguing with Abbie is a futile task. You know that.'

Most assuredly, Bàbá did know that against Abbie's logic, his pleas were futile. Nevertheless: 'I assure you, madam,' he said, now rocking with laughter, 'these old bones do still have some life left in them.'

He was still laughing, feeling very silly and very happy, when he gently drifted off into a deep sleep.

He dreamt that he was back in Òsogùn, in the forests of his boyhood, on the morning of the day the slave raiders pounced on his hometown. He knew it was a dream, but he also knew what was about to happen, and so he was filled with dread.

As he braced himself for the inevitable, however, for the invading army to appear, he found himself drifting further back in time.

He found himself running, with his sister Bọ́lá by his side, on an errand for Ìyá several months before the day of the attack.

He blinked, and could hardly believe it, but there he was, in his father's workshop, sweat-soaked, a full year before the day of the attack.

He saw at once what was happening: instead of growing older by the day, he was growing younger by the hour.

Soon enough, he was a toddler suckling at his mother's breast.

Soon enough, he arrived at a haven where there existed nothing but bliss, an oasis where he felt completely safe, a sanctuary where it was impossible to suffer dread, to feel anxiety, or to know distress.

These conditions did not have a name here.

Here, they did not exist.

His name, here, was not Àjàyí.

He had no name here.

There were no names here.

He knew exactly where he was.

He'd been there before: he was back in the all-swaddling warmth of his mother's womb.

He was back to a time before he was born.

He had never felt so carefree, so joy-filled and carefree, in his entire life.

Abigail held his wrist, checking for a pulse.

'Bàbá!' she cried. 'Bàbá!'

It was quarter to one in the morning. Out on the streets, Lagosians were ushering in the new year; from Broad Street to Pópó Àgùdà, from the Marina to Ìsàlẹ̀ Èkó, sounds of merrymaking issued into the night.

ACKNOWLEDGEMENTS

The Estate would like to thank Olajide Bello, Yewande Sadiku and Chimamanda Ngozi Adichie, with deep gratitude for their open-hearted friendship.